The Song of the Troubadour

Stephanie Cook

For Edna Keller Tonnersen Malik

"Kill them all. God will know his own."

- Abbot Arnald Amaury, head of the Cistercians and spiritual leader of the Crusade, at the sacking of Béziers, July 22, 1209, Feast Day of the Magdalene

"Nearly twenty thousand of the citizens were put to the sword, regardless of age and sex. The workings of divine vengeance have been wondrous."

- Abbot Arnald Amaury in his letter to Pope Innocent III, describing the Crusaders' victory at Béziers

CARCASSONNE

Friday, July 31, 1209

Trencavel

Friday, July 31, 1209, midday

"It's the water. That's our weakness," said Cabaret.

"And they know it," said Trencavel, gesturing in the direction of the river Aude. The descent to the river was steep. At the river bank, the trees were the only green in a landscape of dusty browns. The Crusaders were still arriving. They had been coming for a week, their tents and banners seeming to take over the whole valley to the foothills of the Corbieres. And still they spilled up the old Roman road from the Mediterranean.

The two men continued walking south along the walls, leaving the covered wooden galleries for the entrance to a tower, one of twenty-six placed along the city walls. The men in the tower holding their javelins and crossbows instantly stood to attention as Trencavel and Cabaret passed through. The cool of the stone walls of the tower felt good in the scorching heat of the day. They continued out of the tower and along the walls.

"How many do you estimate?" said Trencavel.

Cabaret paused and stared at the army massed to the west of the city, along the river banks.

"It is the largest army I have ever seen," he said. "Mounted knights, thousands, maybe ten thousand. Plus mounted sergeants, squires, crossbowmen, mounted archers, infantry, engineers, archers, miners, sappers, carters, carpenters, foragers, camp followers. There are maybe 50,000 souls out there waiting to lay siege to our city."

"And don't forget the Abbot and his Cistercian monks," said Trencavel. "Do you know what that mad Abbot said at Béziers?"

Cabaret kicked at a loose stone with his foot before replying.

"They say that a knight asked him how to tell the heretics from the Christians and the Abbot said, 'Kill them all; God will know his own.' "

Both men turned to face the city. Everywhere people worked. Women carted stones to stockpile next to the trebuchets, ready to be used as missiles when the attack came. Children helped the water sellers carry bucket after bucket of water from the river to be stored in the city's cisterns and in the bathhouses, now closed to preserve water. Men continued to build the wooden galleries covering the walls and the towers; these galleries projected out over the walls. They would not only protect the sentries and crossbowmen from the arrows of the Crusaders, but would also be used to throw down stones and fire on the attackers if they came too close to the wall itself. Everyone worked with a grim determination.

"The people are terrified," said Cabaret. "They do not want to be slaughtered like pigs."

"I will not let that happen again," said Trencavel. "I swear it."

Trencavel and Cabaret continued to walk the sentry-route, passing to the southern portion of the city walls which overlooked the Castellar suburb. This suburb was itself strongly fortified, which was vital since it provided access to the Fontgrande spring, the only other source of water to the population other than the river. The water of most of the city wells had either run dry or turned brackish with the drought of the summer. They passed into the first city tower overlooking the Castellar suburb. Here the work of preparation was not as far advanced. The galleries were not finished, and, in some sections, not even started. In the first tower, the guards were resting asleep on the stone floors, their javelins fallen to the ground.

"Is this considered acceptable practice for guards in this sector?" said Trencavel to their stammering sergeant.

"No, my lord," said the sergeant. "But, the heat." He looked at Trencavel's hard face and stopped. "These men are not my best. They are fat and lazy. We are stretched thin. We can't even properly man every tower of the city walls. These towers are behind the Castellar suburb. The suburb is well-defended. Its walls are high and I have some of my best men defending them. These towers need not be well-guarded, I assure you."

The four guards were now awake and had jumped to their feet, faces humbly lowered. Trencavel turned and spoke to them.

"Look at me, men," Trencavel said. "The Castellar suburb will come under attack; the walls may even be breached. That is when you must be ready. This suburb must not be taken. We must have access to the Fontgrande spring. You must be prepared to fight, and fight long and hard. Or you must be prepared to die of thirst. It is your decision."

The guards stared at Trencavel.

"They will be lashed, my lord," said the sergeant. "This will not happen again."

Trencavel and Cabaret left the tower and continued around the southern edge of the city. They looked down at the Castellar.

"They seem ready," said Cabaret. The suburb was a warren of activity. Water gatherers came from the Fontgrande spring to fill the suburb's cisterns. Men dragged siege machines, trebuchets and mangonels, into place near the suburbs' walls.

"They had better be," said Trencavel. "The Crusaders will attack here and the walls are not as high and strong as those of the city."

"But our men are courageous and strong," said Cabaret. "And fighting for their lives, which always gives an army an incalculable advantage."

The two men continued northwards, along the eastern edge of the city walls. Once fertile farmlands stretched eastwards across the plains to where the Black Mountains rose to craggy heights. The fields were blackened and scorched. Trencavel's orders had been followed exactly. No crops were left in the fields, all pigs, goats, cattle, and chickens slaughtered or brought into the walls of the city of Carcassonne. Even the valuable water mills floating in the river Aude had been dismantled to prevent the Crusaders from milling any grain they managed to buy or steal. The Crusaders' army would find it very difficult to feed 50,000 people off the lands around Carcassonne for very long. Nevertheless, foragers from the attacking army wandered through these fields, searching for wood, a forgotten stash of grain, eggs left in empty hen houses. Trencavel wanted nothing more than to see these crusaders miserable with aching, empty bellies in one week's time. Everyone knew that fever followed famine. Maybe half of them would be dead before the month was out.

Trencavel and Cabaret continued their inspection of the sentry-walk and towers along the northern wall of the city, overlooking the Bourg suburb, defended in a similar manner to the Castellar. Here they were pleased with the preparations, wooden galleries were finished, and mounds of stones stood piled next to trebuchets. They walked now southwards, completing their circuit of the city walls and coming back to the castle, where they had started. It stood strong and inviolate, well-maintained and well-defended. Before going back into the castle, they stood looking west across the river Aude at the army continuing to mass just beyond its banks. A garrison defended the route to the wooden bridge across the banks of the Aude, a route protected by only a simple wooden palisade spanning the 500 yard drop to the river. Another suburb, St.Vincent, sprawled on either side of the palisade.

"They will try to take the bridge and St. Vincent soon," said Trencavel. "And if they succeed, our access to the river will be cut off."

"And how do you propose to stop them? St. Vincent has no walls and the route to the bridge is only protected by a palisade," said Cabaret.

"I will do something," said Trencavel. "My city will not be taken and made a charnel house while I stand by watching."

"That sounds like a memorable line in some troubadour's chanson de geste. You would be quite the hero with those kinds of words," said Cabaret. "Just remember that experienced soldiers do not read chansons de geste for military strategy. They read Vegetius. You must remember his best advice on fighting battles. Avoid them."

Trencavel looked at the old man and walked into the castle.

Bernard

Friday, 31 July, 1209, afternoon

My brother Guillaume and I came to Carcassonne, that city of sin, in the days before the siege. We came to infiltrate their defenses, and to aid our brother Crusaders in their Holy battle against the heretic. Guillaume prayed that we would be allowed to serve in a more Holy manner, for he was a simple boy and fearful of our task, but our Father Abbot assured us that our service was just as Holy in the eyes of God as our chanting brothers and just as noble as the warriors called to the Cross. I, of course, realized the importance of our task from the first moment our Father Abbot spoke of it. For God is omniscient and omnipotent, but His disciples here on earth must implement His plans to His greater glory.

I knew that these people had to learn that he who protects the heretics and flaunts the one true faith must be stopped. The death of our martyr would be avenged. Like our Lord Jesus Christ, his blood would serve to cleanse the sins of the others. His death would remove the rot of heresy from this land and he would be remembered as the savior of these people.

As Guillaume and I approached Carcassonne from the bridge over the river Aude, I saw the city rise up from the plains of olive fields that surrounded it. It was placed on a hill, surrounded by walls and impregnable to invaders who have been trying to attack it from days long before the Romans ruled over these lands. Even the great Holy Roman Emperor Charlemagne besieged this city for seven years without it yielding. With the grace of God, we would be part of the army that finally forced it to submit. In the north and the south, suburbs spilled from the city and were themselves surrounded by walls. The tramontano whipped down from the North, rushing to the sea, and setting the windmills to a high speed of frenzy. The trip had seemed much longer than it was, as Guillaume and I fought the hot wind every step of the way, as it lifted great clouds of dust off the fields and into our faces, taunting those of us who worked tirelessly on God's business.

The city was impressive, even to me, who knew what filth and heresy lay hidden behind its walls. The cathedral and many fine houses and towers loomed over the city walls. But the most imposing structure was the castle, home of the Viscount Trencavel, most vile and depraved heretic. Yes, the same Trencavel who forced his choice of Abbot on the monastery of Alet. How did he do this? Did he buy the office or use intrigue to promote his candidate? While these sinful practices were all too common, all of us who have lived in this world understand the ways of power and money. This would have been understandable. No, Trencavel did something far, far worse. His sacrilege was almost unspeakable, and showed only too well his level of depravity. He sent his man to oversee the new Abbot's election with orders for this man to dig up the former Abbot from his grave. He placed the earthly remains of this most Holy man, already wormy and shedding black earth, in the Abbot's chair. And then he told the monks to listen to the choice of their former Abbot. These gentle men of God fainted at the stench of decay, for while their Abbot was a good man, he was not a saint. It was said that his body was bloated to twice the size of normal. The monks elected Trencavel's choice as Abbot in this abbey gone to damnation and decay. And this was but one example of Trencavel's depravity.

My brother Guillaume and I had spent one week with these vermin, these vicious monsters who spoiled the church of God on earth with their evil ways. Over the last few nights, Guillaume whined and cried in his sleep, as he always did in the monastery. But there was no one to spoil and cosset him here. He has spent sixteen years on this earth and finally it was time that he learned that discipline and sacrifice were required to build greatness. I continued my work, despite his weakness, and my Father Abbot was proud of my intelligence and resilience. Guillaume and I watched this week as the Army of God arrived outside of the gates of this modern-day Sodom, this Gomorrah. Host upon host, the golden lion of the Count of Nevers and the blue and yellow diagonal stripes of the Duke of Burgundy. The greatest Christian army ever mustered and all flying banners with that most holy of symbols, the Cross. It was a sight beautiful to see.

I knew in my heart that this city would fall and with it, the heretics who threatened the fibers of the faith. These heretics were a disease in the flesh, weakening the church and all earthly power that descends from it. Plague, pestilence, famine would fall on the land that lost the protection of the Lord. I knew that the lost sheep must be brought back to the fold. It was the decay of heresy that blighted this land and these souls.

Through the power and magnificence of our Lord and his most Holy representatives on earth, the Holy Father in Rome and my Father Abbot, I would make sure that this city would fall. I swore it on the Feast Day of St. Bernard, with whom I share a Christian name and the desire to build a church upon this earth to rival the one we will find in heaven.

Gauda

Friday, July 31, 1209, afternoon

Once, as a girl, my father took me to the wild sea far to the west. I smelled the salt in the air, felt the rhythmic suffering of the waves, forever moving up and down and never going anywhere, only force moving through them, using them, until at last they roared and crashed and died against a cliff. This was how I felt; that my life had stood still while the force of others had swept through it, on to greater and bigger things, leaving me alone in the middle of a vast sea.

In my thirty-fifth year, I chose to no longer wait while others lived their full lives. I devised a plot that would brand me an unscrupulous traitor, were it ever to be revealed. I lived at the court of Raymond-Roger Trencavel, Viscount of Béziers, Albi, Carcassonne, and Razes, a lady-in-waiting to his wife and my cousin, Agnes. For almost two years, I attended to Agnes, jumping at her every whim and avoiding the back of her hand. I played my harp and sang for the viscount and went to his bed, when he asked it of me. I served my lord and lady both day and night, a poor relation grateful for her home in their palace. But they did not know that I spied on them. Every month I sent a letter to a troubadour at the court of the Count of Toulouse, Viscount Raymond-Roger's uncle and his rival. When I finished my service, and I was almost done, I would receive my reward from the Count of Toulouse - my father's lands and castle, stolen from me by my despicable stepsons.

I passed the bitter days dreaming that I would be able to one day recreate the joy and beauty of the court of my father. Troubadours from far lands would come to my castle and would duel with song far into the night. They would sing of my generosity and the skill of my cooks. We would eat wild boar in fine basil sauce; sorbets of cinnamon, ginger, and mint; swordfish with chickpeas and the milk of almonds; sugared peaches with spices of the Orient. We would drink wine with spices and honey and beautiful women would sing and the castle hall would smell of fresh rushes and lavender. I would sing my songs again.

I looked out at the Crusaders gathered outside the gates of Carcassonne. I saw the pennants of the Count of Toulouse flying from his tents down by the green grass near the river. I willed them to victory. I only hoped I would survive to claim my reward.

Bernard

Friday, July 31, 1209, early evening

Guillaume and I walked through the dusty, hot streets of the damned city of Carcassonne. People talked everywhere of the impending siege, fearing not for their souls, as they ought, but for their miserable heretical lives. Supplies were running out in the stores and markets as people hoarded. Houses were packed with three, four, even five families as relatives pored in from the countryside. The city was full of fighting men from Foix, the Minervois, and the Black Mountains. Trencavel's vassals from the plains between Béziers and Carcassonne had seen the error of their ways and the vast might of our most Holy Crusading army and had surrendered without a fight. But the knights and lords from the mountains were popped up with their vanity, their heretical minds too sealed against the truth to realize their foolishness in daring to resist our might.

Guillaume and I went to the cathedral, about which we had heard rumors of great sacrilege. We needed to see for ourselves what these heathen dogs were capable of doing. We entered and found workmen everywhere. The unholy apostates were ripping the very wood from the stalls of the choir. Big, brutish men carried heavy timbers from the stalls, while the most holy reverend fathers of the church tried to stop them. We hurried from the cathedral and entered the refectory of the canons next door. The spacious room was being dismantled stone by stone. A line of men carried the heavy stones as they were pried from the walls. Our men of God struggled manfully to prevent this sacrilege, but they were outnumbered and overwhelmed. We watched as a brother monk, young and strong, struggled to grab a stone from the hands of a big mason. I felt Guillaume move to help, but quietly placed a restraining hand on his arm.

"Do you care so little for your immortal soul that you would destroy the very house of God?" said the monk.

"God does not live here, but only a bunch of fat priests," said the mason. The others laughed as the monk's face turned red. "Better that we use these stones to protect our own city and then we won't be worrying about our immortal souls for a good long while, no?" said the mason, looking round at his coworkers, who were now hooting.

"You will pay for this sacrilege," said the monk, trembling with rage. "You try to build your walls with those stones you ripped from their holy foundations and you will make a wall rotten from within, foul and stinking with your heresy. Your foolish human pride will not defend you. Repent now, while you can, for the time is at hand."

The mason pushed the monk over with his stone and the monk lay stunned on the floor of the refectory. The shouts and laughter of the men echoed over the walls. I had to restrain Guillaume again from rushing to the side of the monk, whose nose bled. He would be fine. We had a more important agenda. I walked over to the mason.

"My brother and I are refugees from the country. We are young and strong. How can we help?"

The mason looked us over.

"You don't look that accustomed to hard work, boys, but we'll take what we can get."

The mason thrust his stone into our hands and we hobbled under the great weight, following the other men as they made their way to the walls of the city just above the Castellar suburb. They did not trust us at first, for no man there would trust any he did not know personally from his own city.

"Where are you boys from?" asked the mason.

Guillaume and I had spent our childhood in a small village not far from Carcassonne, but we knew better than to give the name. There could be refugees from our village here and they would know our family name still and would know of what happened to us.

"We were at Béziers when it fell," I said, which was not a lie.

The men looked up from their work and glanced at us, before quickly looking down.

"Boys, you are welcome here with us. If we can do anything for you..." said the mason. He looked around.

"Thank you," I said, looking down because I was certain he would see the disdain in my eyes. These foul traitors. They would abuse a monk, but open their arms to the foul heretics who escaped from God's justice at Béziers.

We worked all afternoon, our backs aching and sweat pouring off our limbs. The powerful wind blew the dust into our eyes as we carried the stones from the cathedral through the city gates and into the Castellar suburb. Part of the interior of the wall there lay in ruins and the mason led a group of men who were trying to restore the wall's integrity before the siege began.

"Excuse me, master mason," I said. "Will we have time to fix all these walls before the siege starts? It does not seem as if there is time."

"No, there's not enough time, but they don't know that," answered the mason. "This part of the wall is only damaged on the inside. From the exterior it will appear as strong as the rest."

And I knew immediately what I would include in my letter to the abbot that evening. These heretical dogs would pay for their sacrilege. The very stones that they had ripped from the most holy walls of the cathedral would betray them.

Suddenly I heard a yell followed by a low moan. Men dropped their tools and rushed to the wall, where someone lay moaning on the ground. It was Guillaume. Blood poured from his head. His face was white and his eyes were large. I looked around at the men.

"What happened?" I asked, putting my arm on Guillaume's shoulder.

One of the apprentices put down a heavy stone that he carried on his shoulder and spoke.

"He walked towards me when my back was turned," said the apprentice. "I didn't see him as I turned and he hit his head on the stone I was carrying."

"What can I do for him?" I asked.

"You," the mason pointed to one of the youngest apprentices, "bring these boys to the house of the good women."

The mason turned to me.

"The good women will care for your brother. He will be well taken care of there," he said.

I started to protest, but realized in time I would ruin our disguise. I merely nodded humbly and followed the apprentice as I supported Guillaume with my arms under his shoulder. We walked out of the Castellar suburb and into the city gates. We followed a narrow street into the center of the city. We turned to our right and came to a large three- story house, built in the shape of a U, two wings surrounding a central courtyard. The building was clean and white, with baked red tiles on the roof. We walked up to the door, and it was opened by a young heretic girl. The apprentices told her quickly about Guillaume's injury and she beckoned them inside, into a wide room, filled with plenty of light. The floor was covered with makeshift pallets, mostly empty, but soon to be filled with the dying bodies of these heretical dogs if the righteous will of my most Holy Father Abbot came to pass.

The heretic girl directed us to a pallet in the back. My brother groaned deeply. The girl tried to clean the wound on his head with a cloth, her fingers pushing the hair from his face. To allow my brother to be touched by these women was almost more than I could bear. The abbot must truly know the depth of our sacrifice. I would be sure he understood, so that we could be purified of the contamination we would suffer at their hands. For not only were these so-called good women heretics, but they further suborned the natural and good order of all things because they acted as priests in their church of heretical dogs. Their acts of consecration were pure blasphemy, pure sacrilege. Their laying on of hands was a cruel mimicry of that most holy act of the blessed apostles; their giving of blessings a blasphemous imitation of that act reserved to popes, bishops, and priests. I understand that the evil heresy was the same when propagated by man or woman, yet I could not help feel that the women heretics who performed these satanic mockeries of our most holy Catholic rituals were committing the greater evil. Their foul bodies were cesspools of lust and decay, luring men to their eternal damnation through the sins of fornication, adultery, covetousness. Truly, man would suffer almost no sin were it not for the existence of women. All daughters of Eve, all temptresses, only ever to be tolerated when they strove to live the life of purity and devotion modeled on that of the most Holy Virgin mother of our Lord, Jesus Christ.

My anxiety worsened as I watched my brother look at the heretic girl. I could tell already, despite his pain, that he was being seduced by her lustfulness. For it was almost as if the devil himself had decided to create a perfect vessel for all lust and desire and corrupt yearnings. She was probably my brother's age and one who ought to have been safely married or put in a nunnery for several years already. Her eyes were dark with thick lashes and surely Satan himself must have made her hair so that it shone in the light from the window. It was dark, but the light brought out only a deeper luster. I supposed that those men who are weaker and would be attracted to a whore such as herself, so bold and free, would find her figure comely. Though I, of course, felt nothing but contempt for her cheap charms. My whole being felt desire for only one woman, the most holy blessed Virgin, mother of our Lord, and this desire was of a heavenly, pure variety.

Yet Guillaume was weaker than I. He needed to be saved from this witch before she could cast her spells upon him. I realized that I must remove him from her clutches as soon as the apprentice left. I would not leave him there, his tender young soul ready to be plucked by their wickedness. But, then I saw the heretic girl call out to another woman, an older woman, probably also a whore, but probably one of their priests. And I realized that I had the perfect opportunity to see inside their sick and depraved rituals. No one would have trusted me if I had tried to join a group of heretical men, but, here in this home turned hospital, I would be able to observe quietly as my brother's head mended. I could ask questions, for surely this foolish girl would be easily manipulated. For when this Crusade was over, and these lands won for our most holy Pope, there would remain these sinners, these apostates. We would need to root them out, to learn their ways so we could trap them and expose them and burn them to cleanse the rot of heresy from this land. Oh, I would let Guillaume stay. I would watch him closely, but I would learn. And these whores of Babylon would pay for their sins.

Gauda

Friday, July 31, 1209, evening

I walked into the Viscountess Agnes' private chamber and past her bed. Two servants from the kitchen were filling a large wooden tub with steaming hot water and I thought how much I would like a bath. The Viscount had ordered the court to restrict the use of water to only the essentials: drinking, cooking, and watering the horses. Agnes had, as usual, done what she had wanted.

Agnes was sitting in her tub, her face a mask of annoyance.

I only knew that, if it were me in that hot bath smelling of rose petals, my face would show only bliss.

"Gauda, come scrub me," Agnes said.

Attending to Agnes' bath was a new and unwelcome chore for me. Usually, I kept her company at whatever idle amusement she chose - playing chess, gossiping, or reading romances in the long winter nights, for she craved them, but could not decipher the letters. I tried to teach her once, but it frightened her and she preferred that I do it. Agnes always had other maids to care for her clothes and toilet, but she dispensed with them regularly, sending the poor girls off crying to their villages once every few months.

The last girl had been packed off this morning, so I reluctantly sat down on a wooden bench near to the tub. I picked up a sponge and dipped it in a bowl filled with milk and the sap of melon seeds to whiten the skin. The steam rose in the hot August air and I began to sweat. I gently moved the sponge over Agnes' arm and then lifted it to massage the delicate raw skin underneath.

"Viscountess, why do you do this? Your skin is raw. It may fester in this heat," I asked.

"It is what is done," she said. "I would not want to be an embarrassment to my husband. I am sure those sluts who hang about him do no less."

Agnes grimaced as I examined her underarms. They were bright red and raw. The apothecaries mixed a horrid slew of quicklime, goat urine, and arsenic sulfur and sold it to all who followed slavishly the new style of removing all their hair from their bodies except that which grew on their heads. The men brought back the style from the Holy Land and the women quickly followed. I had never understood the lengths some would go to be considered beautiful, but I especially did not understand it of Agnes for she had sworn herself to a life of celibacy two years ago.

After I finished rubbing her body with the soothing melon sponge, I picked up an ivory comb and began to work through her long hair, looking for lice. Agnes' hair was truly lovely, the color of wheat fields and not even from an apothecary's bottle. I pulled the comb through a section of hair and picked at the little creatures I found, neatly splitting them with my thumbnail.

"Stop pulling. You're hurting me, Gauda," Agnes whined. She

reached over and pinched my wrist.

I placed my hand in my lap.

"I am sorry for my clumsiness, Viscountess," I said.

"Well, why did you stop?" Agnes said. "I can still feel them, they disgust me. Get them all."

I moved the comb through her hair again, trying to be as gentle as possible. I did not understand what had happened to this girl to make her such a bitter and mean-spirited shrew. I remembered visiting Agnes' mother, who was my cousin and dear friend, when Agnes was only a girl. Then she had been a dear child, so pretty and always laughing, the joy of her both her mother and father. How had that sweet child turned into this nasty young woman, so beautiful on the outside, yet rotten in her core?

I worked quietly for a while, and allowed myself to dream of having my father's old lands back and being mistress of my own home. Maids would pick the lice from my hair, but I would never slap their face or pinch their wrists. Agnes' harsh voice woke me from my reverie. She was yelling at the kitchen servants, who had shrunk into a corner.

"You foolish girls have let my bath grow cold. If I catch sick, you will be whipped for your laziness," Agnes said. She paused for a second. "Come here, you little fools," she said to the girls.

Cautiously, they came closer to the bath.

Agnes placed her hand on the cheek of the prettier one.

"What were you thinking about that made you forget your duties, you little slut? Some handsome lying troubadour has convinced you to spread your legs for him in return for a pretty song?" Agnes said.

"No, my lady," stammered the girl. "I was not thinking of that, I swear." Agnes slapped her face. The girl cried out and started crying.

"Do not contradict me, you little whore," she said. "Both of you, go, you have ruined my bath."

Agnes waved them away and stood in her bath.

"Gauda, bring me my towel from the fire."

I walked over to the fireplace and picked up a warm piece of cotton that hung from a rack in front of the flames. I draped the cloth around Agnes and dried her body and then placed a second warm cloth around her hair, which smelled of honey. We walked over to chair and Agnes sat down. I brought her a silver mirror and she held it in front of her face. I started to pluck the hair from her brows, making them slim and arched. Then, I plucked the hairs from her forehead, for some were starting to grow in. Agnes had beautiful hair, but her brow was low and she was forever battling to create a fashionable high brow. I saw her look at my face as she winced and knew that she was jealous of my brow. I never needed to pluck a hair from it, for it was naturally high. I anticipated a pinch or slap, but none came. Agnes looked away from my face and stared again at hers in the mirror.

"Do you think my husband still desires me?" she said.

I tried not to show my surprise at her question.

"Viscountess, you are a very beautiful woman. Just think of the many songs written about your beauty by so many troubadours," I said.

"All to gain favor with my husband," Agnes said.

"Well, troubadours often write to please their listener and to keep a warm bed by a fire and rich meals and wine," I admitted. "But, in your case, those were not lies."

"And my husband, do you think he agrees with them?"

"I think he must find you as beautiful as they, but that he respects the vows you have taken. I am sure that he is proud that his wife has received the consolamentum and has become a good woman. He would not want to let lustful thoughts contaminate your purity and the path you have chosen," I said.

Agnes looked as if she were about to cry and then she slapped me.

"How do you know what he thinks, cousin? Do you think you know him better than I, his wife? What do you do with him when he calls you to play for him in the night? I hope, for your sake, that playing your harp and singing your songs is all you do. Leave me, now. I desire to be alone."

I walked out of Agnes' chamber. I had time to deliver one final message to the troubadour at the court of the Count of Toulouse before the city began to close up for the siege. I walked into the great hall and found the young joglar that I had been using for several months to carry my letters to the court of the Count of Toulouse. He was packing his bags, probably one of the few people trying to leave the city as the throngs from the countryside streamed in. I looked into his eyes, which were large and violet and I wondered as I always did if he knew how handsome he would have been had the pox not scarred his young features, leaving his face a mess of pits. Yes, he knew, I was sure, staring into his sad eyes.

"Do you have room in that sack for a letter?" I asked.

"I have room for whatever pleases you, my fine lady troubairitz," he replied, with a slight bow and a sweep of his hand towards the floor. "And I thank you for all you have done for me. I will never forget it, no matter what happens."

I had not much time at my own convenience, but when a banquet ran on for hours, I would sometimes sit with the violet-eyed joglar. I would try to teach him all that I learned from my teacher, the famous troubairitz Azalais de Porcairagues. He would soak up all that I knew about rhyme and meter and would sing me his latest poems, for he wanted more than anything to leave behind his juggling and tumbling and playing of dance tunes for drunkards and become an honored troubadour, one whose songs would be sung across many lands.

I took the letter from the satchel at my belt and gave it to him. He placed it in his sack and then I took both his hands in mine.

"God go with you, and protect you."

"And God protect you here, my lady."

I kissed him on the cheek once and then turned and walked out of the great hall. In the letter I had given to the joglar I had written of the latest musical styles coming from Gascony and included several new songs, but the Count of Toulouse would be able to understand and read what I had really written - everything I knew about the state of the castle and the city. It was difficult to escape from the constant demands of the Viscountess Agnes to do the spying I had been sent here to do, but I found my moments. I would be sent on an errand and linger just a little too long. Agnes never suspected anything other than that I was poorly behaved and the joy she got from pettily punishing me kept her giving me more errands. I spent nights in the hall with the Viscount Raymond-

Roger and his knights and troubadours. I kept my ears open and learned much. Men think so little of the intelligence of women that they will spill the most alarming secrets, thinking the woman too dull to understand. I was sure the Count of Toulouse would be pleased with my information. Perhaps by the time this siege was over, my father's lands would be restored to me and I would be free.

Later that night, I sat down with the rest of the court to a dinner in the great hall. The mood was somber. The meal finished quickly, without the usual singing and dancing. Afterwards a servant summoned me to the Viscount's chambers. Raymond-Roger waited for me beside his bed as I walked in with my harp. I sat down and prepared to play, but he waved his hand.

"Not tonight, your foolish songs of love and romance will only annoy me. Just get into my bed and make me forget so I can sleep, woman."

I did as he said.

There were some days I felt guilty for my spying, but this was not one of them.

DAY 1 OF THE SIEGE OF CARCASSONNE

Saturday, August 1, 1209

Trencavel

Saturday, August 1, 1209, midday

The twenty men sat in the Castle Round Room. They were arranged around a massive circular oak table, in leather chairs that groaned and squeaked under their weight. The ceiling was high, a circular dome. Along the upper part of the walls ran a mural, knights seated on horseback in brilliant red tunics, their shields at the ready, faced their opponents, always at the point of the start of the battle. Pennants flew, all was ready for war.

Trencavel stood to speak. At his side sat his guardian from his youth, Bertrand de Saissac, a wild, hairy man with fists like bricks.

"We must protect our access to the river," said Trencavel. "At whatever cost."

Bertrand de Saissac banged his giant fists on the table until it jumped. Most of the other knights showed their agreement with their fists and feet. These were battle-ready men from the mountains. Lords of castles in the Black Mountains, the Minervois, and the Corbieres. Their towers were perched on hard, rocky precipices where only mountain goats moved with ease. The will to build in stone on these isolated peaks was shown on their determined, sun-lined faces. From these mountain strongholds, they controlled the lands below. Some were blessed with deep valleys that bore vines and fruit. Others presided over ravines and gorges shaped by fast rivers, where only shepherds could eke out a living. These men were too accustomed to their daily battles with a raw nature, wolves and bears and killing frosts and burning droughts, to show much fear over an invasion force cobbled together from men whose commitment lasted only the forty days they believed would send them to heaven, and more importantly, knew would remove any earthly debts from their ledgers.

But from their experience they all feared one thing - the lack of water.

"Listen, men. Let's attack with 400 of our best men and their Arab steeds, before night falls. They are heavy with their baggage and travel. We can take them by surprise and quickly return to the walls of the city." said Trencavel.

The men continued to listen in silence. Trencavel was young, one of the youngest men in the room, but his presence was sure.

"Let's equip ourselves for battle now. We can overcome them, I am sure. We will send them into disarray and make them think before attempting to take the river access. As long as we can hold our water supply, they stand no chance of taking this city. They will be dying of hunger and disease before their forty days of service run out," said Trencavel.

The men began to stand amid calls of agreement. They wanted these invaders off their lands as quickly as possible.

The Lord of Cabaret stood quietly, his hand stroking his neatly trimmed gray beard.

"I would like to speak," Cabaret said.

The men quieted down and retook their seats.

"In my opinion, it is better to wait and do nothing rash," said Cabaret. "The Crusaders are camping across the river. You know what will be the first concern of these sons of Northern bitches. They will try to take the path to the river and cut off the water supply. We should wait until they are exposed in their attack under our walls. Then, when they are weakened by the arrows of our crossbow men, we can counterattack and slaughter them."

"And that will be too late. They will already have taken the path to the river and they will defend it to the end. They are not fools. And they have many more men than us. Our only hope is surprise," said Trencavel.

Bertrand of Saissac stood up, his great shaggy mane spilling over his huge shoulders.

"I agree with the Viscount Trencavel," said Bertrand. "They have the numbers. We have only our courage and their stupidity. We must surprise them. They will never expect that after Béziers. We must fight like men, not hide in the city like a bunch of old women. Anyway, who do they have on their side? Cistercian monks!" Bertrand laughed. "They indulge in vice with their sheep because they are afraid of women. And they spend their days thinking how to disrupt the pleasures of men who are not. We have nothing to fear from these sodomizing whores of the Pope!"

Cabaret slowly turned to face Bertrand. His voice was low and angry.

"Do you want us to be slaughtered like those fools at Béziers?" said Cabaret. "A bunch of impatient idiots, stupider than lice, and covered in maggots by now, for all their thoughts of glory."

Bertrand de Saissac pounded his fist on the table.

"Who are you calling a fool, old man?" he said. Two knights on either side of him tried to hold him back.

"I have fought more battles than you have dreamed of," said Cabaret.

Trencavel's face flushed red. He placed his hand on Cabaret's arm.

"That's enough," said Trencavel. "We have enough enemies to fight outside these gates. We don't need to waste our energies inside. Now, my friends, what is it to be? Do we surprise them tonight or wait until they attack tomorrow?"

The room erupted into noise as the men argued among themselves. Finally, the noise started to subside. The men around the table spoke. Caution would carry the day. There would be no surprise attack tonight.

"Very well," said Trencavel. "You have made yourselves clear. Set extra sentries on all the watch towers. Prepare yourselves for the battle that will come when they attack. They may set the time, but we will still have the advantage of knowledge. We know this land and we are fighting for our homes. Be ready."

Trencavel left the room, followed by Bertrand de Saissac. The two men walked down the hall to Trencavel's chambers.

"I guess we won't fight today, after all," said Trencavel. "You might as well join me for something to eat."

Trencavel called for meats and cheese. A serving girl brought them the platters and filled their mugs with wine, deftly avoiding the hands of Bertrand as she served him. Bertrand watched the girl retreat from the room with something bordering almost on respect. Trencavel thought to himself that some things would never change. A pretty serving girl was never quite safe when Bertrand de Saissac was within reach.

"What I can't believe is that Pierre Bermond is out there," said Trencavel. "I never thought I would see the day when my closest boyhood friend would be part of an army outside my city walls, ready to lay siege to my castle."

"Now, you can't be too hard on Pierre," said Bertrand.

He took a long gulp of his wine and wiped his big hand across his mouth, burping in the process.

"You know better than anyone that Pierre Bermond had no choice," said Bertrand. "Once his liege-lord the Count of Toulouse joined the Crusaders, Pierre had to follow. It is his feudal obligation to fight on the side of his lord."

"I know, I know," said Trencavel. "I would expect the same of my vassals. Their place is to follow me into battle, wherever that may be. And Pierre had to follow my beloved uncle, the Count of Toulouse, whether he agreed with him or not."

"And you can be sure that he didn't," said Bertrand. "Actually, I don't think we have much to worry about from a military standpoint from your uncle or any of his vassals. I think they will be content to sit these battles out from the sidelines of their tents as they did in Béziers." Trencavel ripped off a piece of sausage with his teeth.

"My uncle. I can't believe him," said Trencavel. "The Crusaders came to fight him, not me! And he managed to foist them off with his ridiculous last-minute penance. All he had to do was march naked into that cathedral and kiss the ass of that pompous Abbot. And now he gets to sit back and watch as an army of 50,000 lays siege to my city! The bastard. I bet he thinks he'll take over my lands as soon as these Crusader knights fulfill their forty days and head back north. It's what he's wanted since I was a child."

Bertrand banged his wine mug on the table.

"Well, we are just going to have to make sure that your bastard uncle doesn't get what he wants."

Azalais

Saturday, August 1, 1209, late afternoon

"Betony must be plucked in the afternoon and mixed with oil. See the hairy leaves and purple flowers. It is similar to mint, but is used to cure melancholy, paralysis, and colds," Azalais said.

She bent slowly in the small herb garden in the courtyard of the house of women, her body creaking. At least her hands, Azalais thought, while gnarled, were strong. She gingerly plucked the leaves from the plant and handed them into the basket the girl was carrying.

"Constance, what is the house-leek good for?" Azalais asked.

"For curing jaundice and fevers of the liver," said Constance.

"And why is this so?" Azalais said.

"Because the flowers of the house-leek are yellow and like cures like. The yellow of the flowers will drive the yellow from the skin of the ill," answered Constance.

Azalais stood up stiffly and smiled at Constance.

"Good girl," she said. "We are about done here. We should get back to check on the sick."

Azalais handed Constance the house-leeks she had been picking and they walked through the garden into the house of women. Azalais thought of how peaceful the house had been over the last twenty years that she had been leading the group of good women who lived there. They earned their own way with their spinning. They had no need of charity and were saved from the interference that is often charity's sibling. The good women lived simply and chastely. They often cared for the sick that came looking for advice and medicinal herbs, but with the coming of the siege, Azalais knew that they must do more for the many sick and injured who would soon be coming to their doors. The quiet and simple home had been converted into a hospital. Already there were the injured, those hurt building the defenses and a few cases of fever brought in from the countryside. But most pitiful was an old man whose body was badly burned. He had been one of the few who had escaped from the charnel house that was Béziers. He moaned loudly and shrieked when even a chance breeze swept past his exposed flesh. Azalais had given him salves of the pastes of hops to soothe his burns, but she knew that he would die soon.

Azalais wondered at the hell these Christians imagined, for it could not be worse than the one they created in the name of God at Béziers. Women, children, and old men slaughtered. Even those who ran to protect themselves in the very cathedral blessed by Pope Innocent himself were cut down.

The pope calls himself innocent, thought Azalais, but has hands stained with the blood of Herod's slaughter of the babes. Surely, there is no need for theological debates, she thought, no greater proof for the belief in the evil nature of all earthly matter than the actions of those who called the good men and women heretics.

And now they were at the gates, those foul murderers. Azalais and the good women had watched the Crusaders arrive for a week now, pitching their tents on the banks of the River Aude, leading their pack horses and mules to the river to slake their thirst. Azalais tried to keep her women calm, to concentrate on the preparations for the siege, for surely there would be one and it would be long. The people of Carcassonne would not make the same foolish mistake made by the people of Béziers.

Azalais and Constance entered the house and began moving from bedside to bedside, adjusting dressings, and administering herbs.

Constance walked over to the bed of the young man whose head had been injured while working on the wall. He was a robust boy and handsome. Azalais trusted Constance, but she thought that she would have to watch this one closely, for Azalais remembered all too well the temptations of youth. Next to the injured boy stood a sallow-faced young man, with a tight expression. He must be the brother, thought Azalais.

"How are you feeling?" asked Constance.

The boy blushed.

"Better today, the pain is less, but I still get dizzy when I try to move," he said.

"That is normal, Guillaume," said Constance.

At Constance's familiar use of the boy's name, Azalais froze. She noticed that the boy's brother stiffened as well. Azalais quickly moved over to Guillaume's bed and began to unwrap the bandages from his head. She gingerly moved her fingers around his scalp, tracing the edges of a swollen bump near his right temple. The boy winced.

"Fortunately, the skull does not seem to be broken," said Azalais. "Have you cleaned the wounds?"

"Yes, as best possible," said Constance.

"Very well. Give him a preparation of stinging nettle seeds cooked in vinegar as an analgesic to relieve the pain. He does not need very much attention, just rest," said Azalais.

The brother looked relieved as Azalais led Constance away from the bed and to that of an old woman, sweaty and feverish.

"Good woman," said the old, sick woman in a whisper. "I am ready."

Azalais stopped and grabbed the hand of the woman. She looked at her slowly, taking in her pallid face and watery eyes and wiped the sweat from the sick woman's forehead.

"Are you sure?" Azalais asked.

"Yes. It is time. I am ready to receive the consolamentum," said the sick woman.

Constance looked with awe at the sick woman and took her hand, sitting by her side. The sick woman smiled gently at Constance and squeezed her hand, as if she were the one giving comfort.

The other good women gathered round the bed as Azalais stood facing the woman.

"Do you want to become a good Christian?" asked Azalais.

The sick woman nodded her head.

"Do you promise to give yourself to God and the apostles?" asked Azalais.

"Yes, I promise," the woman said.

"Do you promise to never again let meat, eggs, cheese, or any other product made from the act of procreation to pass your lips? Do you promise never to lie and never to swear? Do you promise to never give yourself over to sexual desires?" continued Azalais.

"I promise," the faint voice answered.

"Do you promise never to abandon the faith, even under fear of death?" asked Azalais.

"Yes, I promise," the woman answered, her voice clearer.

"Do you have sins to confess?" asked Azalais.

"I confess that I feared death and did not trust in the graciousness of God, but I am no more afraid," said the woman.

"Your sins are absolved," said Azalais.

The good women began to pray, and the sick woman joined in, her voice rasping with the effort: "Our Father, which art in heaven, Hallowed be thy name. Thy kingdom come. They will be done, as in heaven, so in earth. Give us day by day our daily bread. And forgive us our sins; for we also forgive every one that is indebted to us. And lead us not into temptation; but deliver us from evil."

After the prayer was finished, one of the good women handed Azalais a Bible. She placed it over the forehead of the sick woman and the good women all laid their hands on the book, supporting its weight. The Bible was opened to the gospel according to Saint John. Azalais began to read:

"In the beginning was the Word, and the Word was with God, and the Word was God. The same was in the beginning with God. All things were made by him; and without him was not any thing made that was made. In him was life; and the life was the light of men. And the light shineth in darkness; and the darkness comprehended it not. There was a man sent from God, whose name was John. The same came for a witness, to bear witness of the Light, that all men through him might believe. He was not that Light, but was sent to bear witness of that Light. That was the true Light, which lighteth every man that cometh into the world. He was in the world, and the world was made by him, and the world knew him not. He came unto his own, and his own received him not. But as many as received him, to them gave he power to become the sons of God, even to them that believe on his name; Which were born, not of blood, nor of the will of the flesh, nor of the will of man, but of God. And the Word was made flesh, and dwelt among us, (and we beheld his glory, the glory as of the only begotten of the Father) full of grace and truth."

One by one, the good women gave the kiss of peace to the sick woman, first on the book resting open on her forehead and then on each shoulder. Azalais removed the Bible from forehead of the woman and closed it in her hands.

Azalais stared at the face of the sick woman and it became relaxed, at peace. No one spoke for several minutes after the consolamentum was done. Azalais finally turned to Constance and spoke to her in a low voice. She knew the next few days were crucial.

"Stay with her Constance. It will not be long now. Make sure she sins not and she will finally be released from this cycle of misery on earth," I said. "Make sure it is as quick as possible. Do not let any sustenance pass her lips. She is almost free now. Let nothing stop her."

Constance nodded and began wiping the sweat from the forehead of the sick woman, who no longer seemed to notice anything material at all.

Azalais walked out of the room and down to her small office by the storerooms. Azalais thought about how she had come to trust more and more in Constance. For while she was headstrong and young, Constance already showed more wisdom and practical sense than all the rest of the good women combined.

Azalais looked out of the windows of her office and saw the soldiers arriving, a greater army than she had ever seen or even heard of in all her life. Azalais did not fear death for herself. In fact, she felt only anticipation for her release, for after all, she was old and had lived through much misery in this life and who knows how many others. Azalais was ready. But she could not stop thinking of all the others who did not know the truth - each generation trapped as the one before. Prisoners of weak flesh, vessels only for the reproduction of the misery that is life on earth. What would happen to all these souls, thought Azalais. She only knew that the Crusaders must not be allowed to defeat them.

Bernard

Saturday, August 1, 1209, late afternoon

"Boys, you're lazy. Get back to work. Do you think the Pope's ball-lickers outside our gates are sitting on their asses?" said the mason. "No, they're working. They're building their machines, their siege engines, their battering rams."

The mason stared at two apprentices who, overcome by the heat and the carrying of heavy stones, had collapsed with their backs to the wall.

"I don't think I need to remind our new friend Bernard here of what these Crusaders are capable of," said the mason.

The two youths flushed red and immediately jumped up. They

started lugging the heavy stone back to the section of the wall we were now working on.

I continued my work with the mason as we rebuilt the walls of the Castellar suburb. This man was truly a heretic, or even worse, for it seemed that he did not even follow the false precepts of that heresy. He was a man completely without faith, without God, and without hope. He must have pitied me, as he believed my family dead at Béziers. He was more patient with my clumsiness, with my questions than he was with the other men who worked with us.

And, I was learning. I was a youth who had spent my boyhood at the scriptorium and I could not keep up with the others for brute force, but I was clever and the mason saw that. After Guillaume's accident with the stone, the mason set me to work mixing the mortar that would be used between the large stones composing the inner wall.

"You have to keep knocking up the mortar or it will not be smooth and uniform. And whatever you do, don't add too much water. You'll ruin it," said the mason.

The work was difficult and the mason kept a close eye on me to begin with, but I slowly learned to judge just when to add a bit more water and when to beat the mortar that had been prepared from three parts sand and one part lime two days before by a master mortar maker. The mason did not leave me alone with this task and kept checking on me, but he was short of skilled workers and had to make do as best he could. There was so much to do to repair all the walls and reinforce the towers and most of the skilled mortar makers had been taken by the Viscount for his works in the city itself.

The sun was hot and my arms and hands, which God had designed for serving him through prayer and the copying of holy texts burned with pain. My fingers were blistered, but I wrapped them in cloth and hid them from the mason, for I knew that I was destined to be here. I knew in that instant that I could do more for our cause than just to report the gossip of the city streets to our Lord Abbot, tidbits of information that any fool could contribute. I would work hard and gain the mason's trust and there would come a moment when I could betray it, betray the very foundations of this city.

For I was growing fond of the mason. I admired his discipline and knowledge and his quest for perfection. I did not want him to burn forever in the eternal hellfire of damnation. I believed he could still be saved. For he was not a heretic, only ignorant of the truth. And how could he help his ignorance when he lived in this cesspool of wickedness? When the Father Abbot took control of this city and this region men like the mason would be instructed in the true Christian faith and they would cling to it, as all men must when they hear the beauty of the truth.

"Good work, Bernard," said the Master Mason. "The consistency of the mixture is very good. We may make a mortar maker out of you yet." He laughed, but it was with good humor.

Yes, I would save this man from the damnation he must surely suffer, but I knew my Father Abbot would not be weak with the heretics, like that girl who was even now trying to steal my brother's soul, as she feigned healing his body. Constance, her name was, or so Guillaume told me. Her name was fitting for I could see that she was constant in her deception, constant in her treachery, constant in her blasphemy, and constant in her heresy. A girl such as she should be married - either as a bride of Christ, as our holy sisters in the monastic life, or to a man who would give her many children and keep her life too busy for sin. I would be glad to see her burn, so that she could no longer drag souls down to hell with her, seducing them with her worldly charms into an eternity of damnation.

I considered again moving Guillaume before he succumbed to her temptations, but instead decided to continue my prayers and to trust in the Lord to protect him. For I was learning too much. I had witnessed their foul consecration ceremony already. I watched a soul damned for all eternity and while I wanted to scream out, to interrupt this foul transaction, smacking of the cloven hooves of Satan, I did nothing. For I knew that I could save many more souls by my silence than by any action at that moment. When I wrote to the Father Abbot tonight with my latest report, I would include a description of this wretched deed. For only by learning of their ways can we destroy them. I thought to myself that I might not survive this task given to me by my Holy Father Abbot but I remained peaceful, sure that the knowledge I gained by placing my brother's soul in jeopardy would not go to waste.

The mason walked over, inspected the mortar, and pronounced it ready. Immediately, the men came with their trowels to take the mortar and continue repairing the wall. I continued stirring, knowing my aching body would earn me a heavenly reward.

Gauda

Saturday, August 1, 1209, evening

I took the Viscountess' undergarments of linen from the red, cracked hands of the laundress. We stood in a basement room of the castle, steaming water rising around us. The smells of ashes and tartar floated in the heavy steam and stung my throat.

"Thank you," I said to the laundress. She was a heavy set woman of middle years with a face pink and sweaty.

"I don't suppose you will be doing much laundry soon," I said.

Her face broke into a small smile.

"I hope the siege is short and we are freed from these wicked invaders soon, but on my soul, I would not regret a few days rest from this toil. The water is only for drinking now. This is my last batch of laundry until the siege is lifted," she said. "Which I pray will be a very short time from now."

Her face grew serious.

"And I pray we are alive to tell of it at the end," she said.

"And, I, too," I said.

I, above all, wished this siege to be over sooner than anyone else in this castle.

I returned to Viscountess Agnes' chambers with her garments, entering in silence. I walked over to the chest by the foot of Agnes' bed and began folding her garments, placing each in the chest as I finished. Agnes looked up at me from where she sat in her bed, hands folded over her stomach.

"So you've heard the news about your little boyfriend?" Agnes said. "So sad."

I looked up sharply. I did not know who Agnes was talking about, but I felt a clench in my stomach and knew I must tread carefully.

"I am sorry, Viscountess, but I do not understand. What has

happened?"

"Your little juggler with the pretty eyes and the pocked face," said Agnes. "He's dead. Set upon by bandits; they found his body today." My eyes welled up with tears and I turned away from Agnes. Let her think he was my lover, the poor boy. I thought of his earnest face as he sang to me one of his songs, crafted so artlessly, but with such passion. He might have been very good one day, but he would have no time to hone his skills now. Then, the clench in stomach traveled deeper to become a chill in my bowels. What of my letter? And what kind of bandits operated outside the gates of fully fortified city surrounded by an army of tens of thousands?

"Where did they find him?" I asked. "Was everything stolen?"

"They found him by the river this morning, stripped naked and robbed of all his earthly goods," said Agnes. "He didn't make it very far, wherever he was going."

I moved from the bed and looked out of a small window overlooking the courtyard. The dull clanging of the blacksmiths in the yard continued as they fixed pieces of armor and shoed the horses. And, in the distance, I could hear the murmur of men's voices as they worked on the walls or towers late into the night. But the city seemed strangely quiet and expectant. For better or worse, we were all locked inside these walls now.

Everyone was waiting - waiting for the call of a lone watchman on a tower. Waiting for the first stone to fly across the city walls. Waiting to hear the thunder of horses' hooves on a charge. Waiting for a sign that it had begun.

DAY 2 OF THE SIEGE OF CARCASSONNE

Sunday, August 2, 1209

Trencavel

Sunday, August 2, 1209, dawn

At dawn, Trencavel rose and went to the ramparts. The Crusader camp was waking. The smoke from their campfires rose against the pink sky. Blacksmiths' hammers rang out on the steel of blades and breastplates, shields and helmets. Already the heat had begun to rise from the earth. Trencavel looked out on this army, greater than any he had ever seen. He turned and looked north to the Black Mountains, where he had spent so much of his youth with his guardian Bertrand de Saissac, after his father had died when he was only nine years old. He had learned to fight in those mountains, defending his father's lands and those of his vassals, but he had never faced a foe such as this.

Trencavel heard heavy footsteps behind him. He turned around.

"It's a good day to fight, no?" asked Bertrand de Saissac, as he joined Trencavel at the ramparts. He sniffed the air and threw back his head in a bellow.

"Cabaret's a pimple on the Pope's ass," said Bertrand. "You were right yesterday. We should have attacked these Northern fools last night while they were fucking their whores and drunk on their shitty wine."

"The men went with him. I could not attack without them," said Trencavel. "And maybe he was right after all."

Trencavel and Bertrand both looked at the endless sea of tents, stretching all the way from the river bank into the hazy distance. They could now see more small figures moving about, saddling horses and sharpening swords. Below them, a garrison of soldiers defended the wooden palisade protecting the path from the city to the river Aude. The suburb of St. Vincent, which sprawled on either side of the palisade, was unprotected by walls. It looked oddly quiet.

"All the citizens left St. Vincent during the night," said Trencavel. "They must be within the city walls now."

"They know they'll be the first target," said Bertrand. "Ah fuck, more mouths to feed, exactly what you don't need."

They stood quietly in the morning sun for a few minutes.

"Find your squire and get ready, Viscount," said Bertrand. "They are going to pay in blood today for their arrogance."

Bertrand and Trencavel went into the castle to prepare for battle.

After putting on his armor, Trencavel's squire brought him his warhorse. Trencavel rode it to the gates of the city wall and now sat on horseback, waiting inside the gates for the sign to come from the watchtower. Trencavel felt the heat of the sun beating down and the sweat trickling down his back. His body was encased in a chain mail shirt, his legs in chain boots and his hands in chain gloves. He wore a tunic of gold and his shield carried the Trencavel arms - yellow horizontal stripes alternated with black against white stripes. His sword felt heavy at his side. His horse stood steady beneath him, caparisoned in the Trencavel colors over armor. They had ridden into battle together many times and knew each other well.

Trencavel turned and looked at the four hundred men seated on horseback behind him. He saw the yellow sun against red on the shield of the Lord of Montreal and the red lion against white on that of the Lord of Termes. The Count of Foix's shield sported red and yellow vertical stripes. The men and horses were a blur of bright colors, stripes, stars, lions, crosses, and crescents. Trencavel turned to his right and was glad to see the white and red horizontal stripes of Bertrand de Saissac.

Bertrand took off his helmet and looked at Trencavel.

"Ready to surprise those bastards?" he said.

Trencavel put his helmet on over his chain mail hood. He looked at Cabaret, who nodded gravely at him. Suddenly, they heard the shout from the watch tower. The Crusaders had begun the attack. In an instant, all the bowmen on the towers let loose with their first volley of arrows. The first screams filled the air. They heard the pounding of hooves and the clanking of steel on steel.

Wait, thought Trencavel, wait. Let them cross the river and come up the slope. Let them think we will let the garrison at the palisade fend for themselves. Let them send more of their men over the river to fight.

The men on horseback inside the city walls were tense, expectant. All talking had ceased, all helmets were in place. Horses neighed and jostled against each other in the pack of men spilling up the city street from the gate.

Trencavel raised his sword. At the signal, men feverishly began cranking on pulleys to raise the city gate. The gate seemed to come up achingly slowly. Wait, thought Trencavel, again, wait. Finally, the gate was open.

Trencavel dropped his sword and spurred his horse forward at a charge. Four hundred men followed. They spilled down the hill, swords in hand. The foot soldiers attacking the garrison halted for a second as they watched the tidal wave of horse-mounted warriors descend on them. Then they fell, their bodies tumbling down the hill by the force of the assault. Heads fell in the dirt and rolled down to the banks of river. A horse shrieked as it lost its footing and fell down the bank, taking its rider with it.

The garrison, relieved, began to cheer. More foot soldiers came from the gates of the city to reinforce the garrison at the palisade.

Trencavel led the charge to the banks of the river and stopped. He looked around him. The bodies of the Crusaders lay scattered on the hillside and the banks of the Aude. In the Crusader camp, all was madness. Squires rushed to arm knights and saddle horses.

On their side of the river, all was eerily still, apart from the shrieks of the dying. The bowmen waited with their arrows in hand. The path to the river was secure and the garrison reinforced. Trencavel gave the sign to return to the castle. He turned to lead the men back up the hill and into the city gate when a thunderous noise filled his ears. He turned back to the river. On the other bank, Crusaders on horseback were charging the city. They roared across the plain, their horses fresh. Only the narrowness of the bridge kept them from a blanket assault. Trencavel led a charge to the bridge and began fighting the knights as they came across. Bertrand let out a roar and followed. They fought in close quarters, dropping many men, but still more came. Then, a rush of foot soldiers swarmed across the bridge and ran up the embankment to the palisade. Men on both sides dropped from the arrows of the archers high up on the city wall. The garrison fought to defend the palisade, which was now burning. The deserted houses in the suburb of St. Vincent also began to burn. The men who had been hiding in them for refuge, emerged on fire, and ran shrieking into the river Aude. Horses caught sparks in their tails and ran off with their riders.

Trencavel looked up and saw another line of knights forming on the other side of the bridge. All was lost. He screamed to his men to run for the city gates and turned to ride up the hill. The other knights followed. Trencavel made it to the gates of the city and watched as his surviving men rode back in. The wounded lay whimpering and howling in the streets just inside the gate. The palisade was lost and the few men left in the garrison tried to run up the hill to the safety of the city. Right behind them rode the latest wave of Crusader knights. Trencavel ordered the gates closed. He looked into the eyes of the men as they saw their exit cut off and forced himself to watch from the tower as they were cut down by the Crusaders.

Trencavel looked down at the smoking ruins of the suburb and palisade, littered with the dead and dying, and knew fear.

Constance

Sunday, August 2, 1209, midday

"You are not well enough to get out of bed," said Constance. She tried to hold Guillaume back, but she was no match for his strength.

"There are not enough beds, and worse wounded than I," said Guillaume. "I want to help."

"I don't think you're going to be much help with your head still wrapped in bandages, but I don't have time to argue with you," she said. "Just stay out of our way."

Constance angrily wiped her hands on her skirt and turned to the patient who had already been placed in Guillaume's still warm cot. He was a foot soldier. His leather tunic had protected his torso from a Crusader's sword, but not his arm. The cut was deep and had severed the sinews of his shoulder. His arm hang at an unlikely angle from, Constance was sure, a broken collarbone. He bled. Constance called to a young girl.

"Bring me cloths," she yelled over the noise of soldiers clanking armor and screaming men.

The girl quickly brought a clean batch. Constance wrapped the wound closed tightly.

"Hold this here with a lot of pressure," said Constance to the girl. "We have to stop the bleeding. I will be right back."

Constance went to Azalais' drying room. Herbs and plants hung upside down from every part of the ceiling. The heady scent of so many mingled herbs in the hot afternoon sun gave the room a fecund smell. The walls were covered with shelves, each filled with glass bottles, stopped with corks. Constance thought quickly. Dried yarrow flowers would help stop the bleeding. She looked along the upper shelf and took a bottle down. She opened it to smell - yes, aniseed, but tannic. Yarrow. And balm. She took down another glass bottle. The dried leaves still smelled slightly of lemons. And blackberry leaves. Constance took the leaves to a large stone table in the center of the room and began crushing them. She brushed the broken leaves into ceramic cup and hurried back to the foot solder.

The young girl's face was red with exertion as blood continued to seep through the bandages. The soldier's face was becoming very pale and he kept whispering that he was cold. Constance stood next to the girl.

"Get me more bandages," she said.

Constance dressed the wound with the herbs, packing them into the bloody slit. The girl returned with more bandages. Constance began wrapping the wound, very tightly, using strip after strip. She finished and placed her hands on the soldier's arms and waited for a minute. No blood seeped through the bandages. She turned to the girl.

"See how I am holding his arm?" Constance asked. "You have to do it with a lot of pressure. It will be tiring, but it is the only way to keep him from dying. Do you understand?"

The girl nodded and Constance allowed her to take over holding the injured arm. She watched for another minute, but no more blood seeped through. Constance grabbed a blanket from a shelf behind the bed and wrapped the soldier tightly. She touched his forehead. He was sweaty and cold, but not too cold.

"Call for me if anything changes," Constance said.

Constance stood up and looked around the room. Azalais and the other women who knew how to heal were working feverishly to deal with the wounded. They had run out of cots and now dying soldiers were being placed on the floor. Constance saw Guillaume supporting a badly limping sergeant. There was nowhere to place him, so Guillaume led him to the foot of the stairs.

Constance saw Azalais look up at her and grimace. They were not prepared for this. The women had set up the hospital for civilian injuries and for the fevers that would inevitably come with a long siege. Constance walked over to Azalais and pulled her to one side.

"We are not army surgeons, Azalais," said Constance. "I have never removed a crossbow bolt from a man's chest or remedied a dislocated shoulder. I do not even have the strength for it. Why are they coming here?"

"The castle doctors are turning men away. The wounded are piling up two or three thick on the floor. They have no choice but to come here. You are going to have to do the best you can," said Azalais. "Stop wasting my time and get to work."

Azalais walked away to look at a man whose skull was bloody and crushed on one side. He softly moaned. Constance stopped and did not know who to turn to next. There were so many wounded, screaming and moaning on every side, their hands pawing the air and asking for mercy. She looked to one side and then the next. Suddenly, Guillaume stood in front of her.

"There are Jews at the door," Guillaume said. "They want to come in."

"Not more wounded!" said Constance.

"No, they say they are surgeons."

Constance looked up and saw ten black-coated men with long beards in the door. She ran over, cleaning her blood-soaked hands on her skirt.

"You are surgeons?" said Constance.

The men nodded.

"Please, please, come in," said Constance.

The oldest man turned and spoke to the others. The surgeons began moving to the patients lying on the cots and on the floor. The oldest surgeon joined Azalais at the side of the sergeant with the bashed head.

Constance turned back to survey the room and breathed. There was hope. She turned to a pale, blond soldier lying on the floor near her feet. He garbled in a guttural tongue. Probably a mercenary from somewhere north. Many still fought for the Viscount Trencavel. His hands were clasped around a crossbow bolt that had pierced his chest. His breathing was labored, but there was no bloody foam on his lips. He might still live. Constance looked around for a doctor and found one right behind her. He was young and strong, with a long black beard and a full head of hair under his circular hat.

"Can you get some tincture of poppies?" he asked. "And a piece of wood, as thick as two fingers, made into a wedge."

Constance ran to the drying room, which was in total disarray. The neat rows of glass bottles were a mess. Several lay broken on the floor. The cutting table was littered with herbs. She found the opium and poured a large swallow into a glass. She ran back and eased it down the throat of the soldier.

Where would she get the wood? Constance looked around and then saw a wedge used to keep the door of the drying room open. She picked it up and brought it back to the surgeon. He took it from her.

"Hold this man steady," he said.

Constance braced the man's head between her legs and held his arms down with her hands. The wounded man's head had begun to loll a bit with the effects of the opium. Constance called for Guillaume and he came over and sat on the soldier's legs.

The surgeon used his knife to cut away the soldier's tunic. The crossbow bolt was embedded in his ribs, sticking out almost straight. The surgeon began to cut away from where the bolt had entered the skin, making a slit above and below the entry point. The man moaned in Constance's hands.

Then the surgeon used his fingers to hold open the flaps of skin. He tried to remove the bolt, but it would not budge. It was trapped between two ribs. Constance could see the white of the bone between the spurts of blood. The surgeon took the wedge of wood and began to insert it between the two ribs, just below the entry point of the bolt. He used a hammer on the wedge to force the ribs open. The soldier began to buck violently, but Guillaume held him down and Constance squeezed his arms.

The surgeon then gently pulled the bolt from the soldier's chest. Two inches, then three. It was finally free.

"He is fortunate. It did not pierce his lungs," said the doctor to Constance. "Dress and suture this wound. You know how, I am sure?"

Constance nodded and went to get more herbs to staunch the bleeding. She added rosemary and St. Johns' Wort this time as well, for the wound was very deep. Constance took her needle and catgut from her pocket and roughly sewed the wound closed.

"Not much of a seamstress," said Guillaume. "Are you?"

Constance smiled at him.

"Good enough for him, I'm sure," she said.

Constance packed the wound with the herbs and then dressed it with fresh bandages. She gave the soldier more tincture of poppies and he began to sleep fretfully.

The wounded had stopped arriving, but still many waited for help. It would be a long day.

Gauda

Sunday, August 2, 1209, evening

"Viscountess, do you really think it is wise to linger?" I asked.

Agnes turned in her bath and looked at me through the steam. I could feel sweat trickling down the sides of my face and down my back.

"Do you really think it wise to ask me that?" Agnes said.

I picked up the brush and began massaging her shoulders. The door of the chamber opened and two sweating maids pushed through, carrying empty buckets. One maid came up to the tub, her face lowered.

"Well, what is it girl? Have you been rendered mute as well as ignorant?" said Agnes.

The maid slowly looked up.

"I am sorry, my lady, but we can get no more water. It is absolutely forbidden."

Agnes turned toward the maids.

"You silly little fools. Imagine the insolence of the servants - to forbid me water!" Agnes said. "Get out here."

The maids quickly left the room. Agnes turned to me.

"I should have sent you, Gauda," Agnes said, her voice getting louder. "They would not dare to do this to my face and not to yours either. I cannot be expected to live under these conditions. The Viscount would never allow me to be treated like this."

Agnes suddenly stopped speaking. I turned to stare at the door, which had crashed open. Trencavel stood there, his hair sweaty and disheveled, blood stains on his face and arms. His tunic was torn.

"What are you doing, woman?" Trencavel bellowed.

He crossed the room in a few steps and grabbed Agnes by the shoulders. She screamed as he lifted her out of the tub, her legs banging against the wooden rim.

"Are you mad? Do you know what happened today?" Trencavel said as he shook Agnes by her shoulders, her long hair whipping against her naked back and her feet skimming the floor. "The river is gone! There is no more water from the river!"

Agnes kept crying and trying to push him away. Trencavel only shook her more.

"No more water! No more baths! If I have to tell you again woman, you will pay for it," said Trencavel.

Trencavel stepped away and Agnes collapsed on the floor, whimpering. I quickly ran to get her towel and tried to cover her. Trencavel walked to the door and slammed it shut. He sat down on a chair and put his face in his hands. He sighed and looked up at Agnes.

"What I don't understand, good woman," said Trencavel, "is why you care. You have received the consolamentum. You are free of this material world of pain and suffering. Yet you concern yourself with your bath and your toilet as if you were some jogleresa or whore. Should you not be beyond these things?"

"I am not a man of spiritual things, but I have tried to protect the good men and women in my lands," said Trencavel. "Even now, there is an army of 50,000 besieging this city because of you and your kind. There is not going to be enough water soon for the sick and dying. Can you at least pretend to live as if you cared more for things of the spirit than the flesh until this siege ends?"

Agnes looked at him, but did not say a word. Trencavel swore and left the room. I picked up a towel and slowly began drying Agnes' long hair, as tears streamed silently down her cheeks.

Bernard

Sunday, August 2, 1209, night

I wondered if these heathens fornicate more at night. Of course, they had no shame, so why would they bother to use the night to hide their lascivious groping? Paul said that if you must sin, marry. But these foul dogs held that marriage was no worse nor better than fornication. Adultery was no sin to them. They rutted like animals, at any time, with any mate. I heard them all night long in the boarding house. I prayed fervently, trying to block out the evidence of their sin. Oh, I how longed for the quiet and purity of the monastery. My father Abbot surely knew how I suffered to do this work for him. That thought kept me strong.

But, oh, how jubilant I was today, watching as the righteous triumphed and the wicked perished. I saw the might of our warriors as they slew the heretics. I watched the river turn to red, as St. John, in his most Divine Revelations, saw the third part of the sea become blood. I rejoiced to know that our victory would come soon and sure, as the heretics were now cut off from the river. But, Satan's power was still strong in this cursed city and all was not yet decided. I still had my role to play to further the most holy and blessed causes of my Father Abbot and the most Holy Catholic Church.

The night was dark, and though there was a moon, it was covered by clouds. The Lord smiled upon my enterprise and hid me from the evil prying eyes of the heretics. Still, I was cautious. I did not want to think what would happen if I were to be found about by one of the guards. Up to this point, there had always been someone to meet me in the busy marketplace. Sometimes a burly knife grinder, sometimes an old woman who sold lavender. I would pass my message to the woman or man and they would slip me a note explaining when and where I was to meet my next messenger.

But this time was different. I crept quietly along the streets, hoping not to encounter a night watchman. The city was under curfew, but various of these fornicators and heretics were scattered about the streets. I believed I could convince a stupid watchman of my need to be about at this hour, if I were stopped. Still, I was uneasy. I made my way through the city towards the eastern wall. This section of the wall was relatively quiet, almost deserted. Most of the Crusader Army was arrayed west of the city, by the river Aude. Most of the soldiers and guards were posted along the western wall or defending the suburbs. The deserted eastern wall seemed the perfect location to pass the message, but I was not sure. I kept to the narrow back streets and finally saw the section of the wall where I was to meet my messenger. It was a quiet section between the tower of Saint- Laurent and the tower of Davejean. Here the city wall was covered by the houses of the poor, wretched dwellings leaning against the thick wall.

I waited in shadow, trying to locate the tavern I was supposed to enter. The houses all seemed identical, shabby and crumbling. There was no sign to indicate which was the tavern. Finally, I saw a drunk stumble out of a low door in a building that seemed to be cobbled together from several. The first floor was sunken under a protruding second floor. Part of the second floor seemed to be spliced by a third floor that seemed to belong to an adjoining building. I imagined that some of the rooms on the second floor would be fit only for a dwarf. As I watched, a woman opened one of these windows and threw the contents of a chamber pot into the street below, nearly hitting the drunk who had not stumbled very far before collapsing on the street in front of the tavern. She was dressed vulgarly and I did not have to work to guess her profession. She spat into the street and then closed the window. I thought not of her, for she that liveth in pleasure is dead while she liveth.

I prayed to ask the Lord for strength before entering such a den of iniquity. I did not fear for my heavenly soul, for I knew I was strong in the faith and the temptations of the flesh did not lure me. But, I feared for my earthly body in such rough company as this. After my prayer, assured that the Lord would protect his righteous servant, I checked for a night watchman and, finding none, darted across the street and into the low door.

I stumbled and almost fell down some stairs leading into the tavern. I grabbed the low ceiling with my hand in time to steady myself and looked around. The room was lit by torches placed in the walls, which filled the room with a smoky haze. There were no windows on any side and I realized that we must be under ground and right against the city walls. The patrons were a motley collection of thieves, beggars, whores, and base laborers - dung carriers and grave diggers for the most part, to judge by the sight and stench of their clothes. They had mostly stopped speaking and had turned to stare at me and I decided that I should do something before they decided to practice their trades on me.

I pulled my cloak tight against my chest and walked over to the bar. The barkeep was a woman who had most likely sold her body for whatever low price she could command for many years, until even the lowliest beggar would no longer squander his pittance for her favors. She was a hag, her teeth gone and her skin pocked and wrinkled, her body bony and sharp through the tattered dress she wore, one cut for a whore that mocked her wretched state of undesirability.

"We don't want any trouble with the guards," she said, as she poured a jug of cheap wine from a keg. The smell of vinegar and piss permeated the air.

"There won't be any trouble with me," I said. "I seek a man who deals with the importing of goods."

She looked up at me with an odd glance and turned her head in the direction of a burly man seated at the end of the bar.

"It's him you will be wanting then," she said. "Go on, he's been waiting for someone all night."

I made my way down the bar, stepping gingerly in the filthy reeds put down probably centuries ago. I heard a rustling and hoped I did not step on any of the vermin crawling through the filth at my feet. As I approached, the burly man watched me, as I watched him. He was of middle age, very strong through the arms and shoulders, with some strings of greasy hair hanging from a balding head. A scar almost neatly bisected his face in two.

"So, it's you I've been waiting for," he said. "Don't keep me waiting next time."

I could not believe this peon, this brigand, would have the audacity to speak to someone of my standing in this way. Truly, these heretics had dismantled the whole right order of society. For if one dared to blasphemy God and his most Holy representatives here on Earth, there would be no fear left anywhere and all righteous behavior would cease. Those dreadful heretics of Béziers knew this well, for they broke the teeth of their bishop and feared no reprisal. Though now they must all be fearing the righteous power of the Lord almighty and regretting their ways as they burned in hellfire for all eternity.

"I thought it wiser to err on the side of caution, rather than haste," I said.

The burly man grunted.

"Come with me. We can discuss your needs more easily in one of the back rooms," he said.

I loathed the thought of following this man into this house where Satan was given free rein to work his evil, but I knew that my mission was of vital importance and that God would allow no one to injure me or impair its success. He got up from his stool and I followed him to the back of the room. He grabbed a torch off the wall and we entered a narrow passageway that curved to the right, yet went steadily down. I was sure that we must be in the bowels of the city wall itself. Still we descended. The air was hot and clammy, and I began to find it difficult to breathe. Finally, we stopped in a small room that projected off the narrow corridor. It was a storeroom, filled with kegs and bolts of cloth, probably contraband brought into the city by a smugglers' route to avoid the viscount's taxes. The burly man turned to me.

"Give the message to me," he said. He held out a gruff, thick hand.

All of sudden I felt chill and knew that I should not trust this man, but what could I do? I had to deliver my message - I knew all the places in the walls of the Castellar suburb where the mason worked furiously to try to repair them before the advance of the Crusaders. This knowledge would be invaluable to the Crusaders and would make my Father Abbot even more respected and powerful. I had to trust that the Lord Jesus Christ would use even this inferior vessel, untrustworthy and blasphemous, to further our cause. I handed over my message, sealed hastily in the narrow room I shared with three other men in the boarding house. The burly man felt the seal and, for a moment, I feared he would break it, but he did not. He placed the letter in his pocket and turned to me.

"Do you know what the viscount does to spies and traitors?" he asked, his ugly mouth curling into a smile severed in two by his deep scar. "He puts the screws on them until they confess all and denounce those who aided them. Then they are drawn and quartered while still alive. Finally, their bodies are tossed to the dogs in the dump."

"I am aware of the risks I run," I said. "I do not need a lecture from the likes of you."

Before I could blink, my body was raised against the wall, the burly man's hand against my throat. My feet dangling beneath me, but my feeble kicks did not even seem to be noticed by the beast.

"Yes, but what about the risks I run?" he said. "You don't seem the type to withstand much in the way of torture. I could care less what happens to your pathetic, conniving soul, but I have myself to watch out for. I run a dangerous business and I need to be compensated. Do you understand?"

I grunted a yes and he let me down to my feet. I slowly massaged my neck and began to breathe normally again.

"What do you want?" I asked.

"Open your letter here and add the following," he said. "I am to be paid triple by your master tomorrow night and in gold. If I don't receive this amount, I will denounce you to the Viscount and take my reward."

I shakily opened the letter and added his demand. I refolded the letter and he poured some candle wax onto the back. I pulled my seal ring out of my innermost pocket and sealed the letter. He took it and placed it again in his pocket.

"You had better hope your master feels generous, my friend," he laughed.

I did not bother to respond to him. He handed me the torch.

"Go back to the tavern, have a few drinks, and try to pretend you're interested in the whores, you faggot," he said. "I look forward to seeing you tomorrow night. Hopefully, this business will be advantageous to both of us."

As I climbed the narrow corridor up to the relative light and air of the tavern, I thought with glee of when my Father Abbot would be master of this city. This city would be swept clean and made a New Jerusalem. These men who were lovers of their own selves, covetous, boasters, proud, blasphemers, unholy, fierce, despisers of those that are good, heady lovers of pleasure more than lovers of God would all be banished. The heretics would burn and the unrighteous would perish. We would create a heaven on earth.

DAY 3 OF THE SIEGE OF CARCASSONNE

Monday, August 3, 1209

Gauda

Monday, August 3, 1209, dawn

I rose very early on the morning after we lost the river. I knew we were doomed to lose this siege and I hoped only that the surrender came quickly before we started dying of thirst and disease. The Crusaders were too numerous, too powerful. For surely, if Trencavel quickly surrendered, they would not slaughter us all as they did the people at Béziers. Surely this time calmer, wiser men would restrain the blood lust. Surely, it would be so.

For strangely, despite my worries, I felt lighter and more at ease than I had in all the time I had been here with Agnes. For once, I did not have to sneak around trying to find out about things about which I really ought to have no interest. I did not have to worry that my letters to the troubadour at the Count of Toulouse's court would be intercepted and that someone would read beyond my pretty words to find the treacherous meanings lying beneath. For during the siege, I could not get my letters out. The city was shut off and so I was free of my obligations.

This also relieved me. For while I did not mind acting the spy during normal times on my dreadful cousin and her husband, who fancied me his plaything and whore, I had begun to feel very uncomfortable in my mind about my role. I did not care whether the Count of Toulouse or the Viscount Trencavel triumphed in their games of power and diplomacy. They were as the same to me, rulers who were more or less fair as long as their wealth and influence increased, and I cared only who could further my plans. But these Crusaders who had come from foreign lands to murder us and force their despotic religion down our throats were another thing entirely. I could not sleep if I thought I were to contribute to their gains. I only knew that my master, the Count of Toulouse, was with them now because he had no choice. His allegiance was false and he would stay at their side only as long as the massive army headed by monks remained in these lands. The Count of Toulouse did not want this city destroyed. On the contrary, he wanted it alive and vibrant, so that he could steal it from his nephew. This I could live with. Yet, I feared that the Count of Toulouse was playing with forces more powerful and shrewd than he had ever before encountered. I hoped, for the sake of this city and for my fortunes, that he could prevail.

After cleaning my face and combing my hair, I entered Agnes' chamber quietly, not wanting to wake her. She was all alone. Her back was to me and she made small sneaky movements with her hands. I wondered what she could possibly be doing.

I continued to walk quietly, my slippers finding the worn places in the rugs that would make no noise. Agnes must have sensed my presence anyway because she suddenly turned and gave me a guilty look. I stared. In her greasy hands, she held a bone that was gnawed until the marrow had been sucked out of it. Agnes' lips had a sheen to them. I stared at her in shock.

"Meat?" I said.

Agnes quickly dropped the bone to the floor, where it was snatched by a small dog. He wagged his tail and ran off to a corner to devour his treat. Agnes looked at me haughtily.

"I was giving a bone to my dog," she said.

"And that's why there's fat on your lips and marrow on your chin?" I said. "I am not a fool, Agnes. You were eating meat. What I cannot understand is why."

"Lower your voice," Agnes whispered. She tried to clean her hands on her skirt, but only succeeded in staining it. Her hands were still greasy and she looked around, finally grabbing some fresh straw from the floor and trying to remove the fat.

I did not lead a particularly exemplary life myself, but I followed the beliefs of the good men and good women. My childhood teacher Azalais had left her life as a troubairitz many years ago to take the consolamentum and become a good woman herself. She now headed a house of good women here in Carcassonne and I tried to visit her as often as I could. I knew that I would make a good end eventually but also knew that I did not have the purity of spirit to become a good woman before I was close to my death. However, I knew enough to know that Agnes had broken a vow that was absolute: the good men and women were never to allow the flesh of animal to pass their lips. I had often wondered at her behavior. Her nastiness was so different from the kindness I associated with the good women I knew such as Azalais. But this was different. This was the breaking of a vow that would render Agnes no more a good woman. I had to say something.

"Agnes, you are a good woman. You have received the consolamentum. What are you doing?" I said.

"Don't tell anyone, please," Agnes said. "I risk only damnation for myself. I have never given the consolamentum to anyone."

"Why do you persist in this if you are not able to keep your vows? Why are you playing at being a good woman?" I said.

Agnes drew herself up and pointed her finger at my chest.

"You have no right to ask me my reasons. How dare you," she said. "I command you to remain silent."

Agnes stared at me, but I stared back.

"I will remain silent, but do not think that my silence will be free," I said. "You will pay for it, every day. And if you are tempted to punish me, remember that I can talk to the Viscount and tell him everything. I do not know why you want this charade to continue, but it will end. The Viscount will be irate that you have kept from him another heir by your false vow of chastity. You will be the one who is punished."

Agnes' face turned red and she lifted her hand to strike my cheek, but she did not let the blow fall. She slowly moved her hand back to her side and sat down.

"Very well," she said. "If that is the way it is to be, then it will be so. You will pay, though, for your ungrateful behavior. I regret the day I took you in, penniless and homeless. I thought I was performing an act of Christian charity, but I see now that I let the snake into the Garden of Eden."

"Go now and see if you can find some water for me to at least wash my face," said Agnes. "I have been forbidden baths, but I will not abandon my toilet entirely."

"Yes, Viscountess," I said.

I went to get her water, but I did not hurry. I had feeling that my life as Agnes' lady-in- waiting was about to dramatically improve.

Bernard

Monday, August 3, 1209, morning

I was dreaming a wonderful dream. I was back in the abbey with our Father Abbot celebrating mass. The candle light illuminated the faces of the chanting monks and the smell of incense permeated the air. I could hear the beautiful tones of my favorite hymn, Veni Sancte Spiritus, written by our most Holy Father Pope Innocent. How I longed for the moment when I felt the Holy Spirit come to me, when I tangibly felt the spirit enter me, the deep, chanting voices of the other monks bringing me the greatest peace I have ever known.

I woke suddenly to the shouting of the other three men in the room. They were rough men, uncouth and amoral drunks, and I loathed sharing this small room in the boarding house with them. But, I had no choice, as the city filled with refugees, the tavern keeper planned to pack as many into his rooms as possible for the duration of the siege. There was money to be made.

I quickly left the tavern and joined the crowds rushing about in the city. The northern suburb, the Bourg, was under attack by our most Holy Crusaders. I could hear the pounding of the horses' hooves as they swept up the hill and the battle cries of the men, but, wonder of wonders, I could also hear the Veni Sancte Spiritus. I had not dreamed that sound. The rumble of the bass voices of thousands of monks reverberated across the valley. Oh, how I had to discipline myself not to open my mouth and join them! One could not escape the beautiful sound of the chanting. I watched in joy as I saw the terror on the faces of the heretic citizens of this town. They knew that God was on the side of the Crusaders. They knew they would lose and they knew that they would burn in hell for all eternity if they did not right the errors of their ways. They knew they would receive the reward of the unrighteous.

I longed to watch the glorious assault, but I could not raise my hand against our most Holy Crusaders and I knew that, if I went to the walls, I would be pressed into action. I felt blessed just to hear the chanting of my brother monks, and to know that we would be victorious and that I had done my earthly part to further our heavenly agenda.

There were other ways in which I must serve the Lord and, even if I were not to be part of the Glory of this day.

Trencavel

Monday, August 3, 1209, morning

Trencavel's body still ached from the battle yesterday when he heard the chanting early in the morning. He quickly dressed and had his squire put on his armor. Now he stood on the Tower of the Marquiere on the City walls, overlooking the Bourg and its walls, currently under attack by the Crusader knights. Cabaret and Bertrand de Saissac stood by his side.

"So we are not the only ones who thought of a surprise attack," said Cabaret.

"Wasn't much of a surprise with the racket all those sodomizing monks were making," said Bertrand.

"It was enough of a surprise," said Trencavel.

They watched as the Crusaders dragged ladders up the hill and placed them in the trenches around the Bourg's walls. On some ladders two knights, on others three, would climb up to level of the top of the wall. Arrows rained down from the defenders on the walls, but many only glanced off their armor. More effective were the stones that the women dropped from the walls, splitting open helmets and crushing skulls. Other defenders used long wooden forks to push the ladders from the walls, always waiting until the Crusaders were almost to the top, so their fall would be hardest. The dull thud that an armored body made when falling from 20 feet punctuated the constant drone of screams, swords clashing, and splintering ladders. And always, underneath it all, the infernal chanting of the monks. Trencavel could see them by the river, hundreds of monks, abbots, and bishops, their black robes fluttering in the hot, dry winds.

The bodies of Crusaders, mostly the less well-armored sergeants and foot-soldiers, kept piling up in the trenches around the city wall, but still they kept coming. For every knight the defenders threw off the walls, two more arrived in his place. Trencavel spoke to a sergeant at his side and ordered more defenders off the city walls into the Bourg.

"And when you have moved all the city wall defenders into the Bourg? What will you do then?" said Bertrand. "They will just keep coming. The only way to defeat these kinds of numbers is with bold strikes. Let's attack now. They are weakened by the strong resistance of the Bourg. We can drive them off."

"And perhaps our attack will be as successful as yesterday's sortie?" said Trencavel.

Bertrand did not reply.

They watched as more defenders streamed into the Bourg, coming to the aid of the exhausted archers and soldiers. More of the defenders were falling as the Crusaders continued to breach the walls and used their swords to fell the defenders. A few Crusaders had made it into the Bourg itself and were advancing under the protection of houses towards the open gate to the city itself.

"I am going to stop them," said Bertrand. "I cannot sit and watch any longer like an old woman. I'll show those fornicators of their mothers what a real knight can do."

Bertrand yelled for his sergeant and knights as he ran down the steps of the tower.

Trencavel and Cabaret watched as Bertrand led his men out of the city gates. The Crusaders were now much closer to the city gates. They were ten men, strong and well- armed, and were cutting down the Bourg citizens quickly. All of sudden, they saw Bertrand leading his men, one large hand holding a shield with red and white stripes, the other wielding a heavy sword. His mane of hair streamed from his helmet and he shrieked like a mad man. His chosen men, all mad as him, shrieked behind him. For a second, they drowned out the chanting of the monks. Bertrand dropped his shield and launched himself at the leader, grasping his sword in two hands and plunging it directly into the chest of the knight, puncturing his chain mail and leaving the man to die. Bertrand bellowed again and his men returned the call. The other knights turned and ran back to the walls, but were cut down by Bertrand's men or by crossbow bolts from the archers on the walls.

The tide seemed to be turning. Bertrand's attack energized the defenders who fought back with renewed force. More Crusaders dropped to the trenches, screaming in agony. The defenders dropped more stones, trapping the wounded and disabling the fit.

All of sudden, Trencavel and Cabaret watched as a large group of horse-mounted knights galloped towards the Bourg sweeping past the main area of the battle and attacking the sparsely defended eastern walls of the Bourg. The defenders did not notice the fresh attack. They were still gleefully defending the western wall, sure that they were winning. These attackers did not bother with ladders, but climbed up over the walls quickly with ropes. The few defenders left on the eastern wall tried to cut the ropes, but they were quickly overwhelmed. Still, the defenders on the western wall did not see the attack.

"You can spare no more defenders from the city," said Cabaret.

"No," said Trencavel. "If they cannot defend the Bourg with the soldiers there now, it is lost."

Finally, the defenders on the western wall noticed the breach on the east, but it was too late. Many rushed to the eastern wall, but this just allowed the Crusaders on the western wall to sweep over unimpeded. A few of the houses in the Bourg were now on fire, and their occupants streamed out screaming. They started to make their way to the city gates, but many were cut down by Crusaders who now marched freely on the streets of the Bourg. The citizens of the Bourg who had not fled to the City yet, now did so. They knew all was lost. The unholy shrieking of the wind and the unholy chants of the monks continued, almost drowning out the sounds of the dying and the fighting.

Bertrand and his men continued to fight, but they now defended the gates to the City of Carcassonne, trying to keep them open as the citizens and soldiers tried to retreat to the safety of the City. The Crusader knights were followed by archers and foot-soldiers, who walked through the Bourg, securing the streets and killing off the dying in the streets, stripping their arms and shields for themselves. A section of the Bourg wall fell under battering rams and sappers' shovels and cheering broke out in the Crusader forces as they streamed through the opening. The monks began to sign even more loudly.

"You are going to have to order the gates closed," said Cabaret.

"I cannot leave Bertrand outside," said Trencavel.

"You have no choice," said Cabaret. "He is a shrewd fighter, he will know when to retreat."

Trencavel ordered the City gates lowered and watched as Bertrand and his men kept fighting. The defenders saw the gates going down and dropped their swords and shields, running for the safety of the city. Finally, when it seemed that the gate could go almost no lower, Bertrand and his men rolled under the gate to safety.

Trencavel breathed. They watched as the Crusaders brought in men to destroy the Bourg walls and used the rubble to fill in the trenches. The Crusaders put out the fires in the suburb and left the houses intact to use as protection as they approached the City walls. The screams of the citizens left behind in the suburb echoed as the Crusaders cut down everyone left in their path.

"So the Bourg too is lost," said Trencavel. "Bertrand was right. We should have attacked earlier."

"Then, we would have ended as did those in Béziers," said Cabaret. "There are simply too many of them. Our best approach is to wait them out. They will grow hungry. They cannot feed so many for so long."

"And, if we run out of water before they run out of food?" said Trencavel. "The fools in Béziers perished because they were not soldiers; they were boys rushing out to play in a game. We must attack and weaken them, or else we sit here passively and die."

"You are young, Trencavel," said Cabaret. "There is sometimes great honor in waiting."

Azalais

Monday, August 3, 1209, midday

The wounded from the defeat of the Bourg began to arrive. The good women were already running out of beds, medicines, and herbs, for many of the wounded from yesterday's battle were still feverish and weak. And today's wounded were not soldiers - they were woman, children, and old men. They had had no battle protection, no armor, and their wounds were vicious and deep. There was no choice. Azalais directed the good women to pile the injured on the floors and even in the courtyard.

Azalais looked around. The Jewish doctors had come back when she had sent for them. They were refugees from Béziers, but had avoided that carnal house. The Viscount Trencavel knew what happened to Jews during Crusades and had taken them with him back to Carcassonne when he left Béziers before the siege. Trencavel thought Béziers could hold out for weeks and that he would have time to come back with reinforcements to lift the siege. No one thought it would end like that - so quickly. In one day, 20,000 dead, the whole city destroyed and on fire with almost no survivors. What Trencavel thought would have been the fate of the Jews became the fate of all the citizens of Béziers.

Azalais walked over to the herb room. A small child sat next to his mother, sobbing and shaking. He appeared to be unhurt, but his mother was obviously dead. She had bled from a head wound and the boy was covered in her blood. Azalais reached down to pick him up, but he started shrieking uncontrollably and attached himself to his mother's skirts with an iron grip. Azalais could do nothing for him now. She picked up the medicines she had come for and left him.

When Azalais came out of the herb room, she saw Constance working on an injured woman. Helping her was the refugee boy who had come to the good women with a head injury. Guillaume, Azalais thought he was called. As she watched, Azalais saw an easy intimacy between the two that she did not like at all. Their heads were bent close together over the woman. Guillaume held the bucking woman, while Constance stitched her face, which was opened by an ugly wound that stretched from her brow to chin.

Constance finished and the woman began to calm down. Guillaume looked up at Constance with a beautiful smile, his right cheek showing a deep dimple that only served to make him more attractive. Azalais could not see Constance's face, but she was sure that her look was not one that was appropriate for a woman who had foresworn the fleshly material world and all its pleasures for a life of spirituality. And Azalais was right. She saw Constance's hand reach out to his and the young man took it.

Now was the time to put an end to this before anything more troubling developed, thought Azalais. She marched over to where they stood.

"Constance, do you have a reason to linger over this woman?" Azalais asked.

Constance jumped and quickly dropped Guillaume's hand. Azalais was distressed to see the guilt on her face.

"I was just," said Constance before Azalais interrupted.

"There is a child bawling over its dead mother in the herb room," Azalais said. "See to it."

Azalais turned to Guillaume. He looked her full in the face and though Azalais was quite old and thought herself inured to the attractions of the flesh, she could not help but stare. When the young man had come to the good women, his face had been bloody from his injury. But now Azalais realized how beautiful he was. Guillaume was tall, broad of shoulder and slim of waist. His legs were shapely and his hands were those of a musician - long fingers, but strong. His face was prettier than that of many a woman, but there was something in it - a thickness, a hardness about the jaw and mouth that kept it from being too sweet. He wore his brown hair long and pulled back, but a strand or two always escaped in a way that Azalais thought must make women yearn to raise their finger to his cheek to place the strand back into place.

Azalais had to shake herself. In her former life, she had been a troubairitz, composing chansons of hopeless love. She had left that life, with its concentration on everything that was material, worldly, and evil. Azalais wanted nothing more than to pass her remaining days preparing herself for the eternity that she would spend as pure spirit, forever freed from her body and this earth that gave only misery and woe. But all Azalais could think of at that moment was which words she would have used to describe this beauty. As if he were my lover, she thought, as if he were one to whom she would be engaged in service forever.

The cry of a soldier, as a doctor ripped a crossbow from his leg startled Azalais out of her reverie.

"Guillaume, go to that doctor," Azalais said. "He needs your help now."

The young man obediently went to assist and Azalais realized that he was a great danger. She had to do something. He would ruin Constance. She would gladly betray any vow to be with him. Azalais knew this already.

The afternoon passed too quickly as the wounded continued to arrive, but the deluge finally slowed. Azalais' bones ached, as she helped to lift yet another lifeless body that the good women and the Jewish doctors could not save. It was always like this in war, thought Azalais. The knights, with all the chain mail and armor that their wealth can buy, almost never died. The soldiers still had their shields and helmets and thick leather tunics to protect them from swords and arrows. The townspeople always had nothing. The strongest had the most protection and the weakest had none. This world is so evil, thought Azalais. She could not wait to escape its injustice and its cruelty.

At that thought, Azalais looked up to see how the woman who had received the consolamentum two days earlier was doing. She was so close to escape. When Azalais had seen her that morning the woman was very weak, her eyes glazed and her breathing labored. Azalais only wished that she could sit with her and pray and watch her as she gloriously slid away, out of the foul body and away from this wicked earth. Guillaume stood beside her and Azalais hoped he was holding her hand for a brief moment. Then she saw what he was doing and ran quickly to stop him.

"Guillaume, stop that!" Azalais screamed and knocked the bowl of broth from his hands.

Guillaume turned to stare at Azalais. The dying woman began again to moan.

"She is very ill and was begging for water," he said. "I only hoped to ease her suffering."

"You are only prolonging it, you fool. Do you want to keep Satan's grip on her forever?" Azalais said.

Guillaume looked at Azalais with confusion.

"She received the consolamentum two days ago and if she dies with no sin committed on her soul, she will break free from the cycle of reincarnation. She will break free from this earthly world and fleshly body and become pure spirit and soul. She will be free for all eternity to be with our Lord in the realm of all that is spiritual and good."

"But you are keeping sustenance from a dying woman!" Guillaume said with incredulity. "Surely, sipping a little broth made from turnips is not a sin."

"No, it is not," Azalais said. "But every second that she is alive she may commit some other fleshly sin, even inadvertently. She may let the broth of the meat of an animal slide past her lips, she may tell a lie. She is doing the endura now. Its only purpose is to speed her death and her release. Promise me you will not tempt her again."

Guillaume looked strangely at Azalais, but he nodded his head and walked away.

Azalais again felt queasy with looking at him and realized she must speak to Constance about the danger he represented as quickly as possible. Azalais found her in the herb room, trying to sweep up broken glass. The dead woman and her screaming child were no longer in the room.

"What happened to the boy?" Azalais asked.

"His grandmother found him," Constance said. "She took the dead woman as well."

Azalais nodded and went to help her clean the table.

"Constance, I am going to forbid you to do something that you may not understand, but you must remember that I am doing this for your own good," Azalais said.

Constance stopped her cleaning and looked at Azalais with a puzzled expression on her face.

"Constance, you are forbidden to speak to the boy Guillaume."

Constance stared.

"But, why?" she asked.

"It is enough for you to know that he is a danger to your salvation," Azalais said. "You cannot trust him. I am taking this step to protect you."

"But what happened?" she asked.

Azalais only looked at her with the face she reserved for those caught breaking a rule of the house of good women. Constance knew better than to question her judgment. That was the end of the conversation and Azalais walked away.

Constance

Monday, August 3, 1209, evening

It was early evening as Constance worked in the courtyard garden. The heat of the day was still thick and the air smoky, as the fires burning in the Bourg suburb still pushed their smoke into the air. Constance tore at the weeds choking their herbs and brutally hacked them out of the ground. Her face was sweaty and her dark hair kept escaping from the simple linen covering she wore. She was angry, angry at seeing all the suffering, angry that she could do nothing to stop it, only be there to stitch up the wounded or prepare the dead for burial.

Constance would not admit it to herself, but she was especially angry that Azalais did not trust her. She treats me as a child, Constance thought. What had Guillaume done to cause him to be ostracized like this? Was the house of woman in some danger from him? Constance could put up with Azalais' pedantic lectures on the herbs in the garden, even though Constance believed she could recite each discussion from memory at this point. Sometimes she wanted to throw the basket of herbs at Azalais and scream "I'm not the village idiot!"

But, Constance knew that Azalais had a tremendous knowledge and she was grateful to be taught. She was grateful to Azalais for many things, especially when she thought about what her life might have been like had she never met Azalais and never become a good woman.

Constance remembered when she first heard the good men speak in her village in the mountains. She was standing in front of the fire, stirring the cauldron, when her little brother ran into the kitchen to tell everyone the holy men had come. The little boy would not stop talking. Constance wanted to go as well, but looked at her mother, her distended breasts, blue-veined and heavy, nursing the cloth merchant's three-month old son. She heard the thin, reedy cry of her baby sister, wrapping in her swaddling on a bed of straw near the fire. Constance picked up the baby and cooed to her. She felt she should stay and help her mother, but her desire to leave the cacophony of noise and odor overwhelmed her and she asked her mother for permission to go hear the preachers. Of course, her mother agreed on the condition that she take most of her siblings with her. The poor woman had been burdened with ten living children, and earned her living by renting the milk of her breasts.

Constance handed her baby sister to her mother and watched as her mother shifted the infant at her breast and took the baby girl, placing her near her other breast. The child's mouth hungrily searched for the nipple and began suckling loudly. The weary woman looked up through thinning hair and pale cheeks at her twelve year old daughter, and told her to go quickly before she changed her mind.

Constance stood in the market square in the sunshine of early spring. The day was a mild one. The crowd pushed against each other, jostling to hear the three men speak. Constance carried the toddler and held the hand of another small brother. The other dirty boys and girls kept darting through the crowd, playing with a stray black dog. The men were poor men of God, thin and humbly dressed like the crowd listening to them. The oldest one began to speak and the crowd quieted down.

"The flesh is evil and the spirit is good," said the old preacher. "We must aspire to live a life of perfection and escape from the mantle of sin and earthly matter. Look at the Catholic priests. They take money from the poor and live like the rich. How can they pretend to communicate with all matter of spirit when their flesh is gorged on goose fat and wine and clothed in the finest silks?"

Voices cried out from the crowd: "What must we do to be saved?"

"You must avoid all things of the flesh," said the preacher. "Eat no meat or any product of the copulation of animals. You must not lie or take oaths. You must be celibate, for to bring more life into this cycle of damnation and evil is truly a sin. You must live as the poor do, without material possessions, passing all your thought and deed into matters of the spirit."

Constance heard a man next to her, drunk and unsteady on his feet.

"I already live the life of the poor, but to be celibate as well, now that's asking a bit much."

"All are not ready in this life to take on the mantle of perfection," continued the preacher. "There are those who are only ready to believe. The believers support the good men and women, giving them shelter and a bit of bread and water to break their fasts. If a believer is strong, he may receive the consolamentum just before death and ascend to Paradise. If a believer is not ready to endure the deprivation of all material things and succor only on the spirit, then he will die to be reborn again into this world of evil, misery and pain."

The toddler in Constance's arms began to bawl. Constance checked his ragged shirt. He was wet and cold. Constance grabbed the hand of the small boy by her side.

"We must go now," she whispered.

The little boy began to cry as well, his shrieks rising and falling in a harmony of misery with the babe in Constance's arms. She turned to go, when she heard the deep, calm voice of the old preacher focused directly on her.

"Young girl, think of what you do. For each one of these little souls that has been born into this world must endure its misery, its pain, and suffer through the cycle again and again until it reaches salvation and achieves perfection. It does not have to be this way."

Constance looked directly into the old man's eyes and saw kindness tinged with a great sadness for all the pain he had witnessed. She bowed her head slightly and turned, pushing her way through the crowd. She walked slowly on the way home, ignoring the screaming of the toddler and the little boy's tugging hand.

When Constance crossed the threshold, she saw that her father had joined them at home for the midday meal. His hands, calloused from field work, ripped the simple bread and dipped it into the vegetable stew. Constance stripped the toddler of his wet clothes and hung them in front of the fire to dry. She held the small body close to her to keep him warm. Her father looked up from his meal and looked at Constance. Constance noticed that her mother was softly crying by the fire.

"It is time you had your own household and were blessed with your own children. Your sister did not live long enough to provide her husband with heirs, but I have now betrothed you to him. You will be married in a fortnight."

Constance felt sick with fear. Her sister had died after only nine months married to her husband, the miller. Constance had seen her come home only twice in that time, a hood covering her battered and blue face. Both times her father had sent her back to the miller. Constance did not understand, but knew that there was a deal involving land and an orchard behind the marriage. Constance's father felt he had profited from the deal and figured he had plenty of daughters to spare, even if took a few of them to cement the alliance.

Constance ran to her older brother that night. Having little chance of any land from a family with so many children, he made his living as a shepherd in the mountains around the village. Constance's brother took her to see the good men that night, before they left the village, and told them her story. They did not want to travel with a young woman, but agreed to bring Constance to a house of good women in Carcassonne, as long as her brother accompanied her on the journey. There Constance could live a life of spiritual purity.

Constance never saw her family again.

As she looked up from her work in the garden and saw the house of good women, Constance knew that her family was now here. Azalais was her mother, a mother who protected her and loved her, as her own mother had never been able to do. Constance resolved to be a better daughter, more obedient and less questioning. She began to gather more herbs to replenish their stocks. She hoped there would not be more wounded tomorrow, but knew that she wished for something she could not control.

Suddenly, she felt herself in the shade. The coolness was almost refreshing, but she felt uneasy and looked up. Guillaume stood looking down at her.

"Can I help you?" he asked.

Constance wanted so badly to say yes. Most of the good women were much older or much younger than Constance and she had truly enjoyed having a companion of her own age over the last few days. Guillaume seemed so kind. He did not speak much, but when he did it was always something that made Constance think. Constance could not possibly imagine what he had done to make Azalais not trust him, but she remembered her new conviction to be a more obedient daughter to Azalais.

Constance said nothing, only kept picking the rosemary. She plucked the flowery white heads and placed them in her basket. Guillaume said nothing, but only squatted beside her and started to pick the flowers and place them quietly in her basket. They worked in the hot afternoon sun for half an hour. When the rosemary was harvested, Guillaume followed Constance to the poppies. They picked the brilliant orange petals, one by one, dropping them into a second basket. Constance thought of how good it felt to just be by his side. Guillaume had such a calming nature - surely, he could not be wicked. But Constance stayed obedient and said not a word.

Finally Guillaume spoke. He turned to Constance and placed his hand on her arm. Constance felt warmth where he touched, even stronger than the heat of the August day.

"I do not know what I have done to offend you, but I wanted only to thank you for all the care you have given me. I have learned much in your company, but I am now well. I must return to my brother. He is helping a mason repair walls and I will be needed. I will pray for your soul, Constance."

With that, Guillaume stood quietly and left the garden. Constance felt a strange emptiness, but only shook her head and continued to harvest the poppies.

Suddenly, a shadow again covered her and Constance looked up expectantly, hoping oddly that Guillaume had returned. She looked instead into the wrathful face of Azalais.

"So you do not trust my judgment," said Azalais in a tight whisper. "You have chosen to directly disobey me."

Constance jumped up, angry and hurt.

"I did not disobey you, I did not speak to him," said Constance.

"Enough," said Azalais. "You have destroyed much of my faith in you, Constance. Do not make it worse with lies."

Azalais turned and marched back to the house. Constance dropped her basket of poppies and rosemary and started to cry, tears of anger and frustration and fear.

Bernard

Monday, August 3, 1209, night

"I do not understand why we must lie," said Guillaume.

"We have been through this before," Bernard said, with a sigh.

"But, I was sure that if I had spoken the truth to the heretic girl, she would have seen the error of her ways. I could have saved another soul from damnation. Instead we lie and deceive. What example are we to these lost souls?" asked Guillaume.

"You concern me, brother," I said. "I worry that your concern about that heretic girl is not about her soul, but about her evil, lustful body."

Guillaume stopped and turned on me.

"Do not speak of what you do not know, brother," he said. "For I have spent several days in the company of these heretic women and, though they may be misguided, they have lives of purity similar to those of our most holy sister nuns."

I laughed and Guillaume stiffened.

"For surely you have been ensnared by this Jezebel, to even think of comparing her to a bride of Christ. You are close to blasphemy, Guillaume, and I will be sure that our Father Abbot knows about this sin of yours," I said. "But, I want you to know that I blame myself. For surely my thirst for knowledge with which to fight these heretics led me to place your soul in jeopardy. Now, be quiet Guillaume, we don't want to arouse the attention of the guards."

Guillaume and I were making our way through the darkened city to the tavern to relay my latest message to our Father Abbot. I was less fearful of the guards tonight because the city streets were crowded with refugees from the Bourg. How I had watched with joy today as these heretics fled from our righteous might! I still shivered when I remembered the power of our monks chanting voices propelling our mighty warriors on to victory.

But all was not yet won. We still had work to do. And now I had an added worry - Guillaume seemed to be slipping in his faith, first questioning our mission, given to us by our most Holy Father Abbot, and then falling prey to the charms of this wicked woman. We soon reached the tavern. Flickering light illuminated two bodies in an open window on the second floor. A whore practiced her trade, but all we could see were her naked legs under the bucking body of a man with his tunic raised above his waist. The man suddenly stopped and, with one hand, reached over and shut the window. I looked over at Guillaume's pale face, for I was sure he had never seen an act of fornication, other than the mating of the sheep and goats in the spring time.

"You take me here, and yet you call those heretic women whores?"

said Guillaume, his face a mask of disbelieving anger.

“It is not for you to question the mysterious ways of the Lord, Guillaume,” I patiently said. “Do not forget your humility. Do you dare to think yourself worthy of judging our Father Abbot?”

“No, of course not,” said Guillaume. He shook his head, as if to dispel the disturbing scene we had just witnessed from his mind.

I felt a rush of affection for the boy that I had not felt for years. I remembered him as a child, so gentle and pure. His mere presence would bring a smile to the face of even the oldest, most dour monk in the Abbey. I reminded myself that I must remember his youth and naive nature and be gentler with him.

“Guillaume,” I said. “The world is full of many things that are evil. There are some times when this evil must be used, bended, to serve a greater, more good and full purpose. It is only for the very wise to know when to do this. This is why we must trust our Father Abbot. For truly, he has a vision such that the glory of our Lord Jesus Christ will reign on this earth. He wants what you do. To save all the souls of these poor heretics. But, sometimes people are weak; they need a strong hand to guide them. This heretic girl and all the others like her will continue to live in sin and misery while their leaders continue to deceive them and lead them away from the one, true way. We must be strong to overcome the evil that is here and to create a new society where the righteous shall flourish and where the sinners can be redeemed.”

“Guillaume, you are young and pure of heart. It may seem to you that we break the very laws of righteousness that we proclaim in order to save these souls, but know that this is because we must do so. We must fight these evildoers using all the weapons at our disposal. This is a battle for souls and we cannot let this heresy spread any farther. There is a time to fight and it is now.”

Guillaume nodded. I could see that he understood the deadly battle we faced and what we must do. I grabbed his arm and pulled him into the entrance of the tavern. I looked around, but did not see the burly man with the scar who took my message last time. I went back to the bar to talk to the old hag who poured wine from wooden barrels, dragging Guillaume behind me. I wondered about my wisdom in bringing Guillaume to this place. He stared around with horror and we were beginning to attract some threatening stares from the idolaters and drunken fornicators who populated the place. The old hag stared at me coldly and then took a long look at Guillaume.

"So you brought your pretty boy, this time, did you?" the old crone said. "I must admit, he's certainly lovelier than anything we've got for sale here." She cackled and tried to run her hand on Guillaume's cheek, but he jumped back, startled.

"He is my brother, you wicked vixen," I said. "If you do not want to be slapped, I suggest that you quickly find the man I came to do business with and bring him to us."

She gave Guillaume a long, searching look that made him blush a violent pink and then went to the back room. She emerged a few minutes later with the scar-faced man. He glanced at Guillaume and spat in disgust on the floor. Nonetheless, he beckoned for us to follow him.

We descended into the bowels of the building as we had done the last time. I prayed that the Father Abbot's contact on the outside had seen fit to pay the man the blackmail he had requested. I did not know whether we were descending to pass another message, as last time, or to be turned over to the Viscount's guards. I had brought Guillaume with me because he was young and strong, and much taller than I, but now I wondered if I had been foolish to ensnare him with me. At least, had he not come with me, he could continue our work. But, I then just as suddenly knew that I was right to keep him with me. For Guillaume was weak and easily swayed. Far better that he stayed with me, whatever the risks to his physical body, than to court the risks to his eternal soul that he would encounter without my guidance.

The slanting hallway and steps were even clammier than I remembered and I felt a sweat break out on my back, chilling in me in the cool underground air. Finally, we reached the room filled with smugglers' good where I had last encountered the scar-faced man.

"You fool," bellowed the man, as soon as we had entered the room and he had closed the door. "As if I do not take enough of a risk dealing with your obvious incompetence, you bring along a boy as well!"

Guillaume stiffened, his pride injured, but he said nothing.

"Have you no concept of stealth? No idea of the risks we run here?" said the man. "Surely, you cannot be so stupid, so you must feel yourself invincible. You're a priest, aren't you? That would explain a few things."

The man chuckled to himself.

"Never have I worked with such an amateur. Well, at least your master puts a high price on your abilities, for whatever delusional reasons that would be. He paid to keep you out of the Viscount's hands, but I do believe my price just went up. My risk has doubled with the two of you imbeciles involved and I want to be compensated." said the man. "This time ask for ten times my original price. For now that I know that you have the wealth of the monks behind you, I plan to profit even more for the risks I take."

I took a deep breath of relief, even though I had been sure our Father Abbot would care for me. I only hoped that he would be able to honor this next request.

DAY 4 OF THE SIEGE OF CARCASSONNE

Tuesday, August 4, 1209

Trencavel

Tuesday, August 4, 1209, morning

This time they listened to Bertrand of Saissac. And this time they were ready.

Trencavel waited at dawn on the walls of the Castellar. They were taking a risk, concentrating their forces here in this southern suburb, but since the loss of the river, the only fresh water available to the city of Carcassonne came from the Fontgrande spring inside the walls of the Castellar. For once, most of Trencavel's knights had agreed on something. After yesterday's taking of the Bourg, the Crusaders would next try to take the Castellar. But this time the defenders would fight back with everything they had.

The morning was still quiet and cool, as Trencavel looked out over the river towards the Crusaders' camp. He could see the black-cloaked monks beginning to drift towards the river bank and knew that the peaceful quiet of the morning would soon be shattered.

The chanting started off quietly, but grew in force as more monks joined the choir at the bank. Soon, hundreds were gathered and the deep voices reverberated off the mountains behind and in front of them, causing strange echoes. Trencavel shivered, in spite of himself. He was glad to feel the warmth of the sun on his back, as it popped from the mountains behind him, blanketing the valley in a warm glow and presaging the heat of the day to come.

Trencavel stood on the parapet of the wall and looked behind him. They had moved most of the city's soldiers into the suburb last night, leaving a skeleton force manning the walls of the city proper. But, the Crusaders would not know that. They would assume the Castellar to be as lightly defended as the Bourg and would expect another victory. Trencavel planned to make sure that did not happen. The Castellar's walls had been recently reinforced with stone from the cathedral and massive piles of stones stood near mangonels, ready to be thrown over onto the attackers. Crossbowmen stood just out of view on the suburb's walls, ready to run to the tops of the parapets and rain down bolts on the Crusaders at the first signal.

Trencavel walked over to the nearest tower and went inside. Cabaret was standing in front of a narrow slotted opening, gazing at the chanting monks.

"You must admit that we have no choice," said Trencavel. "We cannot stand by again while they butcher us."

"There are always choices," said Cabaret. "We will soon know whether you have made the right one."

"While we keep the water from the spring, we can hold out, even without the river," said Trencavel.

"Why do you work so hard to convince me?" said Cabaret. "Is it because you have not yet convinced yourself?"

Before Trencavel could respond, he was interrupted by the cry of a guard on the watchtower. The Crusaders were on the attack. Trencavel and Cabaret grabbed their swords and fastened their helmets and returned to the walls.

The Crusaders again swept up the hill, heading straight for the walls of the Castellar. Knights on horses with fluttering pennants charged towards the walls. When they were close, Trencavel yelled for the bowmen to advance. All of a sudden, the walls of the Castellar were carpeted with archers and crossbowmen. At Trencavel's signal, a deluge of arrows and crossbows flew forth, knocking screaming squires to their feet and lodging in the flesh of stampeding horses. Trencavel gave the order again and another wave hit the Crusaders before they had time to recover from the first attack.

Still they kept coming. There were so many of them and they were drunk on their easy victory of the day before. They pushed forward until they were in the trenches at the foot of the wall. Infantrymen brought ladders and knights started to climb up. Trencavel turned behind him and bellowed to the women and men at the catapults. Each team was ready, a stockpile of rounded stones next to the machine. Each catapult was armed with a projectile, the tension on the beam at the breaking point. Trencavel raised his sword and the catapults all let loose at once. The stones fell as rain on the attackers. Many landed on the earth with only a dull thud, but many more hit the Crusaders in the trenches, pinning horses and men to the ground as they screamed in agony.

Bertrand de Saissac shouted a battle cry and the men at his side poured down burning arrows on the Crusaders trapped in the ditch. Trencavel could sense the excitement in the air. They were beating them back. Even Cabaret fought with the vigor of a much younger man, as he mowed down one of the few knights to breach the wall. Trencavel turned again to his catapults. The teams were working feverishly to crank down the beams and reload the catapults. Trencavel waited until they were ready and ordered another devastating launch.

More Crusaders fell in the trenches. Trencavel could smell their blood and guts in the morning breeze and the smell of burning human flesh. He had never felt more alive.

Bernard

Tuesday, August 4, 1209, morning

I was sickened. My God, my God, why has thou forsaken us? All around me our most noble and blessed soldiers of the army of God were falling, felled by the arrows and stones of these heretic dogs. And I could do nothing.

Why, oh why did they not listen to me? I had sent scrupulous information about the weakness of the walls of this suburb. I had worked on it with my own hands and still they did not listen. I felt as if I were the prophet crying in the wilderness.

They attacked instead with the boldness of men who do not listen to the counsels of God and his emissaries here on earth. And they were paying for it with their blood.

I stood on the ramparts of the Castellar suburb watching the slaughter of our men and the cheers all around me and knew the deepest desperation. Though it tortured my soul to do so, I had lifted my own hands against the Crusaders. I felt the stain of treason, but I knew that I could not do otherwise without revealing my role here. The mason had come for us to help in the defense of the Castellar. Guillaume had disappeared, whispering to me the words "Blessed are the peacemakers," and I had been forced to make excuses for his still lingering injury to his head. In fact, it seemed to me that he had injured something more than his mind in that accident. For he was almost no longer recognizable as himself. He was willful and disobedient and constantly questioning. I would be sure that he received proper discipline from the Father Abbot when we returned to the abbey.

So, I had gone myself with the mason and his heretical workers and brought them stones that they then threw down on the heads of our most loyal Crusaders.

"Don't you want your revenge, boy?" asked the mason, as he handed me a rock.

While the men screamed "Remember Béziers!" I dropped the stone, praying that it would not hit the blessed head of even one of our noble Crusaders. Fortunately, it bounced off the walls of the Castellar and fell harmlessly to the ditch below.

"Well, we won't waste any more on you, boy," said the mason. "But we'll remember Béziers for you, just keep bringing us those stones."

I worked in the blazing sun, praying for forgiveness with every step I took. I tried to feign the joy the others showed as Crusader after Crusader fell in the ditches, but I could not. Fortunately, the mason thought I was remembering the deaths of my family at Béziers and thought nothing of my gloom.

I watched as the Crusaders began to pull back, realizing that their defeat this day was final, when I saw a most brave and inspiring sight. One knight lay wounded in the ditch right beneath me, his leg broken. The other knights were pulling back, but one came back. Under the firestorm of bombardment and arrows, this one brave Crusader risked his own life to save the life of the injured knight. He dragged him back to safety to loud cheers on his side. I could see that even the craven coward heretics on whose side I unwillingly fought were impressed with the bravery of this Crusader.

We might have lost today, I thought, but let this brave action be a lesson to these cowardly heretic dogs. Those who fight on the Lord's side have right and might on their side. This was only a small setback to these great warriors of Christ, one designed to test their faith. They would pass the test and we would achieve victory. I resolved to work even harder at my appointed tasks and to do all I could, no matter the risk to my life, to win this battle for the Lord.

Gauda

Tuesday, August 4, 1209, evening

I had tried to cheer with joy with all the others as our knights and soldiers destroyed the enemy today and drove them away from our walls, but I felt only fear in my heart. The Crusaders would now want vengeance for their slain comrades. Our knights would be drunk on their victory and would not give up easily. I doubted we could negotiate a truce now. I did not know if I would be alive to claim my rewards from the Count of Toulouse, were he to emerge on the victorious side of this siege.

Still, I thought, I must act the role of joyous celebrant, for we would feast tonight and I dared not betray myself. I composed my face into a smile as I entered Agnes' chamber. True celibate or not, I knew that Agnes would want to be arrayed in all her finery for tonight's rejoicings.

Agnes sat in front of her mirror, idly gazing at her face. She turned to face me when she heard me enter the room.

"Gauda, what took you so long?"

I ignored her whining voice and simply walked over to the trunk that held her fine clothes. I pulled out a silk chemise and gently touched the soft fabric.

"I will be responded to when I address you, cousin," said Agnes.

"Please forgive me, Countess," I said. "I was searching for your best chemise."

Agnes frowned, but I sat down next to her anyway and unstitched the sleeves on her simple cotton tunic. She raised her hands so that I could remove it. Underneath, she wore a linen chemise. It was stained and smelled a bit strongly of an earthy smell, but I knew not what. Agnes saw that I noticed and blushed, but she said nothing. I quickly removed the chemise and left it for the maids to wash. I held out the silk chemise, and Agnes raised her hands over her head. I placed the chemise over her head.

I returned to the trunk and searched for her finest tunic. It was blue and made of brocaded silk from Alexandria. I placed it over Agnes' head and she guided her hands through the sleeves. The tunic hung freely around Agnes's slender frame and I went to search for a belt from the trunk. I found a beautiful one made from brocaded gold and tied it loosely about her waist. I sat down to sew Agnes' sleeves shut, to make the narrowest fit for her slender arms.

I remembered my mother dressing for feasts at my father's castle. My mother had worn a tunic that fell to the ground in gentle pleats from a tightly cinched waist. She had appeared svelte and shapely, the curves of her womanly body fully visible. But like all things sensual, this fashion had passed. We wore the same clothes as men now, only longer and trailing on the floor. Our curves were hidden by loose folds of cloth. My mother's tunics had voluminous sleeves. As a child, I could hide behind them when I wanted to play shy. But now the stylish women bound their arms in sleeves fastened with buttons or even sewn together until the garment was removed. I did not follow this fashion at least, for I could not play my harp with my arms bound so.

A fine sweat started to appear on Agnes' brow. The room was stifling in the hot afternoon and Agnes' rich clothes were heavy. At least she did not need to wear the hose that men did, since the skirt of her tunic was so long it dragged on the floor behind her. When I had finished dressing her, Agnes sat in front of her mirror and I stood behind, running the ivory comb through her long, straight blond hair and thought what a shame that I must bind it up behind her in a chignon. Even though I could hate Agnes, I always loved the feeling of combing her hair. I loved separating out the strands as I removed the knots, slowly and gently, starting from the bottom and working my way up to her scalp. All of sudden I was woken from my dreaming by Agnes' voice.

"I know what you do with him, you know," said Agnes.

"I am sorry, Viscountess," I said. "I do not know to whom you are referring."

"My husband," said Agnes. "I know what you do with him each night."

I stopped combing Agnes' hair. I said nothing.

"My dear cousin," said Agnes. "I had long suspected you of being no better than a whore or jogleresa, but I did not want to behave so lowly as to spy on you. But, you forced my hand."

I started to speak, but Agnes interrupted me.

"Don't even bother to deny it."

I began to comb Agnes' hair again, but her hand grasped mine firmly and stopped it.

"I know what knowledge you hold over me, you ungrateful churl, but don't even think of using it, for I will throw you out of this household faster than you can think."

Agnes let go of my hand and I started to comb her hair again, pulling slowly through the locks. I quietly formed them into a perfect blonde chignon at the back of her neck. I wrapped her head in thin strips of white silk that went under her chin, but making sure that her beautiful hair was visible from the back. Finally, I placed a circlet of gold on her head, encrusted with stones. Agnes stood for she was ready. So young, she had no need for powders and artifice. Her eyes were clear and bright blue, her cheeks pale and white.

She was not a good woman, that was sure. She still lived firmly planted in the foibles and luxuries and distress of this material world. But why, I wondered, yet again.

Azalais

Tuesday, August 4, 1209, evening

The good women had just celebrated with great joy the release of another soul from this cycle of suffering and misery, this earthly hell. The endura had finally ended for the sick woman who had received the consolamentum three days earlier. Azalais had watched and prayed as the woman breathed her last, her face calm and serene. All the good women in the house were made joyful by this escape and Azalais was relieved, since they had seen much suffering and death of souls who were not prepared to move beyond in the last few days.

But Azalais' blissful mood was destroyed when she realized that she would have to fulfill her least favorite task as a healer. The woman who stumbled into the house of good women was heavily pregnant. She was supported on either side by two women, who wiped away the sweat pouring down her face. She shrieked and bent double with labor pains and Azalais ruefully prepared a bed for her in a storage room off the main room, still filled with the wounded from the siege.

Well, Azalais thought, that is the nature of life; there is the joy of watching one be released from this cycle of suffering and then there is the misery of welcoming another soul into this life of pain.

Azalais helped the grunting woman to lie down on the simple cot. She would need to keep walking to bring down the baby, but for now she could rest. Azalais could tell that her walk to the house in the heat of the late afternoon had fatigued her greatly. She was very pale.

"For how long has she been in labor?" Azalais asked the older of the two women who accompanied her.

"For one whole day and night and into today," said the woman. "This is her first child."

"And you are her mother?" Azalais said.

The woman nodded and pointed to the other woman.

"And this is her sister," she said. "In this family, we have never taken so long for the baby to come. I worried and so we brought her here. She is getting weaker."

"It is long, but not so long for a first birth," Azalais said. "We will do all we can to hasten the coming. Untie all the knots in this room and take all the pins from her hair. Let everything down and loose and the baby will follow."

The woman shrieked again and bent double, but Azalais could tell that she did not have much strength left. She examined her. The baby was in a good position and her body was sufficiently open. Azalais thought it probable the baby itself was fighting from entering this world of pain. She would have to trick it into coming to join them.

Azalais left the room and went to her herbs. She knew just what would make the baby come - spoiled rye. It was a strong medicine, but it was needed. Azalais brewed some tea of balm to calm the mother and added the rye.

Constance came into the herb room as Azalais brewed the tea. Azalais could sense that the girl remained angry with her, but that only made Azalais surer that she was doing the right thing in preventing Constance from talking with the young man.

"You will thank me some day," Azalais said. "You will thank

me for preventing you from ending up in a dreadful condition such as that poor woman. If you are not careful, that could be you in nine months."

Constance slowly turned her face towards Azalais. It was livid with rage.

"You insult me, good mother," Constance said. "Do you think I would give up all my vows and learning and my salvation for any earthly pleasure? For surely you know me better than that."

"I know you well, my girl," Azalais said. "And I know that you have become disobedient and willful. And with young girls that usually means one thing. Do not think me a fool, just because I am old. Now bring oil and cloths. We must heal this woman who was fool enough to fall into Satan's trap of perpetuating the evil in this world."

Constance picked up the oil and cloth and sullenly followed as Azalais went back to the birthing room and gave the pregnant woman the tea. The flavor was bitter and she tried to spit it out, but Azalais forced it down her throat. She then gave the pregnant woman some hellebore to sniff. She began sneezing relentlessly, but Azalais closed her hands over the woman's nose and mouth. The pregnant woman's face became red as she bore down with great pressure.

"The baby will come soon," Azalais said. "Keep forcing her to push. She is merely a lazy girl."

The mother and sister moved and stood on either side of the pregnant woman, holding her body up as she screamed and pushed down.

Azalais oiled the woman's birth canal, as Constance massaged her stomach, trying to force the baby out and into the world. The pregnant woman screamed again, as her labor intensified. The pains came at only a few minutes apart. The rye was working.

Azalais leaned across and whispered in Constance's ear.

"Is this what you want for yourself? Think carefully, girl," she said.

Constance looked up and stared at Azalais with angry eyes.

"How can you think so little of me? I will tell you the truth, if you want it. I could care less about the boy, but I am sick of this place. I am sick of being helpless as we are destroyed. I am sick of watching the wounded scream in agony, all the while knowing I can do nothing to stop them. You have taught me never to fight, always to live in peace, but what happens when they come to kill us? Will we just stand here and not raise a finger to defend ourselves? What kind of madness is that?"

Constance was yelling and the pregnant woman and her kinfolk were staring at them in silence. All of a sudden, the woman gave one last shriek and Azalais saw the head of the baby pop into her arms. The woman heaved one last time and the baby's shoulders pushed out and the rest slithered free. Azalais grabbed the baby and cut the umbilical cord with her knife, four fingers from his stomach. He let out a full cry and Azalais handed him to Constance. She washed him in a bowl and rubbed his body with salt. She then handed him to his grandmother, who started to swaddle him tightly.

Azalais watched the mother as she expelled the afterbirth and then cleaned the bed. If the new mother survived the night and did not get milk fever, she would continue in this world. Azalais prayed for both the mother and the baby and only hoped they would come to take the consolamentum before dying and would never have to come back to this world again.

Azalais nodded to Constance and they left the room together.

"We have nothing to fear of death, Constance," Azalais said. "You and I have received the consolamentum. If we are killed in this siege, we will be free. It is something you should face with joy, not trepidation."

"Yes, please forgive me," said Constance. "I did not know of what I spoke."

She left the building and went to the garden. Azalais watched her, more worried now than before. Infatuation with a boy seemed a mild threat compared to the blasphemy that Constance spoke today.

Gauda

Tuesday, August 4, 1209, night

That night, the castle hall reverberated with music and song. Trencavel and his men had managed to stop the Crusaders and we still had access to a water source, despite the river having been lost. The wine flowed freely, even if water was still a precious commodity. I sat, as usual, next to my cousin the Viscountess Agnes. She ate only fruit and a simple dish of fish in olive oil, but I watched as her eyes traveled hungrily over the plates spread out before us. To save water, Trencavel had ordered all the livestock slaughtered, so we ate as kings. Tongues of pork in bittersweet sauce, leg of mutton cooked with grapes and wildflower honey, slices of wild boar with basil. I delighted in savoring each bite, watching Agnes struggle to compose herself.

A heavy hand banged a glass of wine down next to me and I quickly moved to avoid the splatter. Bertrand de Saissac sat to my left and so dining was a danger to my best robes. They were simple compared to Agnes' silks, but I still retained some items of quality from my previous life before my fortunes had changed so drastically and I did not plan to allow Bertrand to ruin them.

"So, Cabaret," said Bertrand. "How did it feel to finally fight today?"

Cabaret, seated to the right of Trencavel, leaned forward to answer Bertrand. His neat, gray beard quivered and I could see Trencavel's face tighten. Conversations around the table stopped.

"It felt good to beat those bastards," said Cabaret.

Bertrand let out a hearty laugh and raised his mug to Cabaret, who responded in turn. All the other knights around the table joined them and the drone of conversations again began to rise. Trencavel leaned back and took a long sip of wine.

The hall was immense. More than 400 knights must have been seated around the long, wooden tables, enjoying Trencavel's hospitality in return for their service. There were few women in the hall and those who did sit among the knights and soldiers were, for the most part, women of low virtue - jogleresas, acrobats, and whores. I studied the musicians playing in front of our table, which was raised on a dais in the front of the hall. Despite the fact that no fire burned behind us, the room was very hot and I could see the sweat on their faces. The drummer was an awkward young man who provided a lively rhythm for a dance that was given a joyous melody by a flutist and harpist. The flutist was a very pretty young girl and I would bet that she made more from selling her favors to lonely soldiers than she ever did from her music. An old minstrel, who looked like he must be her father, played the psalterion, providing the base of the chords that underlay the song. Four acrobats danced to the melody in a chain that weaved around the room, in between the tables and occasionally on them. One of the acrobats began to juggle two mugs left on the table and several knights hastily quaffed their wine and threw their empty mugs at the juggler. He nimbly caught the mugs until he was juggling five. A fat knight threw a sixth mug at him and he caught it for a second until everything came crashing down around him. Fortunately, the mugs landed on the soft reeds of the floor and none broke. The juggler bowed deeply and the soldiers madly applauded.

Bertrand turned to me and spoke, too close for my comfort, since he obviously did not follow the proper rules of manners suggesting that one should not speak directly to another unless one were sure that one's breath did not offend. But then I should not be surprised at his uncouthness for he also ate his meat with both hands, instead of just using the first three fingers of the right hand. I sighed and placed my wine glass under my nose, hoping the strong smell of the young wine would dispel his vapors.

"Gauda, you must ask the joglar to sing one of your songs," Bertrand said. "I would love to hear one and I dare not ask you to play for us here."

I smiled at Bertrand. He was a sweet man, for all his boorish manners.

"It is not my place to ask," I said. "Anyway, I doubt these musicians know my music. I do not have wide renown."

"You mean, unlike your first husband," said Agnes. "I am sure any joglar would know Raimon of Miraval's famous chansons."

I felt my face flush, but I said nothing. Agnes took a delicate bite of her bland fish and smiled at me. I did not understand how a face that looked so like an angel's could mask such a vile temper. For surely, our faces are the outward manifestation of all our vices and virtues. Sometimes, I thought she must be a witch to look so innocent and sweet.

"But, I have a better idea," said Agnes, licking her lips like a cat. "Why doesn't Gauda perform for us? I, too, would so love to hear her sing and I almost never have the chance, since she is always playing for you, my husband."

Agnes turned to Trencavel. He reached his hand to his neck to loosen the collar of his tunic and coughed.

"Surely you jest, wife," said Trencavel. "You have Gauda at your command at any time. She can play for you tomorrow."

"Yes, Viscountess," I said. "I will play for you tomorrow, in your chambers. Any song you would like to hear."

Agnes smiled and put her hand on Trencavel's arm. I could see the shimmer of her blond tresses in the candlelight.

"No, I must hear her sing tonight, now," said Agnes. "I have waited long enough."

I looked to Trencavel, but he did not meet my eyes. I began to rise from my chair. Bertrand's big paw shot out and pushed me back to my seat.

"You cannot allow this," Bertrand said to Trencavel.

Trencavel stared at Bertrand, but said nothing. Bertrand slowly removed his restraining hand and I, once again, rose from my chair. I walked in a daze to where the musicians were playing and waited for them to finish another lively dance. I leaned over and spoke to the old man, who seemed to be the leader of the group.

"I have been asked to sing by the Viscountess," I said.

The old man covered his surprise well.

"What will you sing?" he asked. "We know all the songs of the troubadours."

"I would like to use the harp of your joglar, for I always play when I sing," I said.

The joglar who had been singing handed me his harp, with a very curious look. The pretty flutist glared at me. I looked at the drummer and saw pity in his eyes. I seated myself in the chair vacated by the harpist and ran my hands over the strings. A few knights in the front row of tables had noticed that I was now sitting with the performers and quieted down, stunned into silence by the spectacle of a lady performing as a common jogleresa. I felt their eyes boring into me like knives and felt my breath start to tighten. I consciously slowed down my breathing as I had been taught.

"Do you know the canso of Azalais de Porcairagues that starts 'Now we have come to the cold weather'?" I asked.

The musicians nodded. I briefly glanced up at the hall and saw how many people were there. Fortunately, most were not paying any attention to me, more occupied by their drunken stories and the carousing of the acrobats at the back of the hall. I felt my clothes tighten on my body as if they were for a woman smaller than I and felt sweat trickling down my back. I nodded to the drummer, who began a steady, slow beat. The old man played the first chord on the psalterion and I began to trace the notes of the melody on my harp. I began to sing the lyrics of my childhood teacher, Azalais, who had written this song with a broken heart.

I had never performed in front of such a large and undiscerning crowd. I felt first shame, but then a kind of excitement and nervousness. My voice was not very loud and I did not think I would be able to be heard. But, a very strange thing happened. It was almost as if the quietness, the stillness was an irresistible force. Soon, the entire hall was listening to me. I had never felt so exposed, yet this was intoxication better than wine.

I looked up at the raised dais and saw Agnes staring at me, savoring my humiliation. I felt my face flush with shame, but raised my shoulders and kept singing. She may force me to act the part of a jogleresa, but I would not give her the pleasure of seeing me fail. I looked instead at the Viscount. From this vantage point, he seemed so different from the man I had been entertaining for the last two years. The Viscount was still so very young, only 24 years old. He still wore his dark beard and long hair to his shoulders in the old style, though more and more young men shaved their faces and cut their hair short in the last few years. It was a good decision. It made his angular face appear more mature. And, I saw now what I had never seen in all this time. He stared at Agnes with such a longing that I became embarrassed for him. Yes, Agnes was incredibly beautiful, but no man should be forced to display such unrequited desire for his own wife. I knew so well the planes of that face and every sinew and curve of his flesh, but I knew not the man at all.

After the song finished, the hall burst into applause and while I knew I should be humiliated, I felt an intense joy. I decided to play one of my own songs then. How many times had I watched while some other woman mangled my verses and threw in sly winks and kisses during the sensuous passages? I always wanted to scream at these harridans, for turning my words of sensuous, almost divine, passion, into the backroom grunting of whores and piss-drunk groping of villains. I had always wondered what it would be like to sing as the male troubadours did, their own voices singing their own words. To be able to actually sing the words they way I meant them to be sung. I now knew. It was joy.

After I sang my own song, accompanied only by myself on the harp and the drummer, I began to feel uncomfortable. The weight of so many men's eyes on my body and face felt sickening. I started to hear whispers and laughter from some of the tables and knew that the words of the soldiers were not comments on my musical style or phrasing. I quickly got up and handed the harp to the joglar.

"You are welcome to join us any time, my lady," said the leader of the group.

I could not believe the effrontery of the man to think I would stoop to his level.

"I do not think that likely," I said. "But, I do thank you for your accompaniment."

I reached into my pocket for a few coins to give to the man. He would not accept them and I flushed. The pretty flutist laughed at my discomfort. I quickly made my way back to the table, but as I sat down, Agnes rose and left the room. Trencavel followed her. I turned to my left and looked at Bertrand de Saissac. He drained his mug and placed it on the table.

"You sang very beautifully," he said. "But, I wouldn't make it a habit, if I were you." We both turned to watch as the acrobats began to dance again and the joglars started tossing knives and all manner of objects into the air. The hall became steadily louder as the amount of wine increased. I drank more than I should have, wanting to taste again that delicious power of performing and knowing that I must pretend I had never experienced a more shameful event in my life. I must have left the hall very late for I had to step over passed out bodies on the floor of the hall. All

I knew is that I wished Agnes to be asleep before I entered her antechambers to sleep. I did not want to face her again tonight.

DAY 5 OF THE SIEGE OF CARCASSONNE

Wednesday, August 5, 1209

Bernard

Wednesday, August 5, 1209, morning

"You are a man of God, Bernard," said Guillaume. "I cannot believe you raised a hand in violence."

"Guillaume, keep your voice down," I said.

I anxiously looked around, afraid that one of the mason's apprentices had heard Guillaume's words. Fortunately, they all seemed too occupied repairing the damage caused by the Crusaders to pay attention to our mutterings.

The morning after our noble Crusaders' defeat at the hands of these heretical dogs, surely the work of Satan himself, Guillaume and I were back at work in the Castellar suburb with the mason. Though our willfully ignorant forces had not attacked where I had directed, they had none the less done considerable damage to the walls of the suburb with missiles thrown from catapult and trebuchet. Early this morning the mason had surveyed the damage and we now worked on the most damaged section of the wall, in the southwest corner of the suburb.

The carpenters had already built a small ramp so that the mason and his men could work near the top of the wall. The walls here were built of a double thickness, sealed together with a mixture of mortar and pebbles. In this section, the outer wall had remained standing, but most of the inner wall had been destroyed by a falling stone projectile. Already, stone cutters worked to hew the large stones take from the Cathedral. Just seeing those stones, taken from such a holy place to be used in such a despicable manner, reminded me of the sacrilege these minions of Satan were capable of. I resolved yet again to do everything in my power to fight this wave of evil.

I continued to make the mortar, adding the water slowly to my mixture of sand and lime. Now I had Guillaume to help me, which surely aided my sore arms and also allowed me to keep an eye on the boy. When a batch was finished, I sent him up the ramp with the fresh mortar in a basket on his back. I was not sure that he would even join me this morning. After he refused to go with the mason's men yesterday while they defended the walls, he had disappeared. I had not seen him until late that evening, back at the crowded boarding house. He would not tell me where he had gone and refused to even speak to me until this morning.

This was so like Guillaume. He had always left me to do the hard work, the necessary work, the messy work. How were we to continue our subterfuge and spy on these heathens if they did not trust us? I was forced to pretend to defend the city yesterday, though my whole body and soul ached bitterly against the actions I was required to take. Guillaume simply disappeared, heedless of the effects of his action. Then he had the gall to lecture me on my behavior. It is simple to live a pure life if one does not consider that we must survive and vanquish our foes in this tarnished, material world. But, I reminded myself that Guillaume was young and did not yet comprehend the complexities of life. I must strive to be patient with him, nurturing him in his faith and helping him learn his lessons of obedience.

Guillaume came back with his basket empty. He glared at me as he placed it down beside where I worked.

"I can no longer live like this," said Guillaume.

Fortunately, he spoke more softly this time. Between the shouts of the men as they worked and the stone cutters' tools chipping the blocks, we were unlikely to be heard. Nevertheless, Guillaume's stupidity and selfishness annoyed me. I fought to remain patient.

"Guillaume, can we not discuss this matter in a more private location?" I asked.

Guillaume face took on a stubborn set that I knew well. I knew we must discuss this matter here and now.

"I have made my vows to a life of prayer and service to the Lord," said Guillaume. "I cannot stomach the deception, and I do not know how you do so. Truly, brother, I worry for the state of your soul. I would not want to even think this of you, but it seems as if you are even relishing this situation. It seems no more than a game to you."

I continued stirring, but leaned closer to Guillaume so that I could talk quietly near his ear.

"You dare to call this a game, when I am risking everything to follow the Abbot's orders," I said. "Do you not remember how close we came to disclosure last night?"

We had returned to the old tavern, praying that the Lord Abbot had seen fit to pay our ransom, for such it was. I knew in my heart that the Lord Abbot would do that and more for all his children, but the packet of coin was short. Surely, some intermediary had turned thief, for there was only 5 times the amount of the normal pay, instead of the 10 times requested. I had thought that I would faint as the smuggler glared at us. Finally, he decided that it continued to be worth his risk, even at the 5 times pay. I knew we were truly blessed and that God guided our every action and protected us, even to the point of softening the heart of this vile cutthroat. The Lord would do everything to make sure that we succeeded in our most holy mission.

"Close, yes, and it is not surprising, since we are spies. This is not how our Lord Jesus Christ wanted us to preach his Gospel," said Guillaume.

"Guillaume, you talk of your vows, but you seem to find one very easy to break - obedience. It is not for us to question the will of the Abbot. Dare you to say that you know better than our Abbot or even the Pope, how we can best serve the Lord? You have been too long with these heretics, Guillaume, and seem to be acquiring their ways," I said.

Guillaume suddenly moved away from me and began lifting his basket. I turned to see the mason coming over to us. I hurriedly stirred the mortar, which had hardened a bit as Guillaume had distracted me from my work.

"Boys, are you arguing?" asked the mason. "Surely, you must respect the memories of your family. They would not have wanted to see you turned against each other. You have only each other left in this world and you must cherish that bond."

The mason placed his hand on Guillaume's shoulder and patted it. Guillaume looked at me and then looked down.

"Forgive me, brother," Guillaume said. "I was not thinking clearly. The mason is right."

I was glad that my brother had seen the errors of his ways, even though it had taken a heretic to point out that he was wrong.

"I accept your apology, Guillaume," I said and turned back to my work.

The mason looked at us and walked away. Surely, his was a soul worth saving from the hell fires of damnation. Guillaume and

I must continue our work. It was the only way that the mason could be saved.

I scooped out more mortar into Guillaume's basket and he returned to the ramp. I realized that the mason had spoken the truth. For though Guillaume and I had not lost our family at Béziers, we were alone in the world. Our parents had been killed by mercenaries when we were still children. My father and mother had been honest, God-fearing people, who worked hard and lived lives of devotion. And they had been slain by drunken louts, soldiers for hire who cared not for any Lord, earthly or heavenly. They had been caught up in the squabbles of earthly princes over land and wealth, lords like the Count of Toulouse and the Viscount Trencavel, who cared not at all for the Peace of God.

Fortunately, monks from the Cistercian abbey nearby had come to our village after the raid and had found us hiding in the charred remains of our barn. Guillaume had not even yet been weaned. I think he bore no recollection of our mother and father, though I tried to instill a memory of their goodness and the horror of their deaths. I remembered it all too well. The screams of our neighbors, the thick smoke in the air, and my mother's face as she hid us in the barn. It was all madness, the fury of those mercenaries, for they did not fight to gain advantage or even wealth. They wanted only to despoil, to pillage, to lay all to ruin.

The monks sent Guillaume to a wet nurse until he was weaned and then he joined me at the abbey school. So we found a new home. I loved the abbey, with all its rituals. I loved the chanting of the monks in their white robes and the smell of the beeswax candles, so clean and pure compared to the guttering tallow candles we had used at home. I loved studying in the scriptorium as a boy and then working there as an adult, copying manuscripts before handing them over to the illuminators. I was able to read so many treasures in my position as a copyist and I believe I could have been happy there all my life.

Guillaume was not a scholar, but he too found his place in the order. As a child, he was adored by the monks, coddled and spoiled in a manner not befitting those who had chosen an order renowned for the strictness of its discipline. The severity of the regime was eased for Guillaume, who was given meat against all the rules of the order. As a child, I was offered the same cuts of meat and extra portions that were given to Guillaume, but I had studied the Rule of St. Benedict and instead of giving in to these carnal pleasures, I reprimanded the monks who had broken their office by offering this food to me. I followed the rule strictly, but the monks all doted on Guillaume, with his weaknesses and moral laxity. Even as a youth, he did not pray with the devotion and fervor that I did. Guillaume even fell asleep in chapel, but the monks excused it. They said that he was fatigued from his strict devotion to a regime of manual labor. But, I knew better. Guillaume was young and strong and would rather spend his days cutting down trees and clearing land and then napping in the sun after a full, rich meal of delicious meats. It was I who lived an exemplary life of devotion, prayer, and discipline.

I believed that Guillaume and I would have been content to spend the rest of our days in the abbey, but we had been called by the leader of our order, Abbot Arnald of the Abbey of Citeaux, near Dijon. We traveled to the north in France, puzzled by the strange language and customs of these people and missing the sun of our home. Guillaume was forced, finally, to follow the Rule of St. Benedict strictly, now that he was separated from his doting and corrupting favorites at the abbey. I rejoiced in his struggles, for I knew that he would gain greater spiritual strength from them.

I was in awe of the Abbot Arnald from the very moment I first saw him. His was a fiery faith coupled with a powerful intellect. The combination was inspiring. I finally understood so many things. Our small abbey in the south was only a tiny satellite of this vast spiritual empire, leading finally to the Pope, our protector. The Cistercians had a zeal for order, a passion for spiritual perfection, and a rigorous discipline. We despised the laxity of the Benedictines. Not for us their fat bellies and lazy minds. The Cistercians would play a powerful role here on this earth as well as in the heavenly kingdom to come.

When we first arrived, we had been forbidden to shave our tonsures and our hair grew out wild and long. I was terrified. Had we committed some heinous transgression? Had the weaknesses of Guillaume and the monks been reported to this high level? Were we to be ejected from the order? But, then why would I, who had committed no sin or offense, be punished? It made no sense.

Finally, we were commanded to the presence of the Abbot Arnald and our mission was explained to us. We had many questions, but did not dare to ask the august man. It was only our duty to obey. And this we would do, however difficult it proved for my lax brother. We would do our part to make sure that these heretics were destroyed and that the cancer they placed on the land was removed. In a world where our most Holy Pope ruled all powerful, and the order and discipline of the Cistercians pervaded the land, no ragged troop of mercenaries would ever again wreak their havoc.

Trencavel

Wednesday, August 5, 1209, midday

The two sergeants dragged the man into the Viscount's hall, his legs jerking as they bumped along the stone floor. He was thin and his tunic was ripped. His head was bloody and it lolled backward. The line of petitioners waiting to see the Viscount's administrators parted to allow the soldiers to pass. Clerks at their tables looked up from their accounts and stared at them.

The two sergeants approached the corner of the hall where the Viscount sat, surrounded by his vassals. They waited quietly for the Viscount to finish speaking. Their prisoner moaned. Trencavel put down the plans of the city he held and turned to the sergeants.

"Who is this man?" asked Trencavel.

The older sergeant cleared his throat and spoke up.

"We found him at dawn sneaking in to the Castellar," said the sergeant. "He carried coin, a lot of it."

"He couldn't give us an answer as to what he was doing," said the younger sergeant. "So we've been beating it out of him the last few hours."

"At first he said he was just searching for his wife, who had a tendency to go prowling of a night," continued the older sergeant. "But we knew better than that. He finally confessed. He didn't know the name of the man he gave the coin to, but he could describe him."

"And who is this man?" asked Trencavel. "Where is he?"

"Well we went right quick to pick up the man and ask him a few questions. We thought he wouldn't be too hard to find. He's got a big scar across his face and he's always at that whorehouse by the Tour Davejean, but he was gone," said the younger sergeant. "We beat up a few of the regulars, but they couldn't give us any information about him."

"We're sure he's really gone," said the older sergeant.

Trencavel swore.

"So we don't know who the spies are inside," said Trencavel. "He didn't know anything about them?"

"I don't think so," said the younger sergeant. "He only knew the man with the scar."

"Though he did keep mumbling about the monks," said the older sergeant. "How they had so much money. Maybe the spy inside is working for the monks."

"Spies are always the damned priests," Bertrand de Saissac interjected. "You should lock the lot of them up."

"A spy is sometimes quite useful if we can discover who he is without him knowing it," said Trencavel.

"Lock up this man until he regains consciousness," Trencavel said to the sergeants. "I want to know when he does."

The sergeants dragged the man away. Trencavel turned back to the table where he sat with Bertrand de Saissac and Cabaret. Just then the building shook when a large stone launched from a Crusader trebuchet slammed into the Tour Pinte, whose base formed one wall of the hall. Clerks grabbed parchment to keep it from being stained by spilled ink. Some dust from the ceiling floated down to the table where Trencavel sat. The missile bombardment, though desultory, had been going on all morning, but this was the first direct hit to the castle.

"Target practice," said Bertrand. "Fortunately, they know about as much about catapults and trebuchets as my mother."

"I wouldn't be so sure of that," said Cabaret. "The Count of Nevers and the Duke of Burgundy have the gold to buy the services of the best siege engineers in all of Europe. They haven't even begun assembling some of their machines. The ones that are working are still being calibrated. They are only going to get better."

"All the more reason to attack them now while they are still unprepared," said Bertrand.

"They will collapse when the Crusaders' forty days of service is up," said Cabaret. "We need only hold out until then."

"That's still thirty days," said Trencavel. "If we don't keep access to the spring, we won't last until then. Bertrand, what's your plan to attack?"

Another missile hit the Tower and the room shook.

"We need to destroy their trebuchets and mangonels. I want to lead a small party of knights out tonight to set fire to their machines. Our archers have been trying to fire them all day, they've had no luck," said Bertrand

"It's a stupid plan" said Cabaret. "You'll be caught. What will your ransom be? The surrender of the city? Is that too high a price for the guardian of the Viscount, closer to him than any father?"

"The Viscount knows better than to think I would want him to do that for me," said Bertrand.

Cabaret looked over at Trencavel.

"These Crusaders may be dogs, but there are knights like us," said Trencavel. "If Bertrand is caught, he can be ransomed later, after this siege is over. They may slaughter townspeople, but they wouldn't dare kill one of us. Try tonight, Bertrand, and I wish you all the luck in the world."

Cabaret said nothing, but his face showed his disapproval.

"What do you plan to do about the spy?" Cabaret finally asked.

"I have my own spies," said Trencavel. "I plan to find him."

Constance

Wednesday, August 5, 1209, afternoon

Constance heard the heavy thud of the rock and the shattering of cobblestones behind her and stopped in her tracks. She breathed, realizing she was unhurt and then hurried along the road, freezing every time she heard the crash of another stone missile. She started to feel a little dizzy. Another missile landed on the roof of small shed holding a chicken coop. She glanced away as the rooster squawked in terror, his body impaled with the broken pieces of roof tiles, his flock of hens, broken and bleating on the ground. One escaped, unhurt, but mad with terror, and ran across the road, bleating and flapping its wings. A woman ran out of the house next to the chicken coop, crying and trying to save her livelihood.

Constance hurried through the almost deserted streets of the Castellar to the city walls. She hoped she would find Guillaume there. He and his brother had been working on repairing the walls of the Castellar when Guillaume had been injured. Constance ran to the first group of men working near the walls, but did not see Guillaume. She went up to a stone cutter shaping a large rock to fill a gap in the wall. He did not look up at first, but finally seemed to sense that Constance was waiting to speak to him and turned to her.

"Excuse me, sir," said Constance. "I am looking for two young men, Guillaume and Bernard. They are refugees from Béziers and they are working on the walls here."

The man laughed, but without mirth.

"I have lived in this suburb my whole life and I don't know half the people working here today," he said. "They could be anywhere, you had better keep searching."

Constance kept looking along the walls, asking anyone who would talk to her. She felt a little safer here in the shadow of the walls. She could hear the stones from the trebuchets hitting the exterior of the walls and others flying overhead to crash onto the roofs of the Castellar, but few fell in this zone right behind the walls. Constance had only left the house of good women a few hours ago, but already she felt both freer and more terrified than she had ever in her life.

Constance hated Azalais. She still did not understand why Azalais had been so angry at her last night. Constance had been washing herself with a clean rag, lightly dipped in the smallest amount of water and rose oil. The heat had settled on the city like a blanket and Constance wanted so badly to remove the sweat and the blood of others covering her skin. She stripped naked and sat in front of the small window in her cell. There was no breeze to rustle the thin piece of cotton hanging in the window, so Azalais could not think that Constance meant to seduce some man with her naked flesh. Constance gently rubbed the cloth down her aching arms and across the back of her neck, lifting her thick hair and wetting the tendrils that escaped. She moved the cloth across her chest and felt the roughness of the rag against her. She reached down and cleaned herself as she did every night, thinking how much pleasure there still was in this life, though she denied herself all meat and the intercourse of men, when Azalais burst into her small chamber. Azalais stared at Constance's nakedness and Constance felt ashamed, though she did not know why. She felt a heat rush into her cheeks and then Azalais grabbed her by the arm and slapped her face.

The old woman ordered her to dress and then brought her to the hospital room downstairs and ordered her to stay awake all night praying. Azalais accused her of wanting to indulge in carnal pleasure. Azalais then stood in front of her and demanded that Constance beg her for forgiveness.

Constance had lied to Azalais last night. She had lowered her eyes when she had asked for Azalais' forgiveness, because she did not want Azalais to see the truth there. For Constance did not want her forgiveness. Constance did not believe she needed any forgiveness, for she had done nothing wrong. It was the first time Constance had ever lied to Azalais, and the first time she had lied since becoming a good woman. With this action, she had betrayed her vows and this first betrayal had opened the door for all the rest. Despite being forced to stay up most of the night praying on her knees, Constance had awoken early this morning and quietly dressed in her two sets of clothes, ignoring the heat. When the old sister who watched the sick in the night had asked where she was going, Constance had lied again. To get eggs, she said and marveled at how easy it was to speak an untruth. She did not know where she was going, but only that she wanted to do something. To stop having things happen to her. She wanted to fight. Now that she had lied and disobeyed, she would also break her vow of nonviolence.

The more Constance thought about it, the more she realized that she was not ready to be a good woman. There was too much life for her to experience, too many forbidden pleasures that she was not ready to renounce. She ran by the marketplace and stole a small piece of sausage while the butcher stood chatting with a pretty woman. The meaty, gamey smell made her mouth fill with juices. She took a delirious delight in ripping a piece of the meat with her teeth and letting the fat dissolve on her tongue.

For what could happen to her? She would enjoy all the material pleasures the world offered and then she would take the consolamentum on her deathbed. And if she died before she could be consoled, her only punishment would be to do this life over again. Maybe she would be reborn as a countess or even a princess! Constance started to feel giddy, despite the heat, despite the stone missiles crashing into the roofs near her head. She decided that there was only one thing to do. She must find Guillaume. Guillaume was defending the city, doing real work. She could help him. She could fight these invaders and save her home. Constance knew Guillaume would help her. She was sure of it. Now she had only to find him.

Gauda

Wednesday, August 5, 1209, night

I did not hate myself for the pleasure I found in Trencavel's bed. For it was not a sin to couple, if both bodies found pleasure in the coupling. The sin only came when one did not find pleasure but coupled instead for money or position. However, I did surprise myself at the amount of pleasure I could feel in this purely physical coupling. After all, I had written so of the purity of unrequited love. I tried to believe that I dared not resist the overtures of the lord of the castle, but I could not lie to myself.

However, I worried that I committed incest in sleeping with the husband of my cousin. And adulterers were always punished. When Trencavel first commanded me to come to his bed, I had crept back to sleep in the antechamber of Agnes' rooms late at night, hoping that she smelled only the smoke of the fire and wine on me, as usual, and not the scent of her husband. But, now I knew that all was lost. How long had she known? She must hate me so. For surely she expected the Viscount to take women to his bed, servants and jogleresas and whores. She could not expect him to live the life of celibacy she had chosen. But she must never have thought her own lady-in-waiting, her own cousin would betray her. If she only knew how great my betrayal was. Sleeping with her husband was only the smallest part of it.

That night Trencavel took me into his bed and then he did not fall asleep, as I expected him to do. Instead he looked at me and ran one hand down the side of my body. I was slick with sweat.

"I think there is a spy in the castle," he said.

"But, there are always spies," I said. I hoped that my voice was steady and normal, for my heart began to beat quickly.

Trencavel occasionally spoke to me of his worries. I did not flatter myself that he sought my advice. Rather I felt as if he stared into a reflecting pool when he spoke to me at these times. I think it hardly mattered that I was there at all, only that he did not talk to himself.

"Of course, the usual. Priests, whores, and common thieves," he said. "No, I believe there is a spy highly placed in my retinue. The Crusaders know too much. They know where to attack."

"But, it is obvious to take the suburbs first," I said.

"It is more than that. They seem to know which towers are the weakest and which gates may most easily fall. They know where I am dispatching my forces," he said.

I was frightened. He must suspect me. But, it could not be me. I had sent reports, surely, but the Count of Toulouse thought I knew nothing of the details of military matters and would expect nothing of the sort from me. I had kept my reports simple and focused on Trencavel and his immediate group and what I overheard of their plans. Besides, I had not been able to send a single report since the siege had begun. It could not be me.

"I think I know who it is, Gauda," he said.

"Who?" I said. I was sure my voice quaked, but I hoped he had not heard it.

"Cabaret. I would almost believe that he wants me to lose this siege," he said. "I had always thought him a loyal vassal, loyal to me and loyal to my father before me. But, I do not know whom to trust anymore."

I swallowed and breathed.

"Do you believe he would betray you?" I said.

"Any man will betray you for enough gold," he said. "Gauda, I want you to watch him for me. I want to know what he does, where he goes, and who he sees. But do not let him know you watch."

I could not believe my task. Was I to spy for everyone in this war?

"I will try, my lord. But, he may know that I follow him. What do I do then?" I said.

"You will think of something, Gauda, I am sure. You are a very talented woman. Now, go, before my wife's spies see you here again. It would seem I am surrounded."

I pulled my linen tunic over my head before opening the curtains and stepping out of the warm bed. My feet touched the carpet and I searched in the candlelight for the rest of my clothes, looking down to avoid the glare of the Viscount's bodyguard. The bastard. He was always servile when I walked in with Trencavel, but always stared at my breasts through the fine linen as I dressed afterwards. Trencavel was already asleep behind the curtains of the large bed and I was alone.

Bernard

Wednesday, August 5, 1209, night

The streets near the tavern were quiet. I grabbed Guillaume and pulled him into a dark alley as I saw the night watchmen round the corner in front of us. There were many refugees sleeping in the streets of the city, but they did not move at night and the watchmen ignored them. There were more patrols in the streets and I was especially troubled by the appearance of signs, newly tacked up on buildings and on trees in the city:

Spy

This fifth day of August, by the Viscount Trencavel, it is ordered that all men of the city search a spy. A reward is offered for the capture of this traitor. This spy may hide in the disguise of a priest or monk. He may lurk near the city walls at dawn and dusk.

Guillaume and I hardly breathed as the patrol passed within a few feet of us. But, the Lord protected his noble servants in their righteous mission, and we were not seen. For surely, these men watch, but do not know what hour of watch the thief will come. They are as blind men.

We waited another few minutes in the alley and then quietly left. We stepped over the bodies of sleeping men, women, and children and made our way towards the tavern. Here the streets were emptier. Suddenly, an old woman, her face swollen and bruised, came out of the shadows. She clutched her skinny hand around Guillaume's arm. He managed to stifle a shout of alarm, but jumped back out of her grasp.

"You must not go there," she said, again grabbing Guillaume's arm. "They are looking for you."

Though her face was too battered to recognize, I could see the tattered clothes of the old whore who served wine at the tavern.

"Run away, my handsome boy," she said. "Don't let them get you."

Guillaume stood and stared as she slinked back into the shadows. I understood all too quickly what had happened. I tried to pull Guillaume, but he seemed rooted to the spot. I could hear the clank of the watchmen's pikes as they returned from where they had just disappeared. They must have heard the old woman's voice and come to investigate. We could not go back the way we had come. I finally managed to jolt Guillaume out of his reverie.

"Her face," he said. "Who did that to her? We must help her."

"Guillaume, we have no time," I said. "We have to get away."

I dragged him down the street towards the tavern. As we approached the end of the street, I pulled him into the shadows and slowed down. No soldiers appeared to guard the tavern. The street was almost invitingly empty. This alarmed me more than anything we had seen so far. To step towards that tavern would invite capture. But, we could not go back. I could hear the watchmen advancing up the street, their heavy feet in an uneven rhythm.

Quickly, I grabbed Guillaume and pulled him down beside me in the shadows. The street was filthy and as my body sunk into the foul mud I tried not to think of housemaids emptying chamber pots from the overhanging windows.

"Pretend to sleep, Guillaume," I said. "And, for once, just keep your many illuminating comments to yourself."

Guillaume simply nodded, his eyes wide open. I curled on my side, my body tense, willing my breaths into an approximation of the steady, deep cadence of sleep, trying to ignore the odor of decay. Guillaume looked at me. It was too dark to see anything but the flash of the whites of his eyes. I lifted my hand quietly and gently closed his eyes and patted his cheek. Poor Guillaume, he had seen so much in these last few months. He had lived his whole life from early childhood in the confines of a monastery. There was violence even there, but only the blessed blows of self-discipline from those monks who practiced it and the occasional wounded traveler. Guillaume had seen much in these weeks, and had remained strong, but somehow the face of the old whore (and maybe his fears for the preservation of his earthly body - oh he of little faith!) had unhinged him. I could hear him softly crying and when I went to pat his cheek again, my hand came away wet. I pulled my hand away again as I heard the night watchmen getting closer. Hopefully, they would not even see us huddled here.

I was wrong.

The big watchman kicked me with his boot. I feigned deep sleep. The watchmen, unimpressed, kicked me again.

"Get up, you laggards," said the watchman. "Are you drunk?"

"No, sir," I said, in my most servile voice. I would not have to lower myself to these illiterate louts when the Abbot ruled over this city. "We are refugees. We have nowhere to sleep."

"No refugees allowed on this street," he said. "You'll have to move back to the center of the city or the market square."

I stood up and pulled Guillaume up beside me. We started shuffling along towards the center of the city, when we heard a voice ordering us to stop. It was the smaller of the two watchmen. We stopped and turned to face them.

"Why were they here now?" said the smaller watchman to the other. "We cleared this street of refugees around dusk."

"Why were you still here, boys?" said the big watchman.

I cleared my throat.

"We started out the night nearer the walls of the Castellar, but we were chased from there," I said. "We tried to find a spot to rest near the market place, but the crowds were too great. Rough youths from the mountains threatened to beat us, so we ran off. This spot was the only quiet place we could find."

The smaller night watchman turned to his partner.

"How do we know that one of them is not the spy we are looking for?" he asked.

"No, the spy is disguised as a priest," said the big watchman. "One of these two is only a boy. Let them go."

The smaller one stared at his partner, but did not say anything. They turned to continue their patrol and I thought it prudent to leave quickly. Guillaume followed. We did not say anything until we had put several blocks between us. I turned to Guillaume.

"Brother, surely you can doubt no longer," I said. "The Lord is our strength and our refuge, a very present help in trouble. Even as Daniel was saved from the lion's den and Jonah saved from the belly of the whale, were we saved from discovery."

"Thou shalt not lie," said Guillaume and continued walking.

Finally, we reached the chaos of the central market place. Refugee families huddled over their meager possessions, trading anything for food and water. Guards patrolled the edges of the market place. I was afraid to go back to our boarding house that night for fear that we would raise suspicions. We smelled of latrines and the dirt of the street and looked much the worse for wear. Suddenly, I felt a hand grab the back of my arm. I turned around quickly, ready to strike the offending interloper, but it was no more than a girl.

"I knew I would find you," she said.

"Constance," Guillaume said. He smiled, but then looked concerned. "What are you doing here? Why aren't you at the house of good women?"

"I have left," she said. "I could no longer stay there. It is not what I believe is right."

Guillaume started to smile again.

"I want to help defend the city," she said. "I want to fight those evil Crusaders. I am tired of letting them kill us while we do nothing. Take me with you to your mason. I am strong girl, I can help. Only, please help me. Don't let anyone know who I really am. They will not understand and will send me back to the house of good women. No one in the Castellar knows me. I'll be safe."

The smile disappeared from Guillaume's lips, but one began to form on mine. This is exactly what we needed to protect us. Already, Guillaume's youthfulness acted as a decoy. While I alone would have run a good chance of being taken for a spy, I doubted very much that any sergeants or night watchmen would suspect the three of us.

"Of course, Constance," I said. "We are proud of your desire to help us and understand your concerns. Your secret is safe with us, is it not Guillaume?"

Guillaume turned to me and began to speak, but thought better of it. Instead he turned to Constance.

"Truly, it gives me great joy to see you gone from that house," Guillaume said.

Constance smiled at both of us. Oh, she was a wicked Jezebel. And it pained me to have to be so close to her foul female form, but surely it was a sign that she was sent to us, just when we needed a shield.

"We need to find a corner to rest," I said. "We will take turns sleeping so that none of us need worry that our clothes will be ripped off our backs as we sleep."

Constance babbled to Guillaume of her day, her search for us, and her foolish whims. Guillaume listened attentively, and I saw that I would, again, have to watch the boy. Clearly, he was an innocent lamb to her lion. Finally, the girl began to yawn and soon she fell deeply asleep. It was the middle watch of the night and even the guards had dozed to sleep in the corners of the square. We could hear an occasional stone missile slam into the city walls or crash into a roof, rousing the sleepers, but the machines were not in position to reach the central marketplace.

"I know I can save her, Bernard," said Guillaume. He spoke softly. "She has been led astray by this city of heretics, but she has a good heart. But, why did you support her in her deception. Has she left her life of heresy only to become a liar?"

"Guillaume, would you desire that she know the truth about you now?"

Guillaume face flushed.

"You both have your stories to tell and your reasons for doing so. Do not start down that path. It is too dangerous for all of us. For you know, Guillaume," I said. "It is more than likely she will save us. A fair bargain - we save her soul and she saves our skins."

DAY 6 OF THE SIEGE OF CARCASSONNE

Thursday, August 6, 1209

Trencavel

Thursday, August 6, 1209, morning

Trencavel watched the Crusaders. Men were hammering newly-fallen and hewn tree trunks into a structure that looked much like the covered wooden galleries atop the walls of the city where he now stood with Cabaret. The structure seemed as if it would be large enough to hold maybe twenty men. Nearby, wainwrights were creating huge wheels. The noise of hammers and swearing filled the air. Apparently, the monks were taking a day off from their chanting.

"It's a cat," said Cabaret.

"I know," said Trencavel.

Trencavel had seen cats used before, quite effectively. The Crusaders would use the cat to get close to the walls of the Castellar. Under its protection, the sappers would dig out the walls, replacing them with a wooden structure and straw. When they were done, they would light the straw and burn the structure. The wall would usually fall down in that spot or would be so weakened that it could be easily breached.

"They won't be ready until tomorrow, at the earliest," said Trencavel. "There is still time to do something."

"And end up like your guardian?" asked Cabaret.

Trencavel said nothing. Bertrand de Saissac's raid last night had not been successful. They had managed to destroy one catapult, but the heavier siege engines were well-guarded. Bertrand had been badly injured and was lucky to have been dragged back to the city by two of his men. Bertrand's bravery made his men loyal followers. They knew he would rescue them, even if he had to risk his life to do so, and they returned the sentiment. But, Trencavel was starting to wonder if Cabaret were right. Maybe Bertrand's military style was becoming obsolete. Maybe it always had been. For wars were won and lost during sieges, and while a spectacular sortie could temporarily give the defenders the upper hand, the siege was usually won by the side with the most resources or the most luck.

Trencavel barely remembered his father. A busy Viscount had

little enough time for a small boy and Trencavel spent most of his time playing with the other boys about the castle - weaving about the courtyard on stilts in the late summer evenings and playing checkers in front of the fire on cold winter nights. His father's castle was in a wealthy cultured city. Troubadours came from far and wide to perform at the Viscount's banquets. The Viscount fostered intellectuals, rescuing the father of Abraham ben Isaac from prison and installing the scholar at his court. When his father died, Trencavel was only nine and he was sent to live in the mountains with his guardian, Bertrand de Saissac. His whole life changed.

Bertrand de Saissac did not hold with boys being pampered by their mothers and believed that too much learning was not good for a fighting man. His stronghold in the Black Mountains was almost monastic in its severity. Half the town were good men and women, pacifist and abstemious. The other half were fighting men, training in Spartan conditions, though not averse to the pleasures of life and plunder after a victorious battle.

When Trencavel arrived there was only one other boy as small as he, Pierre Bermond. In the beginning, they cried quietly at night, missing their mothers, but afraid lest the older boys hear their whimpering and beat them up. But, little by little, things got better. Trencavel and Pierre began to love their life in the mountains. They learned to swim in the cold mountain streams and climbed trees to pelt apples at the older boys. They jousted and wrestled until they grew big and strong.

And, always, every night, the fighting boys and men would sit in front of the fire and listen to troubadours sing of chivalry. It wasn't all honor and sacrifice. No one laughed harder than Bertrand when a jogleresa pretended to play the shy, young shepherdess who jealously guarded her virginity from the knight, who sang of his torture as he was kept from her charms. Bertrand often took the jogleresa to bed, loudly exclaiming that he would show this shepherdess a thing or two.

A rock missile hit the city walls and shook the gallery, waking Trencavel from his memories.

"I have no intention of ending up injured and out of this fight," said Trencavel.

"Well, what are your plans then?" asked Cabaret.

"I have not yet decided," said Trencavel, which was not entirely true. But Trencavel had no intention of telling Cabaret his plans. Probably it was just good defensive maneuvers on the part of the Crusaders that led to the failure of Bertrand's sortie, but Trencavel could not be sure. Cabaret believed they did not stand a good chance to defeat the Crusaders. Maybe he planned to hasten the fall of the city and profit from a quick shift of allegiance? Cabaret was not known for sticking with the losing side in any war. He was shrewd, that was sure. But was he a betrayer?

Trencavel felt very alone. He was stuck with two advisors in the biggest battle of his life. One he trusted implicitly, but Trencavel was beginning to think that Bertrand's style of fighting was most successful when recounted in song long after the battle. The other advisor was shrewd, but would his cleverness help Trencavel or only himself?

Constance

Thursday, August 6, 1209, morning

Constance followed Bernard and Guillaume as they left the crowded market place and headed to the Castellar where they were helping to fix the wall. She felt tired. And relieved that she had found Guillaume, more relieved than she wanted to admit.

Constance had been used to a life of enclosure in the house of good women. Certainly they went into the streets near the house, to the market place, and to visit the sick, but always in groups. In her neighborhood, everyone knew each other and all accorded some respect to the good women, even the Catholics and those who believed only in their dice or drink.

But now Constance knew no one. The city was crowded with refugees. Men leered at her in the street as she walked past, her head modestly lowered. She had dreaded the coming of the night, as she walked through the streets yesterday. By the time she had run into Guillaume and his brother, she had been almost crying and ready to return to Azalais and beg for her forgiveness, this time for real. But now that she was with Guillaume and Bernard she felt safe. She hurried to move closer to their backs as they walked through the crowds. She did not want to lose them again.

The day was already extremely hot, though the sun was not yet high. There was no wind and the city smelled of unwashed misery. There were so many people packed into the streets and no water to wash with. Even Bernard and Guillaume, who Constance noticed had been very clean young men, were filthy, their clothes stained and smelling as if they had wallowed in the gutters.

As they left the city and entered the Castellar, Constance became overwhelmed by an odor so foul it made the boys seem as if they had been bathing in rose water. Bernard and Guillaume stopped abruptly, coughing and raising their hands to their faces.

"What is that stench?" said Constance. She raised her tunic to cover her mouth and nose.

"A dead cow, festering in the sun," said Bernard. "Why don't these people move it?"

"Inhaling rotten odors causes premature death," said Constance. "No one will dare risk getting too close."

Constance tried not to stare at the cow as they walked quickly past. Its stomach had burst and maggots crawled over its flesh. Unfortunately, there was no wind to dispel the foul humors. Of more concern were the stones that flew overhead, crashing into rooftops and cracking against the Castellar walls. Constance tried to stay close to the edges of the street, but even that would not help her if a stone flew too close.

Bernard and Guillaume followed the streets as if they knew them well and Constance struggled to keep up. Finally, they reached the southwest corner of the wall. A group of men worked by the wall, trying to repair the damage sustained by thrown rocks. Their leader, a strong, squat man, stopped when he saw Bernard and Guillaume approaching. This man must be the mason, Constance thought.

"Do you like the gift the Crusaders sent us?" he asked when Bernard, Guillaume, and Constance got close.

"What do you mean?" asked Bernard.

"You didn't smell it?" asked the mason.

"It was sent by the Crusaders?" asked Guillaume. "But how?"

The man pointed up at the sky. As they watched, another stone flew over the walls and landed in the street near the dead cow, dirt flying in the air. The first days of the siege had been quiet compared to this. The soldiers had fought, but the Crusaders had not yet begun to bombard the city. Now their siege engines were in place. The whole city was under bombardment, but the worst of the attack centered on the Castellar. The Crusaders unleashed their anger at their bitter defeat on the defenders of the suburb. Staying carefully out of range of the archers, the siege engineers launched huge stones from their trebuchets. Fortunately, their aim was shaky, but the large missiles occasionally found their way to the walls of the suburb or crashed through the roof of some poor unfortunate's house.

"They mean to kill us, one way or another," the mason said.

He stopped and looked at Constance.

"Whom have you brought to help us?" the mason asked.

"A refugee girl that we found," said Bernard. "She has lost the rest of her family and has no one to protect her. She wants to help defend the city."

"Good, she can help my wife bring water from the spring into the Castellar," said the mason. "You go, too, Guillaume. They need your strength more there than I do here. Bernard, get to work mixing the mortar."

Guillaume and Constance went in the direction of the Castellar gate that led to the Fontegrade spring. They reached the gate and stepped just outside the city walls. It felt so strange to be on this side of the wall, after the last few days enclosed in the city. Constance felt vulnerable and very small, even though she knew that the archers overhead on the Castellar walls and the natural curve of the land on the path to the spring protected them from a direct attack from the Crusaders. Constance and Guillaume watched as a steady line of women and men moved quickly across the short distance to the spring. The men, from the water carriers' guild, carried their shoulder yokes with buckets hanging from each side. With their practiced steps, they moved quickly, but did not lose any water. They were the initiated and looked down haughtily at the rag-tag bunch of men and women who carried water in any bag or bucket they could find, little wavelets slopping over the edges, wasting precious water every time a foot slipped or the terrain changed unexpectedly.

A short, stout woman with a pretty face, now red with exertion, came up to them.

"You're one of the boys working with my husband," she said. "He said he would try to spare some strong arms to help us. I'm Beatritz."

"It is pleasure to meet you, honored wife of the mason," said Guillaume. "I am Guillaume, brother of Bernard. And this is Constance, a fellow refugee."

Beatritz smiled at Guillaume and then turned to Constance.

"You look familiar," she said. "Have I seen you before?"

"No, I am sure you must not have, madam," said Constance. She quickly looked down at the ground. Constance thought she recognized the mason's wife, too.

"Very well. You look very like a girl in this town, maybe she's a cousin?" said Beatritz. "Anyway, you two better get to work. We don't know how much longer we have to stock up before the next assault."

She handed them each wine skins, one for Constance and two for Guillaume.

"Stay low and close to the side of the hill. Don't dawdle. If you hear the guard's trumpet, turn and run for the gate. We will leave it open as long as we can, but if you do not make it back in time, we will have to shut you out. We don't want to let them in, like they did at Béziers," Beatritz said, then glancing quickly at Guillaume, added "God rest their souls."

Constance followed Guillaume out of the gate. She had to hurry to keep up with his long strides, but she did not want to fall behind. She could not see over the hillock, but she knew that the Crusader army waited on the other side. They were far down the hill, encamped by the banks of the River Aude. Constance knew they were not in battle formation and that all worked on the siege engines or continued to bombard the city with stone missiles. Knights would normally not attack until all was ready, but she kept thinking of Béziers. There it was not the knights who attacked the city on the first day of the siege, but the camp followers, the wretched dregs of their society, harlots, mountebanks, water sellers, and even poor washerwomen. They swarmed through the city, a dirty, desperate mass that stole everything it could and burned what it could not steal.

Constance wanted to ask Guillaume about Béziers, to ask how

he had managed to escape from the inferno, but she did not. She did not want to make him think of everything he had lost. She too had lost her family, even though she had run away from them. She had cried herself to sleep every night at first, quietly, quietly, so that Azalais and the other good women would not hear. Sometimes Constance thought of her brothers and sisters. She wondered what had become of them. Had her father forced one of her younger sisters to marry the miller in her stead? Were her parents even alive? Did her brother still care for the flocks of sheep up in the mountains? Guillaume looked so sad and confused, so preoccupied, and Constance wished only that she could help him.

They made it to the spring and waited nervously while a water carrier filled their skins. Constance felt stifling hot in her two layers of clothes. Sweat poured down her shoulders and back. She could not stand it anymore - she stopped a moment and drank greedily from the fountain. She handed Guillaume the small bucket sitting by the side of the fountain and he, too, poured the cool liquid down his throat with abandon. Constance grabbed the bucket again and poured water over her face and hands, soothing the back of her neck with the coolness. She then filled the bucket up again and threw it at Guillaume. He looked at her, water dripping off his hair and face, and Constance was afraid he was angry, but then he laughed, the first time she had ever heard that sound and Constance only knew that she wanted to hear it again. His face broke into the most beautiful smile, with a deep dimple on one side that made her want to laugh with him. Guillaume picked up the bucket and threw the rest of the water in it at Constance. She shrieked and then laughed harder than she had ever remembered.

"There's a war going on, in case you had not noticed," barked the water carrier. "Your sacks are full, get moving, and stop wasting the water. You won't find your behavior so funny in a week or two."

Constance and Guillaume quickly picked up their sacks and moved along the path with their eyes down, but as soon as they got away from the water carrier, they both started laughing again. Constance looked up and smiled at Guillaume, who looked down at her with a kind smile.

Suddenly, they saw a stone missile approaching through the air. Guillaume grabbed Constance and threw her against the hillside. The stone landed with a heavy thud just behind them. Constance raised her head as she heard an awful shrieking. The stone had landed on the leg of one of the water carriers, trapping him under its weight. The man lay prostrate on the ground, grabbing at his exposed thigh, as the water from his buckets slopped out into the ground. Guillaume quickly jumped up and tried to move the boulder. The man shrieked even louder. Several others came from the line and finally freed the man. Constance went to him. His leg was crushed, broken into innumerable bits that no surgeon could ever piece together again. He was bleeding heavily from where the bone had bitten through the skin. Constance ripped off her head covering and quickly tied it tightly at the man's thigh. He screamed, but the bleeding seemed to ease up. Three water carriers gently picked him up and carried him towards the gate, his screams echoing over the valley.

Constance and Guillaume looked over at their water skins. They sat empty on the ground in a muddy puddle. They grimly looked at each other, picked up the empty skins, and headed back towards the spring.

Bernard

Thursday, August 6, 1209, noon

I worried that Satan would tempt my weak young brother, but never knew how devious the evil tyrant could be. For I thought that I would always be able to be at his side as he faced the seductions of the temptress, her flesh like Eve's apple, ripe for the plucking and ready to destroy man. But, Satan had used his whiles to separate us. My brother was right now in the clutches of the witch, ready to succumb to her poisonous charms, while I stood here stirring this infernal mortar, unable to protect him and fend off her approaches. My mind was fixated on his danger and I could not stop thinking about them, walking together by the fountain, her eyes glancing at him coyly, pretending to be the innocent maiden, when all knew her basest desires.

Suddenly I heard the mason yelling, breaking me from my anxious reverie.

"What do you mean we have no more base stones?" the mason bellowed.

I looked up and saw the head of the stone cutters standing up to the mason.

"There are no more," said the stone cutter. "We have finished with everything we took from the cathedral."

"Well, find some others," said the mason. "Take down someone's house. They won't have it for long anyway unless we fix this wall."

"None of the houses in this suburb are made of stones large enough to be the base of this wall," said the stone cutter. "You are just going to have to make do with what you have."

I looked up and saw the reason for the mason's anger. Over the past few days, I had learned that the strength of a wall was not based on mortar, but on the sheer weight of the stones themselves. The mortar was important, of course. It served to level the uneven faces of stones and worked as a joint between the monstrous cut stones. But, the stones themselves were the force that held a wall together.

We had been steadily repairing this section of the wall, damaged on the inside. The mason directed the laying of gigantic base stones and then built upwards from these goliaths with slightly smaller stones. Though the mortar between them might not harden for months or even years, the stones themselves would keep out the harshest invader.

But all around us different teams worked on sections of the Castellar suburb walls. These walls had been allowed to fall into disrepair in recent years. So much work needed to be done that we had simply run out of the largest stones, so critical to providing a solid base. Most of the other masons' teams were finished laying the largest stones. Their workers had moved on to placing the slightly smaller stones near the top or to filling in the space between the outer and inner parts of the wall with a mix of mortar and small rocks.

Only our mason's team still stood in front of a section of inner wall that lacked a base.

"You're going to have to use smaller stones salvaged from the houses," said the stone cutter, pointing to a pile of rubble. "There's no other option." "If the invaders break through the outer wall here with that cat, an inner wall made from these pieces of crap will crumble," said the mason.

"But what chance is there that they will attack just in this spot?" asked the stone cutter.

He gestured with his arm in a wide circle.

"They have the entire wall of this suburb open to them. They know we're working on the walls all over this place, but they don't know where we ran out of base stones."

"I still don't like it," said the mason. "I have never been responsible for such shoddy work." "Well, you don't have much of a choice," said the stone cutter. "Make it look good and hope they don't get lucky."

I could not believe my ears. This was the chance I had been waiting for - my true opportunity to aid my blessed Crusaders and help them to the victory they justly deserved. But, oh how cruel was my life. Since the scar-faced man from the tavern had been taken by the Viscount's guards last night, I had no way to get this precious information to my lord, the Abbot.

We worked all morning, suffering under the bad temper of the mason. We were all careful not to anger him further, but I could not stop thinking about how I could pass this vital information on.

Finally I had a chance to break free when the master mason called a short break for a noon repast. The other men gathered around as small boys brought bread and cheese, but I slipped away, anxious to head to the spring and protect my brother. If I could do nothing about the information I possessed about the wall, at least I could try to stop the vixen who was trying to steal my brother.

I headed into the maze of streets of the Castellar, hoping to get to the gate to the spring more quickly. I did not want to be gone for too long. A ragged man came up to me and pulled on my sleeve. I thought he was just another ragged refugee and though the Lord Jesus Christ had consorted with beggars and thieves, I did not have our Lord's patience or his time. I pushed him away, but he would not let go. I began to worry that I would be assaulted when the man began to speak to me in a cultured, educated voice with the accent of the French.

"Are you Bernard?" said the man softly.

I glanced around quickly. How did this man know my name? Was this a trap? Had the scar-faced man been taken and talked to the Viscount's guards?

I began to shake. My hands felt sweaty. I did not know what to do. I was sure this must be a test. They were searching for the spy everywhere and someone must have suspected me. I had to get away from this man.

"Excuse me," I said. "I do not know who you are."

The man looked into my eyes.

"We share the same father," he said. "You can trust me. But you must move quickly before we attract any attention."

I made to quickly away from the man, but then I remembered that I had been sent here for a divine purpose. If this man was truly a link to my father Abbot, I had to take the risk. For what was the price I paid here on earth for this risk when my heavenly reward would be so great? And if he were truly from the Abbot then this would be a great miracle, the miracle I had prayed for only hours before. How swiftly work the ways of the Lord!

"Tell me what you know," he said. "Our father needs to know. We know what happened to your messenger and we know the danger you are in, but you must know that your work is vital and must continue."

I looked into the man's eyes and decided that I must trust, trust and obey. I quickly told him of the problems at the wall of the Castellar and where exactly he must tell the Abbot to attack.

He placed his hand on mine and made the sign of the Cross. Then he disappeared into from the Castellar, heading into the city. I did not know whether he was angel or man, but I knew that my prayers had been answered.

Gauda

Thursday, August 6, 1209, afternoon

Agnes slept on her couch, the heat of the day rendering her listless and pale. I thought I would have a few moments to steal to write, but I could not bring my stylus to my wax tablet. I could not stop thinking of the dream that woke me from my bed early this morning, sweat drenching my linen.

In my dream, a young woman walked naked down the street, trying to hide herself in her long hair. Small boys jeered and threw pebbles at her skin. Grown men spat at her feet. Her hands were bound and she followed the steps of the soldiers, for though they were her punishers, they were also her protectors. The young woman walked slowly, careful to listen for any cries of distress from behind her. Behind the woman walked a man. He was chained to her by a light iron tightly placed around his manhood and then wound about the woman's hips.

"Adulterous whore!" screamed a man from the crowd.

"Harlot!" a thin woman yelled.

The young woman stumbled and fell. The man behind her groaned and dropped to his knees. She began to cry, but she stopped for she would not let these people see her weakness. She turned to look at the man behind her and he gazed at her with hatred.

"Bitch," he mouthed.

And then the woman did begin to cry. She stood up slowly and gently and, after turning to make sure the man was standing, she continued onward.

Though I had been awake for hours I could not shake the image of the woman's tear-strewn face from my mind. For this was not just a dream, but also a memory. As a girl, I walked the streets of a town, I remembered not which, with Azalais, my old teacher who raised me when my mother died. We saw this woman, jeered at and despised, linked so cruelly to her lover. For as much as our society raised the ideal of the lover chasing his married lady, it punished the adulterous couples who actually perpetrated the act. Though this was an old punishment, passing out of favor even in my youth, it still troubled me to remember it. And what troubled more was what Azalais had said after she quickly led me away from the spectacle.

"Gauda, always remember what price there is to pay for love. The songs all lie," she said. Her face became hard and we never talked of it again.

It was days like this that I wished I still had a mother, even though I should have been a mother myself by my advanced age, if God had not seen fit to blight me with a barren womb. I could remember very little of my mother, except what I thought was her face, though by this time I am sure that my tangled memories had contrived to make it more beautiful and kind than it was in real life. I treasured one memory of her high forehead and steady eyes, warm brown and speckled with honey, as she leaned over me as I lay sick with fever.

It was my teacher Azalais who had been the mother to me I never had. It was she who had taken care of me at my first bleeding. I remembered handing her the rag stained a light rust in furrows, warm from being pressed to my body.

"I will save this blood and use it to find for you a good husband - noble and gentle," she said.

And it was Azalais who comforted me when these dreams did not come true. I should have married well and richly, but I foolishly married my first husband for love. I could not give him children, and so he gave me away to my second husband, a man with weak knees and weaker will, whose only redeeming feature, in my eyes, was his quite remarkable attachment to me. And while I hated my first husband for his betrayal, I found that I hated the second for his love. Fortunately, he was now dead, though my greedy stepsons had managed to steal my family's lands in the short time since his death. I sued, but my money was all taken by lawyers and the courts, with no end in sight for the case. My case would next come before the Count of Toulouse and, this time, I would win. I had worked hard enough to regain what was rightfully mine. Unless, of course, I died.

But, I would not think of that. I could not die. I had too much waiting for me.

Agnes awoke. She stretched her arms and stood up suddenly. Her right cheek was imprinted with the cross weave of her bed linens. She walked over to her mirror and sat down in front of it, idly playing with her hair.

"Gauda," she said. "Come brush my hair."

I came over to her, but found it difficult to approach closely. Agnes smelled horribly of decay and the marsh rushes. She must be ill. She saw my face and blushed.

"Cousin," I said. "Are you ill? Can I get you medicines?"

"Yes, I think I must be suffering from an excess of bile," she said. "Go to the old Good Woman and get me medicines."

"And shall I pick up some rose petals and jasmine?" I asked. And, I thought to myself, the strongest perfumes Azalais had. For I could not stand her stench much longer.

Agnes colored bright red.

"Yes, that will do, cousin," she said. "And don't take too long. I need you back here quickly."

I left her room and smiled to myself. I would get to see Azalais today. And, I did not care if Agnes screamed at me and threw things when I returned and pinched my cheeks until I cried, I would see Azalais and stay as long I cared to.

Azalais

Thursday, August 6, 1209, evening

Azalais paid the grave diggers who had come for the bodies of those who had died unclaimed in the hospital. The sturdy men carried the shrouded figures out to their wagon, placing them atop a mound of corpses en route to the overfilling church yard. So many dead already and the siege less than one week old, thought Azalais.

In the distance, Azalais could hear the siege machines of the Crusaders shelling the Castellar suburb, but at least it was quieter in this part of the city today. Azalais said a prayer for all the souls trapped still on this earth in their misery and blessed the grave diggers. She turned to head back inside the hospital, but took one last look around, as she had done every time she ventured outside since she had realized that Constance was gone yesterday afternoon. At first, she thought the girl had only taken a quick trip to the market. Then, she assumed she must be sulking in her chamber, but when Azalais went there to search for her, hoping to find her meditating on her impure actions, Constance was gone, as were her only change of clothes. Azalais felt her stomach drop, as if heavy with lead, and knew the girl was gone.

They did not speak of it among themselves, the good women. For occasionally they had lost others. Women who were not ready, who could not live the life of purity required of those who had chosen to forsake this world. These women went away, quietly, and the others pretended that they had never existed. Fortunately, it was almost always the young who went, those who were new to the life and who would never perform the consolamentum. That duty was left to the most senior and committed of the good women or good men, the ones who were iron sure in their conviction. If ever they lapsed into a life of sin not only would they lose their own salvation, but all who had been consoled by them would lose theirs as well. One break in the chain condemned all those down the line back to the agony of an endless cycle of rebirth in this world. No one wanted to think about those who left. No one wanted to think that it could it happen to them or, even worse, to the ones who had consoled them. There was always a particular joy, far beyond the normal contentment, when an ancient good woman or good man, who had consoled many souls, had passed from this earth, still sinless and pure.

Azalais had never thought it would be Constance who would have gone. There were others, feckless young girls, placed by their parents, who Azalais worried about, but she never once doubted Constance's faith. It was too strong, too present, since the day she came to live with them. Azalais took one last look around, hoping to see Constance's dark head, hoping to hear that it was all a mistake. Azalais did not see Constance, but she did see another most welcome sight. Azalais' face broke into a broad smile as she embraced the woman who came across the courtyard to greet her.

"Gauda, my daughter," said Azalais. "It is so good to see you."

"My dear teacher," said Gauda. "It is a blessing to be in your presence."

"We do not see each other often enough," said Azalais. "I take it she finally let you out of her sight for a few hours."

"Yes, but only to get some medicines for her," said Gauda.

Both women laughed and Azalais placed her arm around Gauda's waist as they walked into the house together. Gauda followed Azalais through the large room they were using as a hospital and into Azalais' herb storeroom. Gauda sat in a corner of the room under a small window. Sunlight poured into the room, though it was late in the day. It was still hot, but the massive heat of noon had lightened a bit. Azalais prepared some peppermint tea for them with some precious water. They sipped the steaming, pungent brew.

"This refreshes me," said Gauda. "Though I would have thought the heat of the tea would have enervated me instead."

"Like heals like," said Azalais. "The heat of the tea chases away the heat of your body. And the peppermint soothes away headaches, like those the heat can bring on."

The two women sat in contented silence and sipped their tea for a while.

"So, tell me, my dear," said Azalais. "What did you want to ask me? I can see on your face that all is not well."

"I am ashamed to tell you," said Gauda. "My life has become too much like a sad troubadour's chanson."

"So you are an adulterer," said Azalais.

Gauda blushed and tried to stammer a denial.

"Don't. You forget that I was once a young trobairitz myself," said Azalais. "I may live a life of denial of the flesh now, but I remember all too well the pleasures and punishments the flesh can bring. Who is it?"

"It is my cousin's husband," said Gauda.

"And does she know?"

"Yes."

"Not good. And do you love him?" asked Azalais.

"No, it is only the weakness of my flesh," I said. "And besides how dare I resist the commands of my liege lord, when I am a poor, landless relative, living at his mercy?"

Azalais patted Gauda's hand. They sat quietly for a time. Finally, Azalais stood up and refilled their bowls with tea. The smell of peppermint wafted through the heavy summer air.

"What do you mean to do?" asked Azalais.

"There is nothing to be done," said Gauda. "I could not deny the Viscount my favors, even if I wanted to. And since my cousin has discovered the betrayal, she is doing all she can to make my life miserable."

"I thought that she did that already," said Azalais.

"So I thought," said Gauda. "I did not realize that she could be even more vicious than normal. I do not understand. She was sweet as a girl, always laughing and joyful. I can hardly recognize her as the same person. I think she must be very ill."

"What are her symptoms?"

"She will not tell me anything or let me see her nakedness, but she smells badly," said Gauda. "It is only these last days."

"Maybe she has contracted a fever of the bowels?" said Azalais. "I fear that many will succumb to fevers before this madness ends."

"Yes, that could be," said Gauda. "But she does not seem feverish. In fact, she acts as if all were normal - apart from the fact that she smells of the marshes or the stables."

"I will make a tea for her," said Azalais. "Angelica, I think, to promote digestion and cure flatulence and borage to make her sweat. And thistle is good for the bowels as well. She should apply a poultice of foul-smelling weeds at dawn and dusk to chase away the foul humors."

Azalais began searching for the herbs in her glass jars and took them down from the shelf.

"Tell me about the song you are working on," said Azalais. "The pleasure of a chanson is one earthly pleasure I am not yet denied."

So Gauda told Azalais of her work. Azalais helped her with some difficult phrases, just like she did when Gauda was a girl and just learning her craft. The time passed swiftly and soon the rays of the setting sun were blinding Azalais at the worktable. Gauda jumped up.

"I have been too long," she said. "I will be punished for sure."

"It was good for you, Gauda," said Azalais. "It will be worth the punishment, whatever it is your nasty cousin thinks of next. You should come more often. And keep working on your songs. Your face lights up when you speak of them."

Azalais handed Gauda two packets.

"The larger is for your cousin. See that she follows the regimen exactly. The smaller is for you. It is balm for tea. It will help you feel calm. You must not let these earthly concerns consume you. For many things will pass and all of our earthly bodies will be destroyed by the worms. All that will endure will be our souls and our words."

Gauda kissed Azalais on the cheek and left. Azalais watched

her go and realized how much better Gauda had made her feel and how much more badly she missed Constance than she could ever imagine.

DAY 7 OF THE SIEGE OF CARCASSONNE

Friday, August 7, 1209

Constance

Friday, August 7, 1209, noon

Constance and Guillaume sat in the stifling room at the top of the mason's house, right under the eaves. A small window looked out to the northwest and they could see the Crusader army entrenched on the banks of the river. Constance greedily eyed the cool waters of the Aude, wanting nothing more than to dive into their depths and feel the coolness rush over her. A fly buzzed around their lunch, aged goat cheese and a fresh loaf of bread. They drank new wine in mugs. While water was short in the Castellar, the mason and his wife had laid in plenty of stores before the siege and they took good care of their apprentices and workers. Constance and Guillaume had escaped the throng of boys and men eating on the ground floor and come up to the room where the mason's small children slept in the heat of the afternoon sun. There were three of them. Aude was a pretty little girl of five years old. Her little brother Jacques was a very active 2 year-old who had all the energy and spirit of his father. The baby boy Jean was only 6 months old. Beatritz had nursed them all herself, for she believed that the milk of a wet nurse would sicken a child and kill it. Constance thought back to all the tiny infants who had died at her mother's breasts and thought Beatritz might be right.

"The good woman Azalais would frown on all this procreation," said Constance.

"Is that why you left?" asked Guillaume.

"No, well, not exactly," said Constance. "I felt that the good woman Azalais always doubted my purity and my commitment to the life."

"So you found her way of life to be unholy?" asked Guillaume. He smiled at Constance.

"No, she is the most holy and wise woman I know," said Constance. She felt a little angry at Guillaume. "You do not know what she did for me, for all of us. She leads a life of spiritual perfection. She truly wants to be let free of this earthly cage. It's just that she does not think anyone else capable of her level of purity. She always believes the worst."

"And what did she believe of you?" asked Guillaume.

Constance felt her face grow warm.

"I cannot tell you," she said. "Nothing, except that it was not true. You must believe that. I have left the house of good women, but I still want to live a life of purity. I have lied, and I may no longer call myself a good woman, but I strive to live as many of the ideals as I can. I want to lie no longer. I have done it these past few days and, at first, it was intoxicating, like a honey wine, but now it just makes me sick."

Guillaume looked away from her.

"Now you, Guillaume, know much of me, but I know nothing of you, other than that you come from Béziers and have only your brother as family," said Constance. "Tell me of yourself. What did you do in Béziers?"

Guillaume cleared his throat and stood. He began to walk around the room.

"I am sorry if I have brought back memories that cause you pain," said Constance. "Please forgive me."

"No, it is not that," said Guillaume. "I worked with my hands before. I cleared fields and planted crops. I knew when to sow and when to reap. I loved the feel of the earth on my fingers. I kept bees and collected their honey. It was a good life. We lived simply and close to God. I miss it badly." Guillaume stopped his pacing and looked out the window. Suddenly, he pointed.

"Look, over there, you can see them. They have almost finished working on the cat," Guillaume said.

Constance stood as well, but slowly, feeling her legs and arms heavy and weak with the exertion of the last few days. Never would she take the water carriers' labors for granted again.

Just past the river bank, men were hammering newly-fallen and hewn tree trunks into a structure that looked much like the covered wooden galleries that stood atop the walls. It was large enough to hold maybe twenty men and mounted on four wheels, like a wagon. The noise of hammers and swearing filled the air. The earth and river seemed to shimmer in the noonday heat.

"They will use the cat to get close the walls of the Castellar," said Guillaume. "The mason told me of this device. Under its protection, the sappers can come to the walls of the Castellar and dig them out, replacing them with a wooden structure and straw.

When they are done, they light the straw and burn the structure. The wall usually falls down in that spot or is so weakened that it can be easily breached."

"And the men inside the cat?" Constance said.

"They are not knights, so there life is not considered to be worth as much, but most will escape in the confusion of the attack."

They heard screams from the river. Constance thought another battle had broken out, but then realized that she knew those sounds from the slaughterhouse. She looked closer. The crusaders were killing their pack animals, the butchers taking the skins off the animals and carrying them over to the cat. They placed the bloody skins inside out all over the exterior of the structure and men began to climb into the cat, carrying picks and shovels.

"They are protecting the cat from fire with the bloody skins," Guillaume said. "They will attack soon. Do you hear?"

Constance realized that she had not heard a single stone crashing into a roof or wall for the whole time they had been eating. Now that she noticed it, the lull in the attack and the silence was eerie.

"Hear what?" said Constance. "I do not hear anything."

"Exactly," said Guillaume. "They must be preparing to move the siege engines closer to the walls. They will need to provide a distraction while the cat moves close to the walls."

They quickly finished their meal in silence and hurried past the sleeping children down the stairs. They would be needed at the walls.

Gauda

Friday, August 7, 1209, afternoon

I was reading to Agnes in the afternoon when the Viscount's man came for me. A tall, thin, bald man, I recognized him from the Viscount's hall, but did not know his name. I thought him a lowly servant, but could not be sure.

"Please come with me, Lady Gauda," said the man. "I am Pons, Lord Trencavel's clerk."

Agnes immediately protested. We were in the middle of one of her favorite romances, and she could not finish the book without me, as she could not read. I was glad for once of her interference. I did not know why I was wanted, but could not imagine it would be good news for me.

"You have no right to take my lady-in-waiting," said Agnes. "I will send her to you when I am done with her."

"I am very sorry, Viscountess," said the man. "But, it is the Viscount Trencavel's direct orders that she come right now."

Now I was definitely worried. It was the middle of the day during a siege. The Viscount could not be calling me to play for him or to come to his bed. He never called for me during the day. I was at his beck and call during the nights and at his wife's during the days. It had been like this since I had arrived.

I began to feel sweaty. Had Trencavel discovered my treachery? But how could he have? I had been so careful. No one could think anything of the correspondence between two troubadours. And I had sent nothing since the siege began. It could not be that. But, I felt my legs shake as I stood and placed the book carefully to one side marking where I had stopped reading with a feather.

Agnes glared at me as I stood and I could feel her angry gaze on my back as I left the room. I followed the servant down the hallway, but we did not turn towards Trencavel's quarters as I had supposed.

"Are we not going to see Lord Trencavel?" I asked the man.

"The Lord Trencavel is preparing to repulse the invaders. Just follow me and don't ask any more questions," said the man.

Now I did not know what to think. Who was this servant to address me in such a manner? I made to reprimand the man, but something in his manner prevented me. I did as I was told and continued to follow him about the castle. Men were pouring from the corridors, their squires hurrying behind and carrying their heavy armor. We had to stop many times, our backs pressed to the corridor wall, to allow them to pass. As we made our way into the guest quarters of the palace, the halls became emptier. I had seldom been to this portion of the castle, but I knew this was where Trencavel's most powerful vassals would be honored with a bed and chamber of their own. The regular knights made due with bedrolls on the floor of the hall and the foot soldiers camped out in the courtyard.

We rounded a corner to a dead end. We walked up to a door at the end of the corridor. No squire or servant stood guard outside it, which seemed strange to me. Pons walked quietly up to the door, opened it, and peered cautiously inside. He turned around and beckoned me anxiously inside. I quickly followed, completely baffled by this charade. When we finally entered the bed chamber and the door had been shut, I turned to Pons and spoke to him in a hushed voice.

"What is going on? Where are we?" I asked.

"We are in the chamber of the Lord Cabaret," said Pons.

He drew a long key from a sack at his belt and proceeded to unlock a heavy oak chest that stood at the foot of the bed.

"What are you doing?" I asked.

"We are going to examine the Lord Cabaret's papers to make sure that he is no more than he pretends to be," said Pons.

He began to remove letters from the chest, moving quickly, but carefully. He handed me the first pile of letters.

"You are to read these," he said. "Scan them quickly, but thoroughly. Look for anything that seems out of the ordinary."

"But, why I am to do this?"

"You read more quickly than any of the men who the Viscount trusts for these tasks," said Pons. "You may call us spies, but I prefer to be known as a most loyal retainer, willing to go anywhere and do anything for my lord."

I felt sick to my stomach. I knew the risks a spy ran before I became one, but I had never thought to be doing anything as physically daring as this. My experience to spying ran more to following idle gossip.

"But where are the Lord Cabaret's guards? Where is he?" I asked.

"The Lord's guards have been overtaken by a sudden stomach ailment," said Pons. "And the Lord himself is at the side of his feudal lord, the Viscount. The Crusaders are advancing with their siege engines and the cat. They will be quite occupied for the next few hours."

Pons took more letters out of the chest, carefully laying them on the bed in the order that he took them from the chest.

"Enough questions," said Pons. "You have a lot of reading to do, no matter how fast it is you can do it. Get to work. For the sooner we are done here, the better. If the Lord Cabaret returns to find us thumbing through his personal affairs, you will taste the lash."

"But surely, the Lord Trencavel will not allow us to be punished when we do his bidding," I said.

Pons laughed.

"You are a naive fool, my lady," he said. "If the Lord Cabaret finds us here, the Lord Trencavel will have no choice but to have us tried and punished as common thieves. Do you think he would risk a rupture with one of his strongest vassals to save our necks?"

I spoke no more and bent to my task with an urgent determination, my spine prickling at the least sound. I forced myself to focus as the sweat poured down my back. I wished more than anything for this to be over. The documents were difficult to read, mainly land grants or court cases, correspondence with merchants and inventories of farms or equipment. The handwriting was often crabbed, though fortunately most of the documents were written in our tongue, rather than Latin. I brushed through most of these quickly, handing them back to Pons, who neatly rearranged them in the exact order they had been taken from the chest. Thinking of my own experience, I slowed down, wondering if any of these innocuous-seeming documents could be written in a code. However, if they were I would never be able to figure it out in these few minutes, and I felt my self relax despite the situation, knowing that my own missives would seem just as innocent to any random interceptor.

We began to hear more sounds from the Castellar, shouts and the renewed bombardment from the catapults. Another attack on the Castellar must be underway. I could only hope that it kept the Lord Cabaret and his men preoccupied and away from this room for as long as possible.

Trencavel

Friday, August 7, 1209, evening

Trencavel stood with Cabaret on the walls overlooking the approach to the Castellar. Men and women were loading trebuchets with stones and starting to let them fly at the advancing cat. Most wildly missed their mark.

"These catapults are good for destroying stationary objects," said Cabaret. "But they do not work when the missile throwers try to hit a small, moving object like the cat."

"Well, what else do you suggest that we do?" asked Trencavel.

"You have got to destroy it before they make it to the walls. Try to burn it," said Cabaret. "Better yet, we need Greek Fire."

Trencavel did not want to order his archers to light their arrows. The wind was strong today and he did not want to burn his city down trying to defend it. Even the Crusaders had avoided attacking with fire. Trencavel supposed they regretted the burning of Béziers, for there was no plunder left to take in the smoldering ashes of the town. But the cat continued to advance slowly, but steadily and shakily, blood dripping down the sides of the pelt-covered gallery. The Crusaders launched volley after volley from their catapults, trying to distract the defenders and provide cover for the cat. The monks lined up along the river, first a few and then more joining, and began their chant. Trencavel had to try to stop it any way that he could. He finally ordered the archers to unleash a flock of burning arrows on the cat, but those that fell on the gore-covered roof sizzled out in a smell of burning flesh and hair.

The men in the cat made it up to the wall of the Castellar, despite the bombardment of the defenders. Only a few bodies of those who had fallen to the stone and arrow bombardment lay mangled on the ground between the Crusader camp and the walls of the Castellar. Now, the attack truly began. Trencavel could hear the pick-axes and grunting of the men as they attacked the foundations of the wall of the Castellar. He ordered the guards on the walls to throw down stones, fire, large branches, roof tiles, anything in an effort to break the cover of the sappers trying to dig into their wall. The noise was overwhelming: iron banging on stone, men shrieking in pain, and, always, droning in the distance the chanting monks. Five men maneuvered a large stone up onto the ramparts and pushed it over. It crashed through the roof of the north side of the cat, tearing away the hide-covered roof on that part and shifting the south side of the cat up in the air. Several men fell from the elevated portion and were immediately fired on by archers. Their screams mixed with those who had been partially crushed by the large stone and who lay unable to move, trapped under its weight.

But the sappers kept on working. Trencavel was shocked at how quickly they worked. They were well aware that their only hope of survival was to dig into the wall deep enough to protect themselves from above before the cat completely disintegrated under the strength of the defenders' bombardment. The pace of the pickaxes and hammers became even more frenzied as the men felt their time slipping away. The people of the Castellar began stripping the tiles off of houses, and ripping the stones from the walkways of the suburb, searching for anything to throw at the cat before it was too late.

Trencavel ordered more soldiers to carry a second large stone, this one a cornerstone of a house from the look of it, up to the wall. They strained to carry it up the steps to the battlement on the wall, slipping once. Trencavel was sure they would all fall down the stairs, crushing the people below them, but somehow they managed to keep their balance and continued up. This time they walked to the exact center of the remaining roof on the cat and pushed their missile. It landed squarely on the structure and crashed through, obliterating the roof and crushing the two remaining wheels. Trencavel looked down, expecting to hear the screams of the men, but only heard silence. Even the monks stopped chanting as all waited to see the outcome. Finally, the dust settled and then Trencavel again heard the sound, first a small strike of pickaxe on stone and then many more. The crusaders on the banks of the Aude cheered and the monks started their chanting again.

"We are too late," said Cabaret. "They sappers will tunnel into the Castellar now that they have managed to get to safety in their hole in the wall."

Cabaret turned to walk back to the city.

"We have not lost this suburb yet," said Trencavel. "We will stay and fight them. They will break through only to find that my men will have them trapped and can slaughter them like ducks in a pond." "You really believe that we can defeat this army?" asked Cabaret. "You have been reading too many romances, my young Lord and my friend."

Trencavel stiffened.

"Don't call me your friend if you are not going to stand beside me," said Trencavel. "Would you rather just march out of here now and join the side you think will win? Or do you plan to open the gates for them and thus win this city for them?"

Cabaret's face turned white.

"I am sorry, my Lord, if I overstepped my bounds. I often think of you as the headstrong boy you once were, and forget my place," said Cabaret. "I stand with you as loyally as I ever did with your father. I want these foreign invaders off our lands. But, you must know that I would not honor the memory of your father if I did not dare to tell you the truth as I see it. I would never open those gates of the city for you, but you might be better off doing it yourself. Far better to live another day to fight these bastards when their army disappears in the autumn than to die here for a principle."

Bernard

Friday, August 7, 1209, night

The Lord smiled favorably on our Crusaders this day, for the brave men inside the cat made it to the walls. Though these fool heretics threw all their foulest weapons at them, they marched forward as if pushed by the powerful hand of the Almighty himself. I could hear them even now, for we were so close to them, yet so far, for they were still on the other side of the wall, yea inside its very bowels, gnawing at the innards as a worm destroys the intestines of a dog. The night had fallen while the sounds of their hammers and picks continued unabated.

And, I, myself, was the instrument of the Lord's wondrous will. For the Crusaders had sent their cat directly to the spot I had specified. I was the reason that their hammers and picks knocked at the outer wall just at the worst possible place for these heretic defenders! I knew that I was living to fulfill my glorious destiny.

The mason and his crew had spent the whole day trying desperately to build up the inner wall using the small stones and rubble they were able to salvage from the building destroyed by catapult in the Castellar. I worked harder than ever to supply them with mortar, for they needed much more than normal in their attempt to plug the holes in the small, uneven stones.

We all watched from the top of the wall as the cat made its advance from the Crusader camp. I saw the mason and the other men watch with nervous anticipation as the cat started to move in the general direction of our part of the wall. The mason swore loudly, but then the men started to quietly cheer as the cat veered off towards a place closer to the junction where the walls of the suburb met the city walls themselves.

I began to worry that my message had not reached the Abbot. So much could have happened. The strange messenger in the market could have been taken by the guards or simply killed by cutthroats. Or maybe he was no priest after all and I was soon to be taken into custody myself!

Then I heard the mason swear yet again and I looked up and saw the cat change direction yet again, heading straight for our weak place, following my orders explicitly. I rejoiced inwardly, but knew that I must not betray my true feelings for I was in greater danger now than I had ever been yet.

After I spoke to the Abbot's messenger yesterday, I thought for a fleeting moment that I should escape into the masses of refugees clogging the city. Or try to find a way out of the city itself. After all, if the Abbot's messenger had found a way in and out, so could I. But, I resisted giving into my fears. If the Abbot had wanted me to come out of the city, he would have said so. There must still be work for me to do here.

And, also, I could not abandon Guillaume. For if I were to suddenly disappear and then the cat were to make directly for our section of the wall, suspicion would have naturally fallen on me. In my absence, Guillaume would have born the brunt of the anger of the mason and his men. I could not find my brother at the spring and so I quickly headed back to the wall, to play my role and to pray that one more miracle would be done and that I would not fall under suspicion for my actions.

We worked all through the night, stopping only for short breaks to eat or take a quick rest at the mason's house in the Castellar. Now that the cat had arrived, I knew that we would work again through this night but without any breaks. Guillaume came to work on the wall as well yesterday, but I did not tell him that I had managed to communicate the location of the weak wall to the Abbot. I wanted to share this miracle with him, but I did not trust him to be able to convincingly hide our secret. Yet again, it was left to me to bear the burdens.

"Is the mortar ready?" yelled the mason.

I looked up. A man stood next to the mason, inspecting the walls inside the area where the sappers from the cat worked, trying to break through the outer wall. I recognized him from the blazon on his tunic. It was the dreaded man himself, the Viscount Trencavel, protector of vile heretics and source of murdering mercenaries who scarred the countryside with their evil ways.

Our eyes locked. I wanted to spit in his face, but I controlled myself.

"The mortar is almost ready," I answered the mason.

The mason turned back to the Viscount, talking to him while he pointed at various spots in the weak inner wall. The faces of both men were grim.

DAY 8 OF THE SIEGE OF CARCASSONNE

Saturday, August 8, 1209

Constance

Saturday, August 8, 1209, dawn

Constance woke early, her throat dry and cracked. She wanted more than anything to swig jugs of water, cool and fresh, but there were to be no more trips to the spring unless the soldiers could repel this latest attack on the Castellar. She went to the cistern in the mason's house and slid the cover. Constance allowed herself one small cup of water, but it did no more than excite her thirst for more. She forced herself to replace the cover and turned to go back into the workroom, where she had slept under a large table with the mason's children and his wife. No one wanted to stay in the upper portions of the house as the bombardments worsened. Beatritz woke as Constance returned.

"Have they returned?" Beatritz asked.

"No," said Constance. "They were still not finished when I left a few hours ago."

Constance's body ached from dragging stones into position near the catapults all night long.

The baby Jean awoke and began crying. Beatritz opened her tunic and placed the child at her breast and it quieted down. Constance remembered her mother and felt a small pang. The other two children woke screaming when a stone missile crashed somewhere nearby with a splintering of wood and a cracking of tiles. Constance sat down under the table and tried to comfort them. They sobbed and sucked their thumbs as Constance rubbed their little backs.

"So they have begun again," said Beatritz. "They must mean to attack soon, for I can hear the monks' chanting again."

Constance heard the low chanting faintly in the distance. The sound alone began to make her sweat with fear.

"We must go now," said Beatritz.

"But, where?" said Constance. "What about the men?"

"The mason and I agreed last night that I would take the children and go to my mother's in the city," said Beatritz. "I have no one else. Please help me take the children."

Constance did not want to leave Bernard and Guillaume. She was afraid to go back to the city and afraid she would never see them again. But, Beatritz had been so good to her the last few days. And after the one night in the market place with the other refugees, Constance never wanted to go back again. And she had not had to because the mason and his wife were so kind and generous. They had taken her in like a daughter and she owed this woman a debt she could never repay. Constance just hoped that Beatritz would never learn how Constance had deceived her.

"I will help you, Na Beatritz," said Constance.

The two women stood up. Constance dressed the small children in all their clothes and Beatritz wrapped her small treasures in a sack that she placed on her back. Beatritz looked around at her home, its carefully cleaned walls and floor, containing all her worldly possessions and Constance knew that Beatritz must be wondering whether she would ever see this place again. Constance took the little 2 year-old Jacques in her arms. Beatritz picked up the baby Jean and held her little daughter Aude's hand. They headed out the door and both turned to look towards the wall. They could just pick out the figures of the mason and Guillaume and Bernard, but there was no time to say goodbye. Already, crowds of women and children were pushing through the streets, heading up the hill towards the city gates. The streets were clogged as families tried to escape with all their worldly goods. An old man sat weeping in front of his house, lost and alone. Constance went to go to him, but Beatritz pulled her back.

"We have three small children to care for already," said Beatritz. "He must have family who will find him. But, if not, you will not throw away the lives of my children on a hopeless act."

The noise grew deafening. The monks chanting was louder now, as more and more joined in with their deep voices. The catapults and trebuchets on both sides of the wall unleashed their missiles, which crashed and destroyed. The children were screaming and little Aude suddenly sat down and refused to go any further. Beatritz tried to pull her, but she only screamed louder, her little face red and screwed up, tears coursing down her plump cheeks. Constance handed little Jacques to Beatritz, already weighed down with little baby Jean. Constance then picked up the little five year old girl. Her dead weight pressed down on Constance's aching shoulders and back.

They arrived at the city gates, but were forced into a long line. The crowd pressed to get in the narrow opening, and Constance worried the children would be crushed. She held tight to little Aude and prayed her strength would hold out. People were starting to abandon their carts and belongings. Panicky rumors spread through the crowd that the gate would be ordered shut in a few moments. Young men pushed through the crowd only to be repulsed at the gate by soldiers who ordered them back to man the walls. Constance and Beatritz looked at each other in grim determination and continued to move forward with the surge of humanity. Constance prayed the gate would remain open long enough. Her head rang from the screams of the small children. She did not know what was worse - to stay and fight or to have to fight to flee.

Bernard

Saturday, August 8, 1209, morning

It was shortly after dawn that I heard the blessed voices of my brother monks chanting and I ached again to lift my voice and join them. But, instead I continued my work of weakening the devil from within his fortress, my body sore and tired. I wished I could have slept as did the soldiers, who had passed the night sleeping on the ground behind the inner wall. They began to stir now, one by one, as they heard the chanting of the monks and the renewed activity of the Crusader catapults. I wondered how long we would have to wait for the men of God to break through and take this unholy place.

But, suddenly, with a great joy, I heard the crash of stones on the other side of the barrier wall and the shouts of the men. The sappers had finally broken through!

I looked up and saw the heretic dog Viscount Trencavel call to his soldiers to stand behind the inner wall, weapons in hand. There was silence for a few moments as the men waited and then confusion as the Crusaders began to stream through the hole in the outer wall and over the inner wall into the Castellar itself. The fell as arrows of Trencavel's soldiers knocked them down from off the top of the inner wall. I feared that this attack would be repulsed despite everything I had done to make it a success!

But then I heard a tremendous noise that shook the very ground under my feet. And again, a deep boom and the inner wall began to crumble in one or two places. Still the rhythmic booms continued and small stones from the top of the inner wall began to shake themselves loose and fall on the Viscount's men below the wall. I prayed that God had seen fit to take my small action and use it as only He knew how.

And it was a miracle! For it was as at Jericho and the walls they came tumbling down. A final loud boom and a huge log burst through the inner wall, rammed in by a team of Crusaders. The weakened wall fell of its own weight, crushing soldiers.

I felt as Joshua must have felt at Jericho watching the priests blowing the trumpets of rams' horns and all the people giving a loud shout. And all the walls of the city collapsed and all the people will go up, every man straight in.

I watched from behind a pile of rocks as the mason stared in rage as he watched his work destroyed.

The Viscount lost no time and quickly ordered the rest of his soldiers to the breach, but the Crusaders were pouring through the gap. The clanging of swords filled the air. I watched as the mason, Guillaume, and the apprentices ran behind the line of armed soldiers. For a second, I thought I should not follow them. For surely they headed to the gate of the city of Carcassonne and I did not relish the thought of being cooped up with those 30,000 heretic souls inside the city walls with no water. I had done my duty and paved the way for this military success. In fact, I had made it possible. Surely, I deserved accolades and a well-deserved rest. What further use could I be as a spy now? There was a good chance I would fall under suspicion for betraying the weak spot in the wall.

I started to head towards the breach, but as I got closer I saw a wall of men advancing rapidly, pikes drawn and axes at the ready. They trod over the bodies of the dead and wounded and blood seeped through the ground. I realized the madness of my plan, for I was as the enemy to them, even though I was their hero. They would know nothing of my efforts. I was doomed to contribute in secrecy to success of this great cause. I turned to run.

I sprinted up the street and towards the city gates. Already I was behind, for few people were left in the Castellar, other than the Viscount's soldiers and even they were retreating under the onslaught of Crusaders rushing through the break in the wall. As I watched the main gates of the city began to close, lowering down to only the height of a horse. I knew my time was running out. My sides ached as I pumped my tired legs up the hill. I began to feel as if I would vomit from the exertion, and my breath wheezed out of me. I saw the main group of heretic fighters, led by the Viscount, ride through the gate and I knew it would be closed shortly. I continued running with the heretic foot soldiers just beside me and the Crusaders gaining on us quickly. What madness if I were to be killed by the very Crusaders to whom I had given entry to the Castellar. I did not want to die without performing the sacrament of penance, for I had sinned much, though all in a worthy cause and it would be unfair were I to suffer in purgatory when I should be elevated on high to Paradise. We reached the gate, but it was closed. The foot soldiers and I pushed our way through the small door in the gate, still open, but not for long. We heard the Crusader knights behind us, their heavy horses and clanking armor seemed to thud the very earth to pieces. I managed to push my way into the door, but only a few others after me were in before the soldiers at the gate slammed the small door shut and laid across a heavy beam to lock it. I heard the screams of the few left behind, heard the sick sound of metal slicing into skin and sat trembling on the ground. I had to find Guillaume. I needed to confess and be forgiven of my sins by a priest, even a flawed priest such as my brother. I breathed deeply and prayed for joy that our righteous cause had advanced, even though I knew my own time within these walls was now numbered.

Trencavel

Saturday, August 8, 1209, noon

"What happened out there?" asked Bertrand. He limped to the side of Trencavel and stood next to him in the gallery atop the City gate leading to the Castellar.

"I don't know," said Trencavel. "They knew to come to the one spot where the wall was weakest. I cannot think this was accidental. The mason will be questioned, if he can even be found alive."

Trencavel stood, still panting, his heavy armor drenched in blood. He pulled off his chain mail gloves and took his helmet off his head. Sweat poured down his face and he pulled his wet hair off his face. His squire quickly took his helmet and gloves and began to unfasten the sword hanging at his side.

"Leave it," said Trencavel to the squire.

The young lad bowed his head and stepped backwards.

Trencavel and Bertrand watched as the Crusaders swept into the Castellar, searching vainly for an enemy to fight. Some seemed rather perplexed, but others were too hideously joyful, especially when they found some poor soul who had not gotten out in time, hiding in a feed cellar or in an attic. They dragged him out to the streets and a mob of soldiers would fall on the man, screaming heretic, fiend, demon as they destroyed the life in the person with the very spirits of demons themselves.

"So they've cut us off from fresh water," said Bertrand.

"We could not win this battle, not after that wall fell," Trencavel said. "The Castellar is not nearly as well defended as the city. We would have had to fight them in the streets. We could have lost all our men and killed an equal number of them, but still they would have kept coming. We do much better to hole up here in the city. We can hold out as long as our water lasts or until it rains again. The odds are better than we would have faced below."

Bertrand turned away to watch the scene in the Castellar below.

"You must prepare your defenses for an even fiercer attack because now they will have the houses of the Castellar to use as cover," said Bertrand.

Trencavel looked down at the Castellar. The houses in the suburb sat huddled under the city walls. The roofs of one house were just under the windows of a tower in the wall.

"You can always pray for a miracle, Trencavel," said Bertrand with a bitter smile. "After all, they seem to be happening quite regularly in the Crusader camp."

Trencavel did not smile. Rumors were everywhere. Already some people in the city itself were speaking of the latest miracle that was supposed to show that God favored the crusaders. Trencavel had ordered all the crops burnt or taken in from the land around Carcassonne and all the livestock slaughtered. The mills on the River Aude were destroyed, so the Crusaders could not have milled any grain they managed to bring with them. Yet, the crusaders were not hungry or weak. The foolish and nervous people whispered that the Abbot leading the Crusaders was a wizard and had conjured up demons to fight, instead of real men who needed food and water. However, one could easily see the bread baking in their ovens down by the river banks. The Crusaders had simply managed to go far upriver and steal milled grain from the peasants.

"I don't plan on waiting for heavenly miracles," said Trencavel. "This victory was too easy for them and they will be made to pay for it."

"Do you suspect treason?" asked Bertrand.

"I do not know what to suspect," said Trencavel. "Our enemies seem to know too much about our weaknesses. They know where to attack and when. They know too much."

Bertrand said nothing.

"Have you seen Cabaret?" asked Trencavel.

"He went back to his quarters last night or so my men tell me," said Bertrand. "He did not fight with you this morning?"

"No," said Trencavel. "I fought alone."

Bertrand turned away quickly.

"I did not mean you, old man," Trencavel said. "I want you well again and at my side. Do not play the brave fool."

"I hate growing old," said Bertrand. "I would not have caught this wound as a younger man and I would not have let it keep me from battle at the side of my lord. I am useless now. An old lion that can only roar, but whose claws are no longer sharp and whose teeth have all rotted and fallen out."

Trencavel turned to look at Bertrand and saw for the first time the gray in his beard. It had happened so gradually that Trencavel had never noticed, but the man he thought of as something timeless and unchanging, like the mountains where he made his home, was growing old.

"There is something you can do for me," said Trencavel. "I want to know who is helping the Crusaders. There must be a spy, someone in my inner circle, for they know too much. Find him for me. Find him and kill him."

“I will perform this service for you, my Lord,” said Bertrand. “I will always be your faithful vassal.”

Trencavel and Bertrand continued to watch the Castellar. The sun rose in the sky and the heat started to press down. There was no wind and oppressive warmth lay over the city. The dust did not move, unless stirred by men or dogs. The air itself felt parched. As the day went on, most of the knights and soldiers left the Castellar, realizing that there was little left to take from the suburb. They wandered back to their camp and even the monks gave up their eternal wail, preferring to retreat to the shade under the trees on the bank of the Aude.

In the hottest part of the day when the dogs were sleeping in the streets, Trencavel gestured to his squire to dress him again for battle. He left Bertrand on the ramparts and ordered his fifty youngest and fastest knights to follow him. The gate of the main city opened into the Castellar, quietly and slowly. Trencavel tore into the suburb, leading his men, and massacring the Crusaders left behind to guard the suburb, indolent in the afternoon, lying with their armor off to avoid the heat. They galloped round the suburb, lighting fires to wooden roofs and thatch roofs, destroying the few mangonels left behind. By the time the Crusaders on the bank of the Aude realized what was happening, most of the Castellar was destroyed and all their men lay dead. Trencavel saw the Crusaders putting on their armor and remounting their horses, and ordered the retreat. The defenders were safe inside the city gates before the Crusaders even galloped up the hill.

Trencavel went back up to the ramparts and saw Bertrand, who gave him a grim smile.

“Well done,” Bertrand said. “I could not have done it better myself, my young Lord,”

Trencavel smiled at the grizzled at old man. Then he turned to look at what he had wrought. All that remained of the Castellar was burning buildings and the moans of the dying. Trencavel wondered if he would have any city or lands left to govern, even if he were to win this siege. He turned his back on the Castellar and strode back into his city.

Gauda

Saturday, August 8, 1209, evening

I picked up the harp, placed it on my lap, and put my fingers to the strings. Trencavel sat in the large chair in his bedchamber and I sat on a small stool in front of him, my legs curled beneath me under my tunic. Trencavel absently picked at the gold threads of the brocaded chair cover with his right hand. His head rested in the left hand and his legs were splayed out in front of him. His young face had the look of weariness of an old man. I could not force cheer on him with a foolish pastorelle and I had no stomach for the stirring Crusade songs of old, nor did he, I imagined. But I could play a sad song of love, anything to take the mind of my Lord away from the miserable place where he dwelt, even if it were to think of the misery of another.

I played a song by Guirat ed Bornelh, he who is called the master of the troubadours. Trencavel always loved it, and I hoped to soothe him with its sad, but sweet melody. The music was rich and the poetic images clear, if a bit trite, but I grew tired of yet again singing of the suitor pining hopelessly away for his Lady, who dabbles with his affections, always spurning his advances. Why did these men never cease of writing and listening to this same tale? I felt foolish as a lady singing these words, but no one ever seemed to notice how strange it was, such is the power of a good song I suppose. My teacher Azalais had written some songs in this style, but had changed the suitor for a Lady and the Lady for a Lord. They were beautiful songs and I liked to sing them whenever I could, but they did not feel true to me upon my lips. For I did not know any ladies who hunted their men with falcons and dogs, open in their pursuit and proud of it. No, for us, we had only the weapons of subterfuge and subtlety. We had to give cryptic signs and hope that the man we must have, the one we would die for, would notice.

I watched Trencavel. He seemed far away from this place, but at least his restless fingers had stopped their wandering and pulling. I thought how strange it was that I pitied him only two nights ago when I realized he still loved the fair Agnes. For he did not deserve pity, but, was instead, the luckiest of men! For he loved his fair Lady as a hopeless suitor. He had his desperate passion and he was fortunate enough to be married to the object of his longings. No dangerous adulterous affairs to rock his feudal ties. And, of course, there was no need to deny his base, physical needs. There was always a shepherdess around, or a trobairitz. Most men hated their wives, lusted after some other man's wife, and spent all their money on whores. Trencavel could love his wife, lust after her as well, and never have to actually touch her!

Just once, I wanted to be the hunter. I did not want to be locked in a fortress, under siege, fighting against the thing I most wanted. I did not want to sit quietly, drawing all my resources unto myself to resist the onslaught of a passion that I must deny for convention's sake, though I wanted more than anything to throw myself to it. I had been this object before, many a time, and I hated it. But, what was I now? Plunder, I thought. My castle had been taken, with little or no resistance, and I was a prisoner. I had no force on my side, my capital was spent and I could not even ransom myself.

I forced myself to continue, though the song was starting to enrage me. I forced the anger into my voice and turned into the desperation required of the end of the song when the suitor begs for protection from love itself. When I finished, Trencavel sat in silence a long time, staring at the fire. I said nothing, only waited. Finally, he turned to me.

"Pons tells me that you found nothing in Cabaret's letters," said Trencavel.

"I could see nothing that was not as it should be," I said. "Though I do not know if I have eyes to see."

"True. Betrayal is easy to spot, but true loyalty can never be proved," said Trencavel. "It is always a supposition from day to day, always believed until it is one day broken in a way that can never be repaired."

"But what choice have you other than to trust?" I said. "Otherwise you will be isolated and just as broken as a man betrayed."

Trencavel sat quietly. He looked young again, despite his exhaustion, and somehow fragile even though he was a big man, strong through the chest and shoulders.

"I want to keep fighting," he said. "This city has been in Trencavel hands for hundreds of year. I have already lost Béziers for my family and at what a price. I do not want to be remembered as the Trencavel who lost the all the lands in the Viscounty. What will be left for my son? He will have no lands, no pride."

"I grew up hearing stories of how Charlemagne himself laid siege to this city for seven years without taking it," said Trencavel. "I know I could hold out against these invaders until the winter winds forced them home, if only I were commanding a fortress city filled with knights and soldiers instead of a city teeming with refugees. And, I am left with a choice that I would like to see Solomon make. Either the people die from thirst while the siege continues or they are slaughtered if the Crusaders take the city in battle. But to surrender means that all is lost for the Trencavel name and how do I know that these vile bandits will not slaughter all of us anyway? They have already shown that they cannot control the bloodlust of their rabble."

"Play again for me, Gauda," he said. "Just the harp. I do not want to hear about castles under siege or broken hearts. I do not want to hear or think of anything at all."

I played for him for a long time until the candles in the room guttered and finally blew out. Trencavel sat quietly for a while as I continued to play in the darkness, my hands feeling for the strings, knowing them as well as a blind woman knows the face of her husband. I finally stopped.

"Go, Gauda," said Trencavel. "Check on my wife, for she has not appeared in the great hall for a day now, and I worry after her."

"Yes, my lord," I said and I left him there, sitting quietly in the dark.

I walked the halls of the castle, lit by flickering torches. It was very late and the castle was quiet. I made my way back to Agnes' chambers. I quietly unrolled my mat in the antechamber and placed my harp beside me. I could hear the soft breathing of the two maids and the gentle rhythm lulled me to sleep. I did not dream at all and it seemed only minutes later when I heard loud voices and slowly lifted my sleep-numbed head from the mat. One of the maids stood at the entrance to Agnes' bedchamber, a pile of linens in her arms. I recognized Agnes' voice shouting from the bedroom.

"Don't you dare enter," screamed Agnes. "I gave you orders. No one is to enter this room."

A bone comb came flying out of the room and struck the maid on the face. She began to cry and ran off. The other maid ran after her. I stood up and rubbed my eyes. The early morning light fell on my face and hurt my eyes. I walked to the entrance to the chamber and looked in.

Agnes lay in her bed, covers up to her chin, despite the heat. She looked pallid and was sweating.

"I am coming in, cousin," I said. "You have nothing left to throw at me, so don't bother."

Agnes madly looked around for something at her side, but she could find nothing and seemed to give up suddenly, falling back on her pillows with a sigh.

I walked slowly into the room. It was dark and, despite the incense burning everywhere, I could still smell the sick odor of decay. I overcame my revulsion and walked up to her bed. I laid my hand on her forehead. It was sweaty and burning hot. Her face was completely white, but a red spot burned in each of her cheeks. Her beautiful hair lay on the pillow, stringy and dirty. I looked for a cloth to dry her skin, but all the ones at the side of the bed were soaked.

"Agnes, you are very ill," I said. "We must call for a doctor."

Agnes' eyes shot open and her hand clenched mine in an iron grip. On her face was a look of pure terror.

"No, no doctor," she said. "I would rather die."

I gently unclenched her fingers from my hand and took her palm into mine, stroking it gently. I remembered seeing Agnes as a young girl in her father's palace in Montpellier, when I went to visit her mother, my cousin. How had Agnes become so bitter, so mad at such a young age? What had changed her from that sweet little girl, laughing as her mother combed her pretty blond locks?

"But what of your son?" I asked. "Would you that he be raised without his mother?"

"I want nothing to do with him," she said. "Let my mother keep him until his father wants him, when he's ready to be the next Trencavel."

She must surely be mad with the fever. For no mother would want to die instead of living to watch her child grow and assume his place in the world. My nurse told me that my own mother cried as she died, knowing that her infant would never know any mother at all. But, maybe she cursed as well. Maybe she cursed me.

"I will go to the house of good women. Azalais will come to see you and you must let her care for you," I said. "We may hate each other, but you are my blood and I will not see you die, if there be something I can do to fight it."

I stood up to go, but waited as Agnes spoke one last quiet word.

"You think you know that living is always worth the toil, but I know better."

DAY 9 OF THE SIEGE OF CARCASSONNE

Sunday, August 9, 1209

Azalais

Sunday, August 9, 1209, morning

The tiny, old woman approached Azalais, her skin wrinkled like a baby bird. She looked as if she weighed no more than one as well. The oldest woman in the house of good women, Eleanor was respected by all the others.

"Sister, if I could speak with you for a moment in private," said Eleanor, clasping her gnarled old hands in front of her skirts.

Azalais nodded and led Eleanor into her herb drying room. Azalais sat at the stool in front of the table and gestured to Eleanor to sit across from her, but Eleanor declined with a nod of her head and remained standing. Only her shoulders and head were visible above the table. Azalais sat quietly and waited.

"The other women and I are concerned about Constance. It has been five days and we have had no sign of her," said Eleanor.

"We are all concerned about the soul of Constance," said Azalais. "I pray for her constantly, hoping she will see the error in what she has done and come back to us, asking for forgiveness."

Eleanor folded her arms in front of her.

"Yes, of course, we are all praying for Constance's soul," said Eleanor. "But the other women and I believe that more should be done to find her earthly shell. She could be sick, injured. She may not be able to come to us. We want to send some to look for her."

Azalais stood up from her stool quickly and it fell to floor with a clatter.

"You speak of her earthly body as if it were more important than her everlasting soul," said Azalais. "Azalais has betrayed everything our community holds valuable. It is a blessing that she is so young and has never given the consolamentum or she would have taken others with her in her fall from grace. How could we take her back now, knowing she has fallen once? We would never be able to trust her again."

Eleanor stared straight at Azalais before turning to go.

"Do not leave yet," said Azalais. "Make it known that I forbid any women in this house to go searching for Constance or to send others to search for her."

Eleanor nodded her delicate little head once, but her mouth was set in a line of grim determination. She said nothing and left the room.

Azalais sat back on her stool and began to idly crush a few rose petals left on the worktable, watching the papery pieces turn to dust under her fingers. Her back ached and her mouth felt dry and scratchy from the thirst. Azalais looked around her. There were so few medicines left and they were running out of everything-food, linens, water, of course, always water. The good women were already on strict rations and, fortunately, the very sick or injured did not need much to eat. Azalais always thought it best to balance the humors with fasting and soups and herbal tisanes. But they did not have much water for the soups and teas. The cistern in the courtyard was full, but their well only produced brackish, dirty water and rains in August were a rare occurrence. Azalais did not know how much longer they would last. And now that there would be no more fresh water from the spring by the Castellar, the sick would start to multiply. Azalais did not know why that was so, but it was true. Maybe when the people drank more water they flushed the evil humors of fever from their bodies? Or maybe the miasma from which came all plague was the antithesis of the force of water and the two kept each other in balance until one was pulled away and the other triumphed?

Azalais sighed and stood up. There was no sense in wasting her time philosophizing. She must use her wits and energy to find a way to feed and care for all the sick that would soon flood their home. Azalais walked into the main room. The other good women were respectful, but Azalais felt their anger directed at her. So these women thought she was too harsh with Constance, thought Azalais. Let them. Constance deserved to be cut off from their community after her betrayal.

Azalais heard a familiar voice near the door and looked up. She smiled. It was Gauda. She walked over to the door.

"So, I am to be blessed with your presence yet again this week," said Azalais.

Azalais placed her hand on Gauda's shoulder and kissed her on each cheek.

"Unfortunately, I come not to visit, but to beg you to come

with me to the palace," said Gauda. "The Viscountess is very ill and she will not see a doctor."

"But, I have so much to do here," said Azalais. "We are short on everything and more sick and wounded arrive every day. I cannot keep vigil at the bedside of a fainting Viscountess, whose major sickness is ill temper, in my opinion."

"No, she is very ill now," said Gauda. "Please come. You do not have to stay long. Just please tell me what to do to care for her. And, you will be paid. There are many stores at the Viscount's palace. You'll be able to feed and care for your patients for weeks."

"And is there water?" asked Azalais.

Gauda lowered her voice.

"The wells of the palace have not run dry," she said. "But the Viscount rations as does everyone else. He does not want it widely known for fear the palace will be overrun in a panic. But, I will see to it that you receive water, if at night in stealth. Only the heavens know the reason, but the Viscount cares greatly for his wife and would do most anything to save her."

Constance

Sunday, August 9, 1209, noon

Constance held the crying baby on her lap, trying to rock it gently and get it to quiet down. She and Guillaume sat against the wall of the kitchen in the house of Beatritz' mother. Little Jacques was crawling around the kitchen and Beatritz' sister kept jumping around trying to keep them from falling into the fire or tripping on the hearth. Only the little girl Aude sat quietly.

There were people everywhere in the small house that usually held only Beatritz' parents and their daughter, a little slow in the head and still unwed. Only Beatritz' parents, the mason, and Beatritz were seated at the small table. The sister brought them bread and cheese and some sausages. A wine jug stood on the table and the mason was pulling long gulps from it. The two apprentices and the journeyman mason who lived with the mason were all seated on the floor or standing near the hearth, trying to get out of the way of the sister. The boys looked shocked. They had outrun the

Crusaders in the Castellar, but their comrade, the littlest apprentice, had not made it. He was cut down almost as soon as they had turned to flee by the arrow of an archer. The other boys looked stoically ahead, but their eyes were red and tear stains streaked their cheeks.

The four sitting at the table had not said a word. They grimly tore off hunks of bread. Beatritz sat still, not eating, with tears in her eyes. She ignored the cries of her children as if they were not even in the room. The mason slammed down the wine jug.

"Wife, get up and take care of those infants," he said. "And, someone feed those boys. They are wretched with what they've been through."

He nodded to Beatritz' sister who quickly went back to the cupboards for more cheese and bread and brought it to the silent apprentices who fell on it with a ravenous hunger. Beatritz sat immobile at the table, crying softly and fingering her rosary.

"Who do you think we are?" said Beatritz' mother. "Do you think we are made of money and have a storehouse fit for a king? Where are we going to get enough food to feed all these people?"

She gestured at the room. Constance wondered as well. There were now 3 children and 11 adults in the room and most of them were hungry working men or boys. Beatritz' mother turned to her.

"I agreed to take in you and the children," she said. "Not this army of men."

Beatritz did not answer her mother, but continued to sit in silence. The mason turned to his mother-in-law, took another swig of wine, and placed the jug heavily on the table.

"Woman, you were more than pleased to take our money and gifts when you needed them," he said. "You will help us now when we need you. We will find the food to feed everyone. You are just going to have to dig up those coins you have hidden under your floorboards."

The two apprentices stopped their loud chewing and started to listen closely, their eyes sweeping the wooden floorboards of the kitchen.

Beatritz' mother's face turned red and she began to bleat.

"I don't know what you're talking about," she said. "This must be a fantasy you've come up with when drinking too much wine because we are poor people and have nothing to spare."

"You lie, old woman," said the mason.

"You will not speak to my wife in my house in that manner."

Everyone turned in surprise to hear the first words all morning out of the mouth of Beatritz' father, an old and frail man. The mason looked down, staring at his bread.

"Yes, father, you are right. I apologize for my disrespect," said the mason. "It has been a terrible morning for all of us."

"And, you wife," said the old man. "You will behave with more honor towards our guests."

Beatritz' mother humbly nodded. Everyone continued to eat in silence. Constance waited silently for her turn, her mouth watering from hunger. Their flight from the suburb this morning had been physically exhausting and Constance felt weak with hunger. She watched the apprentices continuing to eat. Guillaume and the journeyman had joined them and it seemed as if they would never stop. Constance hoped some small morsels would be left over for herself and the sister.

Beatritz started to whimper audibly. She began mouthing the words of the prayers, quietly, over and over.

Suddenly the mason stood up.

"Will you shut up?" he yelled.

"We have lost everything, our home, our workshop, our money," said Beatritz. "Would you take from me my only comfort?"

"You are a fool, woman," shouted the mason. "It is your precious priests and Pope who are responsible for our misery. It is they who sent these soldiers to destroy our home. They who killed our apprentice. And yet you would continue to pray to this monstrosity of clerics? You are mad."

"No, it is you who are mad!" screamed Beatritz. "It is your blasphemy and all the heretics around us who have brought this punishment upon our heads! And I am guilty as well of tolerating your sacrilege! That is why I am being punished. I will tolerate it no more."

Beatritz stood up and left the table, tears streaming down her face. She picked up the two smallest of her children and gestured to Constance to grab the little girl Aude and follow her as she went up the stairs to the bedroom. Constance followed her slowly, wishing more than anything that she could have filled her stomach before being sent to care for the children. In the bedroom, Beatritz and Constance placed the children down to sleep, calming them by softly patting their little warm backs. By the time the children had fallen to sleep, Beatritz' tears had dried. She turned to Constance and grabbed her arm.

"I betrayed my soul when I married that man and I will pay for it dearly. Do not make the same mistake, my girl. You may go now."

Constance nodded and went down the stairs. Everyone had left the house and only the slow sister sat finishing the last of the bread and the final few crumbs of cheese. She looked up guiltily at Constance and offered her the final piece of the loaf. Constance ran over and ate it, gratefully, in one gulp. She was so hungry, but there was nothing more to eat. She would just have to wait until supper and, if there was anything for anyone to eat, she might get a few more bites. It would be a long wait.

Gauda

Sunday, August 9, 1209, noon

I stood aside to let Azalais enter Agnes' chamber. Agnes looked even worse than she did earlier this morning and she did not even seem to fight our presence. It was this resignation that made me realize how sick she had become. Azalais walked over to the bed and put her hand on Agnes' cheek.

"How long has she been like this?" asked Azalais.

"She has been confined to bed, sweating and pale, since yesterday afternoon," I said.

"Close the curtains, Gauda," said Azalais. "I am going to examine her."

Azalais pulled back the covers, exposing Agnes' slim body in a linen chemise, soaked through with sweat. Agnes shivered, even though the heat of the August noon made the room like a furnace. She tried to claw the covers back over her, but Azalais gently placed her hands back at her side and Agnes did not resist. I pulled back involuntarily as the sickly odor of decay wafted up from the bedding. Azalais did not seem to be affected by it, but then she was used to nursing the ill.

"Help me take off her chemise," said Azalais.

I held my breath and moved closer. Azalais gently rolled up Agnes' chemise from her legs and I lifted her torso as Azalais slipped the linen over Agnes' head. Agnes moaned, but seemed too unconscious to feel any pain from our manipulations. We laid Agnes gently back on the bed and Azalais began to examine her body, searching for the source of the fever. She did not have to look for long, for it was obvious that Agnes was bleeding from her womb. The sheets were stained under her.

"Is it only that she bleeds?" I asked. For many women had severe bleeding, but I had never known it to result in a fever such as this.

"No, I am afraid not, Gauda," said Azalais. "Were that she only were bleeding, but it is much worse. I have seen this before in women who have had a difficult childbirth or one assisted by a butcher. She is torn inside and her wastes escape slowly from her womb. It is a miserable curse. I do not know how she has hidden it so long."

"Her baths," I said. "She bathes all the time."

"We should bathe her now," said Azalais. "And clean her linens. I will give her valerian for her fever and thistle to help her sleep through the pain. And chamomile to stop the bleeding."

I called for the maid to fetch water and linens. Azalais and I cleaned Agnes as best we could and sent the filthy sheets away with the maid. Agnes seemed to rest easier and I walked with Azalais to the bed chamber door.

"I will see that you receive the supplies you need," I said. "Thank you for coming."

I kissed Azalais goodbye and walked back to the side of Agnes' bed. I opened the bed curtains and tried to air the room, but the smell of the illness still lingered. I stood looking out the window for a long time, but eventually the fresh air must have awoken Agnes, for she began to stir. I went back to her bedside and put one hand on her cheek. She looked up at me.

"So, now you know of my shame," Agnes said.

I nodded my head slowly.

"So this is why you stayed a good women, even though you sneak meat when no one is looking?" I asked.

"I never wanted it," Agnes said. "But it has saved me. I almost died in childbirth. You have never given birth, have you?"

I nodded no and lowered my head. I had always cursed my barrenness, but, at this moment, I was wondering if I had been the blessed one.

"Then you do not know how fortunate you are. I have never been the same since. I was badly injured by the child; he did not come out in a normal way. I still have pain. I am so ashamed. You would not know," Agnes said softly crying.

"When they thought I was dying, I was given the consolamentum in extremis. Though I am no holy woman and never wanted to be, they were sure that I would die. When I survived, I at first thought that I would renounce the consolamentum. It is often done by those given the sacrament on the death bed who then recover. Why should I live a life of denial when I am a Viscountess, when I could have anything? But then I realized that I would never have to endure childbirth again. So, I pretend. I try to live the life I am sworn to live, but I am too weak. I cheat. There is only one desire that I no longer have," the Viscountess said.

"And your husband?" I said.

"He wanted me to receive the consolamentum. He did care for me and wanted me to be free," Agnes said. "Now he regrets, of course, since we have only one heir. He thought, of course, that I would die and he would remarry. And when I survived, he assumed I would renounce my vows. He never expected that I would continue as a good women, but he respected what he thought was my newly acquired holiness of spirit."

"And, you?"

"I love my husband. I wish more than anything to be able to be with him, to produce more heirs, to be anything but this burden I am. He will repudiate me when he finds out how I have tricked him. He must. I wish I had never known a man at all."

Agnes turned her head from me and cried softly into her pillow.

I stroked her hair gently.

Suddenly, we both heard the door opening as Trencavel crashed into the room. He looked as young as a boy and as ebullient. He ran over to Agnes' bed and grasped her hand and kissed it.

"We are saved!" he cried. "The King of Aragon has arrived! He has brought reinforcements! We are saved!"

Trencavel

Sunday, August 9, 1209, afternoon

Trencavel sat in the courtyard of the palace, protected from the midday sun by a tent. Bertrand stood at his right and Cabaret at his left. Trencavel had spent so much time in his armor the last few days that he felt almost naked in his finest tunic and coat, a coronet of gold on his head. The wind whipped around the courtyard, throwing up dust in the faces of the soldiers standing at attention on all sides of the open space. The fabric of the tent flapped in the wind like the sails of a ship in a fresh breeze.

Into the courtyard of the castle, rode three men mounted on fine horses, but without armor and carrying no shields. The man in the lead was large and prepossessing. He rode his mount as if traveling between two armed camps without sword or shield was something he did every day. The two men who followed him were equally proud in their saddles. No one would dare attack him, thought Trencavel. He is my liege lord, the King of Aragon, and he will be my savior.

The three men jumped off their horses and squires ran to take the reins of the beautiful animals. The King of Aragon walked over to Trencavel's tent, followed by his men. Trencavel stood at his approach. When the King came near, Trencavel kneeled and kissed his hand. It was a fighting man's hand, big and strong and the rings on his fingers showed all the wealth of Aragon and Catalonia that would back that strength. Trencavel was no longer alone. He rose to his feet.

"My Lord, you have come," said Trencavel.

"Yes," said the King. "And it seems that you have gotten yourself into a predicament in which you have need of aid. You have the armies of all France, Nevers, and Burgundy camped at your door. Even your beloved uncle appears to have suddenly seen the error of his blasphemous ways and felt the need to repent by turning Crusader himself."

"My beloved uncle would sell his mother out to avoid a battle," said Trencavel.

"Be careful of your words, young Trencavel," said the King. "Your beloved uncle is also my beloved sister's husband. And before you mock him too severely, I should inform you that I just dined with him in his commodious tent, festooned with golden fabrics. We supped on the most luscious lamb and drank the finest wines. He hasn't even donned his armor and he's managed to end up on the side that is currently winning. A man in your position should be careful of whom he mocks."

Trencavel felt his face color and stiffened his back and shoulders.

"My Lord," said Trencavel. "We beseech you to come to our aid. You cannot allow this injustice to happen to your vassals. Do you know what these fiends did at Béziers? Old men, women, children slaughtered in the streets. Even those who sought refuge in the cathedral burned to death in a funeral pyre. The city is destroyed. Your city, my liege Lord, is destroyed. Everywhere they go these Crusaders sow destruction, ruin, and fire. Our country is dying. We must chase them from its borders. They are worse than barbarians."

Trencavel realized he was shouting and quickly stopped talking. His hands were shaking with rage.

"You have been on noble Crusades to save the Holy Lands from the infidel," said Trencavel. "How can you allow this travesty to continue? This Crusade kills the very Catholics it claims to protect. It's a Crusade on the cheap for those who want their debts cleared, both earthly and heavenly, but don't want to bother with a dangerous trip to the Holy Land."

The King interrupted Trencavel with a flick of his hand.

"Enough," said the King. "You risk infuriating me with your blasphemy. You are the only one to blame for this dirty affair. If you had banished the heretics from your lands, as I have told you to do many times, you would not be in this mess. It makes me incredibly sad to see you in danger of terrible misery because you tolerated a bunch of crazy fools."

Trencavel opened his mouth, but the King raised his hand and Trencavel did not dare to speak.

"I do not see any other remedy out of your situation," said the King. "You must negotiate, my son. An honorable accord is your only hope."

Trencavel felt his bowels turn to ice. His heart felt like a lead weight. How could this be happening? How could his Lord not come to his rescue? How could it be that he would lose all his lands in less than two weeks? Trencavel saw Bertrand's face turn ruddy with anger. He placed a hand on his arm, for the last thing he needed was for the old man to go off and enrage the King. The King was their only ally, as seemingly useless as he was. Trencavel glanced at Cabaret and saw him nodding in agreement with the King. Trencavel wanted to strangle him. He was a traitor, even if only in spirit.

"If you insist on running to the battle and banging your shields," the king continued, "the worms will be soon nesting in the orbs of your eyes. The Crusaders are too strong. Believe me. I just traversed their camp. You cannot vanquish them. Your walls are, I admit, are strong, tall, and high. But, reflect, this city is encumbered with women and children. Tell me, how are you going to feed them all? Your misfortunate is making me miserable, for I love you much. Let me save you. Speak to them. I will do anything, as long as it is honorable, to see you content."

Trencavel looked around at the knights and soldiers lined up around the courtyard. He did not want to lead them to surrender and defeat. He would lose his lands as would they. So many had fought and died already for this city and to give up now made him want to rage madly, to plant his sword in the skull of every Crusader who had come to destroy his people and his lands. But, then Trencavel thought of his people who sought refuge inside this city. So many. So many weak and young and vulnerable. They would not withstand a long siege. There was no honor in ruling over a city of the dead.

"Very well, I will negotiate." said Trencavel.

The knights in their ranks seemed to stiffen, but no one uttered a sound.

"Sire," Trencavel continued. "Take into your hands this city, and all within its walls. Long ago, your father and mine loved each other. In remembrance of this, I entrust all to you."

Trencavel bowed down and kissed the ring of the king again. He stood and watched as the king and his two men walked to their mounts. They rode out of the courtyard. Trencavel ordered the gates of the city shut tight. Trencavel breathed again. He did not know for how much longer, but the city was still his.

Bernard

Sunday, August 9, 1209, evening

Did Judas feel a marked man after he had kissed our Lord in the garden? Did he wonder how long it would be before his treachery was discovered? How long he would be able to live before he was punished for his betrayal? And yet, he who betrayed our Lord Jesus Christ and sent Him to His death was allowed to live, while I, who had betrayed only heretics and blasphemers, was likely to be driven to my death for my acts.

Though it was evening, I had just awoken. I had spent the day hidden in the cathedral and had finally fallen asleep. I had been walking the city streets all yesterday since I escaped from the Castellar and all last night. I searched all the refugee faces, but could not find Guillaume anywhere. I did not even know if he had managed to escape the carnage of yesterday morn. I was sure that I was being followed late last night by two night watchmen, but I disappeared down a narrow alley and managed to escape from them, the drunken foolish louts. But, I did not know how long my good fortune would last. If the mason had escaped, he may have guessed that it was I who had betrayed the weak spot in the walls. In his rage, I was sure that he would hunt me down himself, if the guardsmen did not succeed.

I knew what my fate would be. I suppose that I had been preparing for it ever since I was first given these orders by the Father Abbot. I will not lie. I prayed that the Father would pass this cup from my lips, but, like the most Holy one whose life we can only try to emulate, I, too, drank the bitter dregs. I did not mind my fate, now that I knew that my purpose here had been served. How many souls would be saved by my actions? It would be like counting the grains of sand on a beach. But, I wanted one thing only before they took me. I wanted to see Guillaume and I wanted to confess to him. I wanted to go to my death pure and absolved of all sin.

I headed to the marketplace and found a stall that sold cheap wine at mad prices. My throat was parched and my tongue swollen from thirst. The wetness of the liquid grapes filled my mouth with joy, but nothing I drank could quench the deepness of my thirst. I tried to ignore my fellow patrons, but their incessant drivel filled the night air. But, soon I heard the most joyous news and cocked my ear to listen to an old man rumbling on.

"It may all be over by tomorrow," he said. "The King will save us all. He will slaughter them all in their beds and drive off these invaders."

"Not a chance," said another grizzled man. "My sister's aunts' cousin is in the Viscount's guard and she heard the King advising the Viscount to surrender. Even the King of Aragon is afraid of this army."

There was still a glimmer of hope for my earthly existence, if these rumors were true. I could be back with my Father Abbot tomorrow evening, if I could just stay alive until then. I imagined myself honored and feted at the table of the Father Abbot. Maybe I would travel to Rome as the Abbot's personal secretary and maybe even meet our Lord's representative here on earth, the Holy Father himself.

An old man put down his wine glass and began to cry.

"If he surrenders, we will be butchered!" said the old man. "Remember Béziers!"

"But, we are not going to fight," said the first man. "Surely, they will not be too hard on us."

"They have many dead already," said the old man. "They will not forget those who have died. We will be butchered in recompense. There is no hope."

The old man spilled his wine as he began to sob uncontrollably.

I stopped short my reverie; I had just been imagining myself in cardinal red, gracing the offices of the Vatican. How mad! I must keep my head clear. If I were even to see my Father Abbot ever again, I would need to avoid being killed by the Viscount's men and then by the Crusaders themselves.

Suddenly, I heard the clomp of the guardsmen's feet as they marched along the cobblestones streets of the marketplace. I hurriedly threw down the last of my wine and pulled my cloak closer around me. I left the wine stall and tried to move away from the guards quickly, but without attracting too much attention.

"That's him," cried a voice. "He's the one I saw talking to the spy."

I started to run, my heart pounding. I knocked over a young man as I quickly turned into an alley and I could hear the man swearing at me.

"Catch that man," yelled a guard. "He's a spy."

I looked over my shoulder and saw that the young man had joined in the pursuit and was gaining on me. My breath was becoming labored and my side ached with exertion. I did not see the cobblestone that tripped me, but only felt the wind knocked out of me as I fell forward to the dirty street with all the force of forward momentum. I struggled to get back up quickly, but it was too late. The young man landed on my back and pinned his arms to my side.

"You thought you could run, you bastard spy," said the young man. He spat on my face. "That's for my dead brother, you murdering fiend."

I felt my captor's hands tighten their grip on my arms, twisting the shoulder until I winced. I was glad to see the two guardsmen catch up with me. I was whipped to a standing position, with a beefy guard on either side. The young man spat again in my face.

"Let me spend a few minutes with him before you take him," begged the young man.

"We would be more than glad to let you, and might even give you a hand," said the older guard. "But the Viscount has given strict orders that all men taken as spies are to be brought to the palace for questioning. The last one had an unfortunate accident before we could get him to the Viscount's man and we were brought to account for it."

A crowd had begun to gather. I sweated as I heard the word spy bandied about. Some of the young men at the edges of the crowd had picked up stones and pieces of brick. The angry young man was scowling at the guards, but said nothing. I felt hugely relieved when the guards finally began to move me out of the alley, pushing aside the crowd with their staffs. A group of men followed the guards, muttering and swearing, but they did not dare to attack me while the Viscount's men were guarding me. I never thought I would be glad to be taken to jail, but I preferred the Viscount's justice now to that of this crowd, who looked as if they would like to rip me from limb to limb.

DAY 10 OF THE SIEGE OF CARCASSONNE

Monday, August 10, 1209

Constance

Monday, August 10, 1209, morning

"She wants you to help her in the courtyard," said Beatritz.

Constance did not know how Beatritz could decipher her sister's words. The slow woman could speak, but it was a guttural language that Constance could not follow. Gratefully, Constance got up and followed the slow woman down the stairs. Beatritz' constant crying and moaning had begun to irritate Constance. She felt bad for the woman, who had lost her home and her husband his livelihood, but she did not wish to hear the keening anymore. The children were miserable as well, hot and thirsty. Their mother's fear spread to them and they cried as well. It would be a relief to go downstairs and help the sister with her chores.

Constance followed the sister to the kitchen. A basket of vegetables sat on the trestle table. The sister handed Constance a knife and the two women sat down and began peeling carrots and onions. Constance threw the chunks of carrot in a heavy iron pot that hung over the fire. They poured a little precious water into the pot and continued to cut vegetables for the stew. Constance wondered how long the house's supply of vegetables would last. She hoped they had a deep root cellar.

The heat in front of the fire in the hot August morning was stifling and Constance could feel sweat pouring down her back. She stood up and opened the door leading into a little courtyard behind the house in the hope of maybe finding a small breeze. In the courtyard, the two apprentices and the journeyman sat under the shade of a small apple tree. They were sharpening their tools and idly eating apples plucked from the branches of the tree. Constance came back into the kitchen and sat down again at the table. She could still hear the crying from upstairs, but it sounded more remote. A bee droned in the air. The voices of the young men wafted into the kitchen.

"The mason is going to have to pay for this disaster even if it wasn't his fault that no stones were left to make the base," said the journeyman. "He'll have a hard time getting work once everyone knows it was his wall that fell and let in the invaders. A reputation is a delicate creation - you can work your whole life for a good one and see it destroyed in a day."

"But, what will happen to us?" said the older apprentice. "I have almost finished my apprenticeship. Will I have to start over again with someone else? I don't want to eat the scrapings of the pot and work my back to the bone again for yet another master."

"We'll be ruined," said the youngest apprentice.

"Boys, it doesn't have to be like this," said the journeyman. "When this is all over, come away with me. We'll go to another city, and I'll pass their guild test to become a master. I have some gold coin saved up. I'll take you on as my apprentices for half the normal time. We can become a masonry shop."

"And we work for you for free for all those years, even though we're trained men and almost journeymen ourselves," said the older apprentice. "That sounds like a good deal for you, but not a very good one for us."

"Take it or leave it, boys," said the journeyman. "You don't have any money to set up on your own and no guild will let an unfinished apprentice start in their town. You'll be run out of the city in no time. You can always wait around here, but I don't think your current master is going to have much in the way of business soon. If he even manages to avoid a prison cell."

Constance listened intently. She worried for the mason, who had been so kind to Bernard, Guillaume, and herself. She wondered if she ought to say something to him about his treasonous workers, but did not know if she would do more damage than good. Anyway, the mason was probably smart enough to guess what his journeyman was up to. Even in the best of times, these men were always scheming for a way to get their own workshop. More than one mason's widow was all too quickly married off to the journeyman who shared her roof. Maybe Guillaume would know what to do.

Constance also worried for Bernard, but she knew he must probably be dead. Guillaume had not spoken of his brother, but his face was lined with worry and the dark circles under his eyes were surely a sign that he did not sleep. But, then who could sleep? Rumors were flying around the city. The Viscount would surrender. They would all be massacred. The Viscount would fight with the King of Aragon and they would all be saved. Constance did not know whom to believe. She only believed that, whatever decision the Viscount made, it would not go easy for the common people of the city. Their homes and coins were to be the spoils of this battle. If their Viscount could not protect them, all would be lost.

The door to the street opened and Guillaume walked in, followed by the mason. The mason's face was livid with rage. He slammed the door behind him and the timbers of the house shook.

"They don't have need for men," said the mason. "My ass, they don't have a need. You could see the holes in that wall. They need every proficient, hard-working mason in this city to repair the damage to those walls. And now is the time! While the King of Aragon is here and they're negotiating, we've got precious time to do these repairs before the bombardment starts up again."

"Perhaps, if we are fortunate, there will not be a need to repair the walls," said Guillaume. "If the King can negotiate an honorable surrender, we may all be free of this violence by tomorrow."

The mason turned on Guillaume and slammed his hand against the table.

"Are you a fool, boy?" said the mason. "Do you expect those murderers to behave with honor? They slaughtered everyone in Béziers. They even burned down the cathedral where the idiot Catholics thought they would find refuge! There is no refuge. There is no trusting the word of those madmen. They want us dead and they will come and slice us down in our beds, our homes, our churches. Now they have come to convert us and we will never be free of their violence."

The mason turned and went up the stairs. Constance could hear him yelling at Beatritz. The children started their crying again. Guillaume came over and sat next to Constance.

"I worry for him," said Guillaume. "He is a broken man. They needed help today at the wall, but they did not trust him to do his job correctly. I don't know which he fears more - that they think him a traitor or merely incompetent."

Constance lowered her voice.

"The apprentices and the journeyman have been talking," said Constance. "They are scheming to leave him."

Guillaume' face clouded. He looked down.

"I am sorry that you have not heard from your brother," said Constance. "He could have escaped. He would not know where to find us here in the city."

"I do not know what to make of my brother anymore," said Guillaume.

He looked strangely at Constance. She did not know how to respond, so she said nothing.

"I worry for us all," said Guillaume.

Azalais

Monday, August 10, 1209, noon

Azalais finished organizing the load of supplies that had been delivered from the castle this morning. Gauda had kept her word and the Viscount had sent water, grains, and meat to the hospital in the early hours of the morning. The porters had arrived under a heavy guard, even at that hour, and well they should have, for soon water would be more precious than gold in this city. Azalais stopped and stretched her back slowly. She was too old to be doing this, but there would be no rest until this siege was over, one way or another.

The brief respite from bombardment had done the patients well, thought Azalais. The most seriously injured would surely die and she gave them medicines mainly to ease their suffering. But those who had suffered less severe injuries were showing signs of improvement. There were some wounded arms and legs that were festering, despite the good women's best efforts, but they could be amputated to save the life of the patient. Though, for what, Azalais sometimes wondered. A life begging on the steps outside the cathedral, most probably. Those who were not strong or rich had no other recourse than to beg for charity in this world. What a misery. Far better that they escape, but Azalais only performed the consolamentum on those who asked for it. It always surprised her how tenuously most clung to the last shred of their earthly existence and left it, wanting only to come back for more.

"Sister Azalais, there is a man calling for you," said Eleanor. Eleanor turned and left the pantry without waiting for Azalais' reply. The ancient Eleanor was barely respectful of Azalais these days and the younger women took their cue from her. Eleanor had not spoken to her again of Constance, but she commented frequently on the blessings of forgiveness in one or another context.

Azalais often came upon a group of good women talking in low voices among themselves, only to have them abruptly stop as soon as she approached within earshot. So, if this were to be a mutiny, so be it. Constance had brought her shame upon herself and she could come begging for forgiveness if she truly felt repentant. It was not the place of Azalais to go to her.

Azalais left the pantry and walked through the main hospital room. A man stood at the door, supporting a pale woman at his side. She was doubled over, moaning.

"Yes," said Azalais. "You wanted to speak with me."

"Please, good woman," said the man. "I have heard that you can heal with herbs and draughts. My wife is very sick."

"Can you not care for her at home?" said Azalais. "We have many injured to attend to and there are not enough beds as it is."

"She became ill so fast," said the man. "I fear for her life. We are alone here in the city and there is no one I can turn to for her care."

"You are refugees?" asked Azalais.

"Yes, from the countryside," said the man. "We feared the army."

The woman moaned again and Azalais could see that her face was white and sweaty.

"Very well," said Azalais. "Bring her in."

Azalais guided the man to an empty cot in the back of the room, whose previous occupant had died from a sword wound this morning. The man helped his wife to lie down. Immediately, she doubled up in pain and her bowels loosened. Azalais stared at the sheet with a sense of resignation mingled with fear.

"The bloody flux," said Azalais.

Azalais called over one of the other good women and together they began cleaning the woman as best they could. Azalais prayed that the rumors of surrender were true, no matter the outcome. She did not think a marauding, victorious army could do half the damage that this bloody flux would do. Of one thing Azalais was sure. This woman may have been the first stricken, but she would not be the last.

Trencavel

Monday, August 10, 1209, afternoon

Trencavel sat again under his tent in the palace courtyard in the midday sun. All was exactly as it had been yesterday. The soldiers were standing to attention on each side of the courtyard. The flags whipped in the breeze. Cabaret and Bertrand stood to either side of Trencavel. The three of them watched the approach of the three lone horsemen. The only thing changed was Trencavel himself. Yesterday he had watched the King of Aragon approach with hope and even joy. Today he waited with resignation. Trencavel was about to hand over his city and lands to these foreign invaders. At least he would be able to keep his people from dying of hunger and disease and negotiate for their safety. And Trencavel was young. He could escape to the mountains with Bertrand. They would retake this land and this city when the time was ripe. All was not lost, thought Trencavel, except his honor.

The King of Aragon arrived and stepped off his horse, as before. He solemnly walked over to Trencavel. Trencavel stood up, kneeled, and kissed the ring of the King.

"I have spoken to this Abbot laying siege to your city, my son," said the King. "He offered to let you live and let you leave the city with ten of your men, but without any arms or baggage. He offered no more."

Trencavel felt as if he had been slammed in the stomach. Did they think so little of him that he would leave his people to this fate? Did they think him so weak so as to be toyed with in this manner?

"I would rather see my nearest flayed alive in front of me, after which I would embrace their corpses and then die myself, the last," said Trencavel. "On my life, my sire, know that I will never abandon my people here."

The King of Aragon looked Trencavel squarely in the eyes.

"I told him that you would accept such an infamous offer when donkeys learn how to fly," said the King. "I knew that you would not abandon your city to this fate."

Trencavel looked again at his king, hoping for some sign that his lord would now realize the injustice of his position and come to his aid. But, even as he looked, Trencavel realized the truth. The King of Aragon had not risen to his lofty position by backing the losing side. Trencavel was alone and there was no hope of rescue.

"Go back to your lands, my sire," said Trencavel. "And let me fight."

The King of Aragon made as if to place his hand on the younger man's shoulder, but seemed to think better of it. He inclined his head slightly toward Trencavel and turned away. The King and his two attendants mounted their horses and rode out of the courtyard without looking back.

Trencavel sat on his chair under the tent and stared after the retreating figures, not saying a word. The knights and soldiers standing at attention in the searing sun began to fidget, wiping the sweat from their brows and beginning to talk softly among themselves. Cabaret and Bertrand stood on either side of Trencavel, waiting for a word or sign from the Viscount, but Trencavel just stared woodenly ahead. Knights and lords from the mountains began to break away with their knights, milling about.

"My lord," said Cabaret, leaning over to speak into Trencavel's ear. "You must say something. The men are waiting for their orders."

Still Trencavel said nothing, staring ahead and watching as the drawbridge closed behind the retreating figure of the King of Aragon and his men.

Bertrand placed his big shaggy hand on Trencavel's shoulder.

"We don't need him," said Bertrand. "We have the best fighting men in the mountains and now they are fighting for their lives as well as their lands. This city has never been taken. We can defeat those bastards or at least hold out until they all get tired and go back to their damned homes, may the pox follow them always. Your father would not have let these dogs defeat him and I know that you will not let them take the Trencavel lands from you. You have too much pride and honor and courage. Stand up, my lord. Fight."

Trencavel did not say anything for a minute, but then he slowly stood up. He raised his right hand and the soldiers fell silent and stood to watch him.

"So, we are on our own," said Trencavel. "I hoped for more, as did you all, but that was not to be our lot. The siege will continue. It will be a hot, thirsty, merciless siege, but we will outlast them, they who come merely to steal and pillage. Know this, that while I am yet alive I will fight for my city. I will never abandon it. I call on you all to continue this fight. Make these invaders pay in blood and pain for their assault on our fortress, our lands, and our people. Make them dream of their homes at night and cry in their death agonies knowing their corpses will rot far from their native soil. We will drive these invaders from our lands. We will persevere. We will never surrender."

The soldiers lifted their shields and screamed their loyalty. Trencavel stood grimly, but surely over them, forcing his rage into a finely honed sword of desire - desire to make these invaders pay. There would be no more talk of surrender.

"Now, go, all of you, back to your stations," said Trencavel. "We have a city to defend and a siege to win."

Bernard

Monday, August 10, 1209, evening

Did Paul of Tarsis grow to fear the stomp of the guards' feet along the corridor, as I did? Or did he hope for that sound as a deliverance from the hell of a crowded prison cell? I did not know where the guards would bring me, or to what new hell, as they hoisted me up from the crowded floor and dragged me down the corridor. I feared what would be done to me and wished only to be left unnoticed in a corner of that nasty, putrid cell. For I had seen the men brought back by the guards in twisted, bloody heaps, moaning softly as they lay in their own blood in the darkest corner of the cell.

But, yet part of me longed to escape this confinement, no matter what hell would come next. I did not know how long I had been kept in that cell, crawling with cutthroats, thieves, and murderers, but it felt as I had been consigned for an eternity already. I prayed constantly for my deliverance. I had done nothing wrong and, yet, here I was consigned to a cell with these base criminals. I, who had done nothing but work in the most Holy name of the Father, following the dictates of my Father Abbot. I had been obedient and brave and righteous. And what was my reward? I was crammed into a cell filled with monsters who had already stolen my shoes and bag, their leering faces laughing in my mine as they cuffed me on the side of the head. I itched everywhere for I had been contaminated by the vermin thriving in this hell hole. I tried mightily to pray for the souls and deliverance of even these basest of creatures, for the Lord Jesus Christ even deigned to save the soul of the thief, but I was not worthy of the magnificent mercy of our Lord and I wanted nothing more than to consign these rotten creatures to the basest ranks of Hell.

I wondered if I would see them again, as the guards pulled me from the cell and, for that matter, if I would ever seen anyone again who mattered to me - my Holy Father Abbot, my brother Guillaume. I prayed fervently that the siege would end soon - that the rumors I heard of surrender were true. But, no one knew anything in that wretched cell. Even when a new prisoner was thrown in, bloody and broken, his news would contradict the news of the one thrown in just previously. I spent however long I had been in that cell of damnation swinging between joy as a rumor of surrender arrived and desperation as the next newly arrived prisoner contradicted that news.

I marched down the long corridor, the guards flanking me on either side. I assumed that we were deep in the bowels of the palace for I could see no natural light and everywhere torches flickered on walls. I could hear screams coming from the closed doors of rooms we passed and I felt my body begin to sweat and my bowels clench. We stopped in front of a door and one of the guards produced a key. He turned it slowly in the lock and then pushed the heavy wooden door, reinforced with leather and nails, open. I felt weak and my legs buckled under me.

"Finally scared are you?" said the heavier guard. He laughed. "Well, you've every right to be."

I quickly stood tall. I refused to let these heretics see any weakness in my bearing. I had the righteousness of the Lord on my side and I would not give these Satanic dogs the pleasure of watching my fear - they who had everything to fear from my Lord Abbot. I would see them smoking in the ruins, writhing in agony on the day of judgment. Those proud and foolish heretics in Béziers had paid with their lives for their arrogance and so would these vermin.

The taller, slimmer guard kicked me in the back of the legs and pushed me into the room. It was a small room, lit by torches with soot staining the walls. I choked with the force of the bad air - smoke and sweat and another smell I could not define, but knew was the smell of human fear. A thick slab of a man stood by the wall, naked from the waist up. His chest and arms were a knotty mass of muscle and his face was hard, a cruel smile playing on his lips. Another man, richly dressed and quite young, sat in a chair raised on a platform against the wall. A thin, bald servant stood by his side.

I was thrown in the room. I fell to the hard stone floor, but was quickly raised to my feet by the muscled man. I could feel the man's fingers clench around my upper arm like a vise. The bald man to the right of the richly dressed man spoke.

"Viscount, this is the man that was seen speaking to the spy in the tavern out by the Davejean tower. We have been searching for him for many days, but he was only found by the guards late last night. We kept him for you, as you requested," said the servant.

I stared. I recognized the viscount from his visit to the wall in the Castellar suburb, but I prayed that he did not recognize me.

"The Viscount has some questions for you, spy," said the servant. "And I suggest you answer them quickly and truthfully. The man who is holding you down likes to hurt people. The Viscount finds him useful to keep around, but he would so prefer not to see him do his work."

The Viscount stared at me, but then shook his head.

"Spy who are you working for?" said the Viscount.

"I am not a spy," I said. "I am a poor refugee come to this city to escape the fires of Béziers."

The bald servant nodded at the muscled ape that held me. I felt my arm almost twisted out of the socket as the brute deftly grabbed my elbow and pushed upwards. I gritted my teeth, but would not scream. The servant nodded and I felt the pressure relax, though ebbs of pain wafted through my body from my shoulder.

"Let's try again, shall we?" said the servant. "We know you are a spy. We have witnesses. You went to that tavern and you disappeared with the spy, several nights in a row. Spare me your stories and spare yourself a lot of pain. You can tell us what we want and we will give you a quick death or you can choose to take a lot longer to die."

I felt myself wet with sweat. My stomach was pinched in tight knots.

"Who are you working for?" asked the Viscount. "It's a simple question."

"I am simple refugee. I work for no one," I said.

Even as my words came out, the thin servant again nodded and I felt my arm wrenched out of the shoulder socket. I screamed and felt bile rise up from my guts.

"Wait," said Trencavel. "I knew I had seen this man before. He worked on the section of the wall that collapsed in the Castellar. He must work for the mason. That is the man we must find. This fool is no more than a go-between."

Trencavel stood up.

"Pons, order your men to search everywhere for that mason. We thought him an incompetent fool, but he is a brilliant spy and saboteur," said Trencavel.

The thin servant nodded and left the room. The two guards who had brought me from the prison cell entered and grabbed me by my arms. I screamed again and jumped quickly to my feet. I looked into the face of the brute that had injured me and the blasphemer gave me a deep smile and blessed me as would a priest. I spat into his face, immediately regretting it as a powerful fist tore into my guts.

Blessedly, I fell to the floor and remembered nothing else.

Gauda

Monday, August 10, 1209, night

Agnes slept fitfully, her body wracked with fever and dreams torturing her liar's soul. I doused a rag in the lavender water Azalais had prepared and wiped the sweat from her pale face. Suddenly, Agnes reached up and grabbed my arm with a claw-like hand.

"Does he know?" she asked. Her voice was low and raspy.

I slowly removed her hand from my arm and placed it gently on the covers.

"I had to tell him," I said. "We needed water to care for you and he forbade any water to be sent here. I had no choice."

Agnes' eyes filled with tears as she blinked.

"He will repudiate me," said Agnes. "He will realize what I have done and he will repudiate me. I should have died that day my son was born. I should have died."

I placed the covers more closely around Agnes, who shivered, though the day was the hottest yet of this cursed siege. I left Agnes in the care of her maid, for I had been called to play this night for the Viscount. I picked up my harp and walked into the corridor. I had not walked five steps when I became aware of something, a presence behind me. My skin prickled and I stopped to turn and look, sure that I was hearing ghosts.

"Do not turn around," said a voice, muffled and low. "Keep walking, but slowly."

Something in the voice was familiar, but I could not place it. I wanted to turn around with all my will, but something in the tone of the voice made me sure I would regret it if I did. I continued to walk along the corridor, my hand clenched tightly around my harp.

"Gauda, we know what you have been up to," said the voice.

I froze and stumbled, but a sharp prod in my back from my shadow got me moving again.

"I don't know what you are saying," I said.

"I know everything that is going on in this palace," said the voice. "Very clever of you, sending letters to your fellow troubadour, but not clever enough."

I felt a sick coldness in my bowels and I began to sweat.

"I am sure that the Lord Trencavel would find it quite interesting that you had so much information to report to his beloved uncle," said the voice. "You know how fond he is of spies. But, of course, a spy that betrayed him from his bed, I am sure he would want to think of a special punishment for this kind of betrayal."

I kept walking slowly, trying to keep my wits together.

"What do you want of me?" I said. "For surely, if you cared for the Viscount, you would go directly to him and let him take his revenge on me. What is it you want? Gold? Influence? Just tell me and I will make sure it is yours when this cursed siege is over."

The voice laughed, but so softly that it sent chills down my spine.

"You think I need gold or influence? You are a very foolish woman. And I had estimated your talents at such a higher level. You cannot deal for my favor, for you are the pawn now. You will do as I say or I will tell the Viscount Trencavel of your activities."

I kept walking silently, my legs shaking.

"For now, continue as always," said the voice. "You will be watched, so do not try anything. Though what you could possibly do, I couldn't imagine. You are certainly not going to complain to the Viscount about me."

Again the voice laughed, ever so lightly.

"I will come to you again when I need you," said the voice. "Be waiting."

I kept walking slowly, forcing one trembling foot in front of the next. I sensed that the creature with the horrid, quiet voice had walked away in the direction we had come from, but I dared not turn to be sure. Finally, I reached the threshold of the Viscount's chambers. I walked in, forcing my hands to stop shaking.

Trencavel sat in his chair in front of the empty fireplace, his hunting dogs at his feet. He looked up at me blearily, a goblet of wine in his hand. It was tilted at an angle and some wine dribbled to the carpet at his feet. Trencavel was drunk, his eyes bloodshot.

"Gauda, my sweet Gauda," he said, none too clearly. "Come sit here and play for me."

I took my harp and walked across the rushes to the fireplace. I sat on the cold stone and tucked my feet beneath my skirts.

"What would you like me to play, my Lord?" I asked.

His head swayed on his neck a bit, like a baby's before it gains control of its muscles. He leaned forward and exhaled and I could smell the wine, almost turned to vinegar, on his breath. He reached out and pulled the cap off my head. My hair fell forward onto my shoulders and he started playing clumsily with the loose strands.

"Oh Gauda, my Gauda," he said. "You are the only one I can trust. My wife is a lying fraud and I am surrounded by spies. My uncle betrays me, my liege lord deserts me in my hour of need, and my counselors are incompetent old men who think only of themselves. Why am I treated so?"

I could say nothing. I only thought of how young Trencavel seemed, consumed by pity for himself.

Trencavel stood up suddenly and threw his goblet into the fireplace.

"Why am I treated so?" he yelled.

We heard the metal goblet ricochet around the stone of the empty fireplace and then the room fell eerily quiet. Trencavel turned to the young servant at the door.

"Don't be a fool, get me some wine," he yelled.

The servant dashed off down the corridor.

"And what are you staring at?" Trencavel said to me. "Play for me, or get out of here."

I placed my harp in my hands and began to quietly pluck the string. I sang, the softest, sweetest song I knew for to calm us both.

DAY 11 OF THE SIEGE OF CARCASSONNE

Tuesday, August 11, 1209

Constance

Tuesday, August 11, 1209, noon

"He's burning up," said Beatritz.

Constance walked over and placed her hand on the cheek of the baby boy. They were all hot, stuck in this stuffy attic as the sun rose over the city. But this baby's cheek made Constance's hand feel cool in comparison.

"What is going to happen to my little boy?" asked Beatritz. Her eyes were wild and red- rimmed, her hair escaping from her kerchief in untidy clumps. Constance could not believe she was the same woman who had warmly welcomed them into her cheerful, orderly home only a few days ago.

"He has a fever," said Constance. "I know something of herbs and curing. I will do what I can."

"This is all the fault of that foul heretic, my husband," said Beatritz. "May he rot in hell for his blasphemous ways."

Beatritz started to wail again, setting off the cries of the other children, who clustered around her skirts, terrified. Constance's head felt as if it would burst from the cacophony of screams. She walked over to Beatritz and began to shake her roughly at the shoulders.

"That's enough!" screamed Constance.

Beatritz looked up in shock, but she stopped crying. The children still sniffled and whined beside her, but their cries were also shut off.

"You are upsetting the children," continued Constance. "All your cries will not make the little one better. If you care about him, go to what's left of the market and see if you can find anything - thistles, antimony - to get this fever down."

Beatritz walked down the stairs, still shaking, but at least quiet. Constance stood next to the feverish infant, wishing she had cool water to bathe him in and try to bring down the fever. What else could she do while she waited for the herbs? The oldest little girl, Aude, stood close by Constance's side, her little brother sucking his thumb, his face still wet with tears.

"Is baby sick?" asked the little girl quietly.

"Yes, he is not feeling very well, but we are going to try to make him better," said Constance.

The little girl walked over to the bed and gently touched the baby's head, smoothing his sweaty hair into place. Beatritz' sister walked up the stairs.

"My sister went to the market," said the women, in her slow, garbled voice. "I can tend to the baby while you get something to eat."

Constance looked at the thin, timid girl and nearly started to cry from this display of kindness. Her head was aching, she was exhausted and hungry and so very thirsty. She just nodded mutely to the girl and grasped her hand in thanks. Constance practically ran down the stairs to kitchen. The mason and Beatritz's parents were eating around the table. Guillaume, the journeyman, and the older apprentice sat near the hearth eating moldy cheese and old roots. Constance walked over to them and sat by Guillaume, who offered her cheese and a radish. She sunk her teeth into the decaying cheese and felt that she had never tasted anything so good in her whole life. But, as soon as her belly was a little full, she began to feel the deepest ache for water that she had ever experienced. She had been thirsty before, but the salt and whey of the cheese seemed to scour her mouth with an rabid thirst that made her want to jump to the table and rip the jug of wine from the hands of the nasty old woman, even if she had to hurt her to get it.

"What is the matter, Constance?" asked Guillaume.

"It is nothing," said Constance. She shook her head, shocked at the thoughts that had been passing through it. "I am just thirsty, as are we all."

Guillaume stood up and went to the table, before Constance could stop him.

"I am sorry to make yet another demand on your great hospitality, sir," said Guillaume to the old man. "But, the young lady who has been caring for your grandchildren has a great thirst. I beg of you just a small bit of wine for her to slake it."

The old woman's face turned red.

"We feed you and give you a place to sleep, and you have the nerve to ask for more!" the old woman yelled. "You ungrateful cur!"

The old man placed a hand firmly on her arm.

"I am an old man and have not much either of thirst or hunger," he said. "Please take the rest of my jug for the young lady, to keep her strong."

The old lady looked like she was going to speak again, but the old man looked at her and she said nothing. Guillaume gratefully took the jug and brought it to Constance. She placed the jug to her lips and felt the blessed liquid go down. She wanted to drink it all in one gulp, but after a huge initial gulp that made her cough and her eyes water, she forced herself to slow down and savor the acidic wetness.

"Thank you," she said quietly to Guillaume.

Suddenly, the door to the house slammed open and the younger apprentice came running in, out of breath.

"They'll come to take us all! We'll be strung up and killed!" he screamed, his words coming out in a squeaky high soprano.

Instantly, the room erupted into chaos. The mason stood up and placed his hand on the boy's shoulder, forcing him to stand still and calm down.

"Speak clearly, boy," the mason said. "What has happened?"

The boy took several quick breaths and then one long one.

"The soldiers," he squeaked. "They are looking for you. At all the sites. The Viscount wants you taken as a spy!"

No one spoke. Constance looked around the room and saw only terrified faces. Into the stunned quiet, Beatritz' sister ran down the stairs.

"Come quick, girl," said the sister. "The baby, he has the flux. Help me!"

"God help us all," said Guillaume, softly.

Trencavel

Tuesday, August 11, 1209, afternoon

Trencavel stared at the man cringing before him, trembling on his knees, his face pressed to the floor. The man slowly raised his miserable face.

"Have mercy on me, Lord Trencavel," said the man. "I would never desert the garrison. These men are liars."

The sergeant standing over the man kicked him.

"Shut your mouth, you foul deserter," said the sergeant. "I swear, my Lord, I saw this man trying to leave his post at night and escape over the walls."

"That is enough, sergeant," said Trencavel. "Stand back and let me question this man."

The sergeant moved back. The soldier began to cry and clutch at Trencavel's boots.

"I knew that your Lordship's mercy was great," said the soldier.

"Quiet," said Trencavel. "I want you to answer my questions and know that a truthful response will make me see your case in a more merciful light. If you do not want to suffer, do not waste my time with lies."

The soldier stopped crying and looked up at Trencavel.

"Why did you do this?" asked Trencavel.

"I am thirsty, my Lord," said the man. "And scared. My cousins were killed at Béziers. These Crusaders, they know no mercy."

"But what makes you so sure that we will lose?" asked Trencavel.

"Any fool can see that," said the man, and then realizing what he had said, he quickly lowered his head. "I beg your pardon my Lord."

Trencavel grimaced.

"Continue, you fool," said Trencavel. "But watch what you say. My interest in your motives is the only thing preventing me from ordering you whipped for insolence."

The man groveled his thanks and then timidly lifted his head.

"My Lord, the people are starting to die in the streets. Our defenses are crumbling under their siege engines. And there is hardly enough water to live. I stare all day at the river as I guard the walls under this wretched sun, watching our attackers slaking their thirst, pulling buckets for their animals, even bathing. I could not help myself - the water called me. I wanted nothing more than to drink until I could drink no more and then, if they killed me, so be it."

"Did you desert alone or were others involved in your plot?" asked Trencavel.

"It was only I, my Lord," said the man.

"Very well, I am finished with you," said Trencavel.

"Your gracious mercy knows no bounds, my Lord," said the man, his face wet with tears.

Trencavel did not look at the deserter. He gestured to the sergeant.

"Take this man and make an example of him," said Trencavel.

The hall resounded with the cries of the condemned man as he was pulled from the room by the sergeant. Trencavel sat quietly. Bertrand de Saissac raised his hand and placed it on the young man's knee.

"The siege has been easy until this point," said Bertrand. "It is now that your strength and honor will be tested."

Cabaret stood on Trencavel's left.

"The man was a deserter and he needed to be dealt with harshly," said Cabaret. "But, you would be a fool not to listen to his words. He is not the only one who feels that way. There will be more, no matter what spectacle you make of him."

Trencavel turned and stared at Cabaret.

"Leave my sight, old man," Trencavel said. "I have had enough of your cowardice, always counseling me to surrender. Whose side are you on anyway? Would you see my honor, my family's honor, destroyed before you stood willing to fight? My ancestors have been the lords of this city since the time when your family were peasants, following your sheep through the mountain passes. Troubadours were writing of the glories of our exploits when your forefathers were scraping dung from their sandals. We know the meaning of honor and courage. I listened to you when the King of Aragon came and was humiliated. The monks heard the cowardice and fear in my offer to negotiate and took advantage of it, as is only just. I will not make that mistake again. They will only listen to strength and courage and that is what I will give them."

"You are young," said Cabaret. "But someday you will learn that the path of greater courage may sometimes appear that of the coward."

Cabaret turned and walked from the room.

DAY 12 OF THE SIEGE OF CARCASSONNE

Wednesday, August 12, 1209

Gauda

Wednesday, August 12, 1209, morning

I ran the comb through Agnes' beautiful locks, once again golden and shiny. She sat up in her bed, wearing a clean white chemise. A tray of sweetmeats rested on her lap and her delicate fingers placed the succulent morsels in her pink mouth. A beatific expression radiated from her. She sighed with pleasure.

"I had forgotten the pleasure given by the leisurely eating of the flesh of animals," said Agnes.

"It is a delight," I said.

I thought that Agnes must also be delighting in the pleasure of no longer having to keep up her elaborate hoax. For to keep a secret is fatiguing beyond belief. I knew that only too well myself. How I longed to escape this castle and the double-life I was forced to lead. I only hoped that I would not be exposed against my will, as Agnes had been. For her betrayal had been innocent compared to mine.

Agnes turned to me and smiled.

"Thank you, cousin" said Agnes. "For your kindness."

I smiled back and remembered the pretty little girl I had once known, sweet and joyous and always so beautiful.

Suddenly, the door to the chamber opened and Trencavel barged in, sending the two maids scurrying to the corner. His breadth filled the room and his face was livid with anger. He marched over to Agnes' bed and swept the tray away with one hand. It clattered to the floor. I felt Agnes shrink into me as I stood beside her, comb frozen in my hand.

"You eat the finest delicacies of my storerooms and engage in foolish pursuits while my city is dying!" yelled Trencavel. "Do you even know or care what happens in these lands? People are dying in the streets of thirst or the flux! Soldiers are deserting and walls of this very city are crumbling! And you know nothing, you foolish, vapid creature!"

Agnes straightened her spine away from me and placed her hands squarely on her coverlet.

"My Lord," she said. "I have betrayed and deceived, but not for my own gain, but for my protection. I will devote my life to charitable works, but I know the measure of my weak soul. I will ask again for the consolamentum, but this time on my true deathbed. I have made my peace with my God for what I have done. Can you not forgive me even if you must repudiate me?"

Trencavel stepped back and stared at her. He came forward and his hand reached out to Agnes. She flinched, but did not move. Trencavel lightly touched the golden curls cascading over her shoulder.

"What fool me," he said. "One should know better than to fall in love with the vision of beauty that is one's own wife. For I have pined, like the most foolish troubadour, only after you. It has clouded my vision, caused me to place the very lineage of my family in jeopardy. How I secretly hoped that you would repudiate your vows and come back to my bed. And, now I learn that it was all a lie. You could never come back to my bed or bear me more sons. I was truly pining after the unattainable lady, forever out of reach, forever far from that glorious consummation of our love."

Trencavel let Agnes' hair fall back to her chest. He gently touched her cheek and bent down to kiss her forehead.

"I must repudiate you," said Trencavel. "I have no choice. You must understand."

Agnes nodded slowly. She smiled at him gently, though her eyes were filled with tears.

"After I win this siege," said Trencavel. "I will give you a settlement of lands so that you will live comfortably the rest of your days."

Agnes nodded, the tears now falling freely down her face. Trencavel held her hand tightly. He turned to the maids.

"Clean up this mess, and leave us," said Trencavel. He turned to face me.

"Gauda, go now and get more sweetmeats. Tell the cellarer to provide anything Agnes asks for, the finest wines, the best sugared ginger from the East. Gauda, you will continue to care for your cousin until she needs you no more. This is the task I charge you with. Go now."

I felt as if I had been slapped. I followed the maids out the door and down the hall, but stopped after turning a corner and tucked myself into a small alcove by the stairs, hidden by an old, moth-eaten tapestry. I tried to curl myself into the smallest ball possible as silent sobs racked my body. I stuffed my hand into my mouth and pinched my hands, but I could not stop the tears from welling out of my chest. I had always known that I provided nothing more than a physical release for Trencavel, so why did my guts feel as if they had been torn from my mouth? The Viscount was a young fool and his wife a shrew. I wanted nothing more than my due, my family lands, and a comfortable life, free from the fear of hunger or the humiliation of poverty. I was the betrayer in this little triangle. I was the one who had enjoyed the lustful pleasures of the handsome, young Viscount's bed, knowing they were temporary and that I could replace his attentions with those of a handsome young minstrel when I was finally lady of my own lands. So, why did I cry?

I do not know how long I stayed there, but finally my tears subsided and my body felt cramped. I gingerly moved my frozen limbs and peered from behind the tapestry. A shadowy figure stood in front of me. I started to scream, but he clamped his hand over my face and slid behind the tapestry with me.

"I was wondering when you would be finished with your hysterics," said the man.

His face was covered by a hood, but I recognized the hushed whisper. It was my tormenter, the man who would betray my betrayal. He pressed a vial into my hand.

"Your task has been chosen," he said. "This is poison. You must slip it into the wine glass of the Viscount when next he calls you to play for him. He will take wine from you, even if he does not from any other. If you do not, I will divulge your secret and you will go to the rack. Do not think of trying to warn him for I have my spies everywhere and you will not succeed. Anyway, I do not doubt that you want this to end as badly as the rest of us. For if he dies, the city will surrender. You will be free to claim your spy's recompense. If Trencavel continues this foolish defense, the city will eventually fall and when it does the Crusaders will wreak vengeance on all of those who inhabit this city, all of those left alive that is."

I took the vial and placed it in the small sack on my belt. The hooded man left and I waited in silence behind the tapestry, willing my heart to beat more slowly. I felt the small glass cylinder in my purse. It felt strangely like freedom and damnation all at the same time.

Constance

Wednesday, August 12, 1209, noon

"Your son is dying," screamed Beatritz. "Would you have him rot in purgatory to pay for your sins?"

The mason took a step towards Beatritz, attempting to place a calming hand on her shoulder. She launched into him, her fists flailing against his chest.

"Don't touch me, you foul heretic!" she shrieked. "Don't you dare defile me with your blasphemous words and your sinful ways! Find me a priest so he can baptize your infant son and maybe you will be forgiven for all the damage you have caused!"

"You idiot woman!" said the mason. "It is your foul priests who destroyed our home, ruined my craft, and are now killing our children!"

Beatritz stomped away from the mason and back up the stairs. Constance shrunk into a corner as Beatritz passed, next to Guillaume. They were the only people left in the house besides the mason, his wife, and her family. The journeyman and the two boy apprentices had been gone when Constance awoke this morning. She supposed that they had finally decided to cut their losses and try to get work elsewhere in the city before the Viscount's soldiers came to take the mason. The mason stood alone, trembling with anger, his hands clenched into fists.

Constance heard weak cries from upstairs and remembered that she had come down for more straw. The little boy and Beatritz's father had also fallen sick with the same bloody flux as the infant. Constance had nursed the ill before, but never without water or the other good women to help her. She tried to keep the sufferers as clean as possible and tried to ease their fevers with valerian, but they cried for water, their bodies parched from the fever and drained by their fluxing bowels. The baby's cries, which shrieked all last night into Constance's ears, had now become weak. The baby was dying.

The little boy had been taken so quickly by the flux. Last night he had played with his older sister in front of the hearth, but now he lay listless and depleted on his filthy straw pallet. Constance had seen death from illness many a time and could see the signs of its approach. The baby did not have long for this world. She gathered up straw from the courtyard, apologizing to the poor donkey for stealing its meal. The donkey, thirsty and miserable itself, did not even look up from where he had collapsed, too weak to even stir the flies covering his coat. She absently looked into the buckets sitting alongside the donkey's manger, hoping to see a drop of water that had been missed by every other being, human or animal, but everything was baked dry in the scorching midday sun.

Constance walked past the mason, sitting blankly at the table, and walked up the stairs. She entered the stifling and foul-smelling bedroom and stared. There were so many people in the small room. Beatritz' mother sat next to her sick old husband, mopping the sweat from his brow with a dry rag. Beatritz and her sister stood with their backs to the staircase, staring over the cots of the baby. Beatritz' little girl clung to her skirts and Constance could hear Beatritz quietly crying and speaking to her mother.

"God has made a miracle manifest," Beatritz said. "I prayed for this and the mightiest Lord delivered a miracle from heaven, a miracle to soothe a poor Christian mother's heart."

Constance wondered if the baby had suddenly gotten better. That would have truly been a miracle, for all the signs of death had been on his face when she walked away just ten minutes ago. Constance dropped her straw and quickly walked over to Beatritz. She stopped and stared, for she did not understand. The baby was still dying, the death rattle vibrating his poor chest as he struggled for his last breaths. But now Guillaume stood over him, sprinkling precious drops of water and speaking words in a language Constance did not understand. Constance screamed and tried to leap towards the water, but Guillaume held her back.

"Guillaume, what are you doing?" said Constance. "How can you waste what we so dearly need?"

Constance turned to Beatritz, whose face bore an expression of rapturous joy.

"Beatritz, what is happening?" asked Constance.

"It is the greatest miracle I have ever heard of," said Beatritz. "For my baby was dying and I prayed only that he would be baptized before he is delivered back to his Heavenly Father. And, behold, my prayers were answered! All I had to do was renounce the husband who had brought heresy and disaster to this house and my answer came from heaven. And surely this is a sign that I am now under God's grace again and all will improve."

Constance still did not understand. She thought that Beatritz must surely have gone mad. Constance looked at Guillaume. He had finished speaking his words and had closed the eyes of the baby, who had finally drawn his last breath. Beatritz fell on the baby, and took his lifeless body into her arms, where she cried and cooed as if she were only rocking him to sleep.

"Guillaume?" asked Constance.

Guillaume turned to her with a gentle expression.

"There has been enough of falsehood," said Guillaume. "I cannot lie any longer. I never wanted to and I was convinced against my better judgment of this folly. I am a monk, Constance. Bernard and I both. We are here to send information to the Lord Abbot who waits outside this city with the Crusaders to rescue all of you from eternal damnation. I could not allow this soul to die without baptism. I am sorry for my deception. Please come to us, see the error of your ways. You can still be saved."

Constance screamed and turned to run away. She ran right into the imposing form of the mason, standing at the top of the stairs. His face was completely red and Constance could see the veins popping from this forehead. He advanced on Guillaume, who did not make a move to defend himself.

"I am ashamed of our behavior, good mason" said Guillaume. "You must know that we only wanted to help you."

The mason answered with his fists, pummeling an unresisting Guillaume until he fell to the ground. Beatritz screamed and tried to pull the mason off of Guillaume, hissing and pulling at her husband's hair. The mason flicked her off like a fly. The little girl screamed in terror. Then Constance heard the pounding of heavy boots on the stairs. Two soldiers spilled into the fetid, crowded room.

"We have orders to arrest the mason," said the older. "Who is the mason?"

Beatritz stood up and pointed at her husband.

"Take that man, and may he rot in your jails and in hell for all eternity for what he has done."

The soldiers finally pulled the mason off of Guillaume, who sat bloody and confused on the floor.

The mason stopped struggling with the soldiers.

"I am an innocent man," he said. "But, I know you must follow orders and take me now. But, take this man as well, for he truly is a spy! I will not go alone to pay for what I did not even do!"

The soldiers stopped to confer with each other for a second, but then the older nodded his head and the younger went to grab Guillaume. Guillaume did not resist. The soldiers led the two men away. The mason did not look back, but Guillaume turned and spoke to Constance.

"Please forgive me, for I knew not what I did," said Guillaume.

The room seemed strangely quiet after the big men had left. Constance did not know why her heart hurt so much, but she did not think on it, but only went to the side of the little boy and tried to clean his messed cot. She did not know she was crying until she saw hot tears fall on the face of the little boy, who lapped them up eagerly with his parched tongue.

Azalais

Wednesday, August 12, 1209, early afternoon

Azalais dropped the pestle she was using to grind mustard seeds. The heavy stone implement fell on the table in the herb drying room with a dull thud. She felt very faint and weak all of sudden and stepped backward until she found the chair in the corner. Azalais thought that she must have been overexerting herself these last few days, for she was not young anymore. The sick had not stopped coming, more and more sufferers of the bloody flux and fevers, and still the wounded came, for the bombardments had started up again after the failed negotiations. Azalais and her good women had nursed and cared for the sick as best they knew how, but without much water there was little they could do to replenish the bodies of those drained by the flux and sweated out by fever. The dead were piled in the courtyard garden, for there was no one to come and collect them anymore.

Azalais started to sweat and when she lifted her apron to sweep her brow, it came away soaked. It was this heat, thought Azalais. This day had seemed to Azalais the hottest yet of the siege, with the sun baking this city full of the dead, the stench rising to encompass them all in its unhealthy vapors. Azalais stood up very slowly. She just needed some water - that was all that was the problem. The tail end of the supplies that Gauda had obtained from the Viscount still stood in the good women's storerooms underground. Azalais had carefully rationed them, with a bit extra each day for the good women, who needed to keep their strength to care for the sick. Of course, so many did not need the water, for they had taken the endura, the better to speed their release from this carnal hell. If there could be any one blessing from this siege, it was this - facing death focused many a man's mind on his eternal soul. Azalais had performed the consolamentum countless times over the last two days and each time she watched the blissful relief on the believer's face as they knew they were to spend eternity free of this earthly yoke.

Azalais felt lightheaded and tried to grasp the table as she suddenly fell to the floor. When she awoke, several good women were standing over her.

"The flux must have taken her," said one. "The smell of rot is everywhere. The miasma was too strong for an old woman to bear."

Azalais felt the wetness of the flux on her clothes and cringed in shame, though she knew from caring for the sick that they could not control themselves as the flux passed through them, expelling all the foul humors with cramps that caused the sufferer to double in pain.

"She needs to be cleaned and moved to her bed," said Eleanor.

Two of the stronger good women picked up Azalais and bore her gently to her small room. Azalais felt her whole body burning and was glad to feel the women's hands strip her of her filthy tunic. They cleaned her as best they could and then lay her in her own bed, covered by a light blanket for, though Azalais burned with fever, she felt a sudden coldness deep in the core of her body. Eleanor stepped closer to Azalais and laid her delicate little hand on Azalais' forehead.

"My dear sister," said Eleanor. "Will you want to start the endura? I know how you yearn for freedom."

Azalais remained quite for a minute. What joy would await her if she just let go! All the bliss of heaven, forever free from pain and hunger and the ache of her all too human heart. Azalais turned to Eleanor, ready to give her assent, when a small, dark face entered her thoughts. Constance. What would happen to her? How could Azalais think of her own bliss when the one she loved as a daughter was lost, maybe sick and terrified, thinking she was all alone? Azalais had passed the last few days so sure that Constance would turn up at their door, begging to be taken back. All would be as before, but Constance would have learned her lessons. She would not be so haughty or so sure of herself. Azalais always believed she would see Constance again in this world. And, if not in this world, then surely in the world to come for Constance was one of the chosen, those who knew young that their salvation was assured. But, who knew what could befall Constance out in the world? When one of the chosen fell, their path back to salvation is surely much longer and rocky than that of a simple believer. Constance needed to be here, surrounded by her sisters.

Azalais looked up at Eleanor.

"I must see Constance before I leave this world," said Azalais. "Please send someone to find her. My pride kept me from taking care of her as I would any wayward sister. Forgive me, Eleanor, I hope it is not too late."

Eleanor took Azalais' hand and placed it on her heart.

"We will do everything we can, both to find Constance and to keep you alive to see her and take her back to us."

Azalais breathed deeply and closed her eyes.

Trencavel

Wednesday, August 12, 1209, afternoon

Trencavel sat in the interrogation room, Pons at his side. The three men in front of him disgusted him. He hated nothing more than a spy, those cowards who refused to fight in the plain air like honorable men. Holding himself as if he had nothing to be ashamed of, the insolent mason stood tall and proud. Trencavel would see that false pride beaten out of him before the day was through. The other two men were much younger than the mason. They were obviously brothers, though one had the fine bearing of a young knight and the other the mien of a furtive clerk caught tipping his hand in the accounts. Who were these men and, more importantly, who did they all work for?

"Shall we begin the questioning, my Lord?" asked Pons.

"Yes, start with the mason," said Trencavel.

The brutish guard moved the mason forward. His face was bruised and it was obvious he had put up a fight when he was taken.

"Who do you work for, spy?" asked Pons.

"I am no spy," spat the mason.

Trencavel signaled to the guard and he began to twist the mason's arm. The mason deftly pulled his arm loose and gripped the guard's wrist in his strong hand. The guard whimpered. Pons ordered the other two guards to hold the mason back and free the red- faced guard.

"I am no spy, but I can tell you who is," said the mason, struggling against the two guards who held him back. "These two double-crossing Papist scum!"

The two brothers stood still, their faces drained of color.

"Very well," said Trencavel. "Tell me your accusations and then we will hear what these two have to say of you."

It was always like this, Trencavel thought to himself. Thieves and spies have no honor. It took only to bring them together under the threat of death and they all began blaming the others to save their own skins. Usually, Trencavel could sift out the truth from the lies and learn enough to condemn them all. It was more effective than torture which did give many answers, if one was not bothered to look for the truth.

The guards loosened their grip on the mason, but stayed warily close to their prisoner.

"I took in these two bastards, who claimed to be refugees from Béziers," said the mason. "I pitied them and fed them and taught them skills I usually only give to an apprentice whose parents have paid dear for the privilege. I welcomed them into my home and how am I thanked? They told their masters where to attack our walls and my wall fell under the assault. Now I have nothing - not even my good name! I didn't want to think it true, but I saw the younger one with my own eyes baptizing my infant son with his Latin gibberish! This one is a popish priest and probably his brother too, damn them all to hell!"

The mason lunged towards the brothers, but the guards quickly moved to hold him back.

Trencavel thought for a moment. Priests were always used as spies. That was nothing new, but who had sent them? That was what he needed to know and he was no closer to the truth. Plus, he doubted that the mason was innocent. How could he shelter spies for a week and not know? It was all too easy.

"What do you have to say for yourselves to this accusation?" asked Pons.

The older brother stepped forward. His face was sweating and his eyes moved wildly from side to side.

"We are just innocent refugees, who have lost our whole family," said the older brother. "This mason took us in and cared for us, this much is true. But, I know nothing of masonry or walls. How could I do anything to sabotage the wall when I am ignorant? I did everything exactly as the mason directed. I believe he took us in only to have a scapegoat were his perfidy to be discovered. It is too easy to blame a poor refugee with no family or friends to defend him. As soon as he was taken by the guards he began to make up all manner of lies to confuse you! But he is to blame, my merciful lord, not us!"

The mason jumped away from his guards and began to choke his accuser.

"You lying, scheming popish fiend!" screamed the mason. "I will kill you for your lies!"

The older brother began to turn blue in the face.

"Enough," yelled Trencavel.

Pons opened the door and the two guards from the hall came

into the cell. Along with the other guards, they managed to subdue the mason with kicks to his kidneys and groin. He finally sat moaning against the wall and the guards placed shackles on his legs and wrists.

"It is true," said the younger brother, in a quiet, calm voice.

Trencavel looked up at this boy, who had not yet said a word.

"What is true?" asked Pons.

"It is true what the mason said," said the younger brother.

The older brother leaped to his brother's side.

"He is mad from heat and thirst," said the older brother, "Do not listen to him."

"Guards, restrain that man," said Trencavel. "I want to hear what this younger brother has to say."

The guards led the older brother to the wall and began to shackle his wrists as well, as he begged his younger brother to be quiet.

"Continue," said Trencavel, thinking that he might actually hear the truth in this room, for a change.

"I have betrayed all my beliefs in my God," said the younger brother, in a calm voice. "I can no longer live as a liar and so I must tell the truth. My name is Guillaume and my brother is Bernard. We are Cistercian monks and have been sent here by Abbot Arnald to further the cause of our most holy father in heaven. We are here to save you from the heresy that will make you burn for all eternity and we only meant for good to come from our actions. But I am ashamed that I did not trust to preaching and openness to convert the wicked and save souls. For surely, when those who have been blinded by the ways of the devil hear the most blessed words of our lord Jesus Christ, they will come back to the fold. There is no need for subterfuge or force, the most blessed words of our father will suffice. I beg the forgiveness of the mason and all whom we have deceived, but mostly I beg the forgiveness of my Lord Jesus Christ for not trusting the power of his truth."

Trencavel watched in astonishment as the brother called Guillaume dropped to his knees and began to pray. The older brother called Bernard sat with his head in his hands, softly moaning. And the mason glared at both with hatred in his eyes.

So, it was the Abbot, after all, thought Trencavel. The bastard. This was good information, but how to use it? And how to use the men who sat in front of him? Trencavel needed time to think.

"Pons," said Trencavel to his servant. "Keep these men detained, for I do not want them executed yet. There is more I may need to learn from them."

Trencavel stood to leave the room.

"My Lord," said the mason. "You have heard this man. I am innocent. Will you order me freed?"

"Just because they are guilty does not mean you are innocent," said Trencavel. Trencavel turned to Pons. "Make sure the mason is held with the others, but keep him shackled. I don't want him killing these other priestly spies before I am ready to do it myself."

Constance

Wednesday, August 12, 1209, evening

Constance cursed herself for her foolishness. Why had she ever left the side of Azalais and the comfort of the home for good women? Constance wanted to return with all her soul, but knew she must stay here and care for these people until this was over, one way or the other. Constance had watched as the little boy and Beatritz' mother and sister had all succumbed, so quickly in the hours after the baby's death. Beatritz and Constance were the only ones unaffected by the flux. Perhaps Beatritz' madness protected her, for she had descended into an even deeper lunacy, leaving Constance to care for the old man and the little girl.

Constance despaired. She had no herbs or clean clothes and very little water. How could one heal the sick in such a situation? Constance knew she had to search for stores one more time in this house. There had to be something. She turned to Beatritz, who sat on the floor, counting the beads on her rosary and softly moaning. Constance put her arms on the shoulders of the shaking woman.

"Beatritz, listen to me," said Constance. "I must go search for food and water. We have nothing left. You have to watch the others. Your father and your little girl need you. Beatritz, do you hear me?"

The woman turned her lifeless gaze towards Constance, but she did not respond.

Constance turned abruptly and went over to the old man. In the short time Constance had stayed in his home she had already seen what a good man he was, kind and just. She leaned over and spoke into his ear.

"I have to go search for more supplies," she said. "I will not be long. If the little girl wakes, tell her where I have gone."

The old man nodded his head and clutched Constance's hand tightly, once, before letting go.

Constance walked to the head of the stairs and headed down. She covered her face with a rag as she descended into the kitchen. It was eerily empty, the door to the street bolted securely. Constance dared not head to the streets, filled with desperate, mad refugees. She thought to hunt again for food in the garden, but did not have the courage to go out into the small space where they had left the dead. The heat was too strong and the stench of decay permeated the kitchen. She headed instead for the cellar. There were no candles in the kitchen, so Constance left the cellar door wide open and descended slowly. The blessed coolness enveloped her as she went down, her hand holding onto the floor of the kitchen and moving delicately forward until she could grasp hold of the post rising from the bottom of the stairs.

When she got to the last step, Constance sat for a moment to give her eyes time to adjust to the darkness. It was the first rest she had had in days. She placed her hands in the small of her back and stretched like a cat, hearing the small bones in her back crack into place. Unbidden, Guillaume's face popped into her mind. She could almost see him in the darkness. But, no, it was just an old tunic hung in the opposite corner of the cellar.

Besides, why did she want to see him again? Constance chided herself. He had lied to her and used them all to destroy everything she believed in. A monk! One who lived off the backs of the poor as drunken gluttons laying up treasures of gold on earth. And she thought him a poor boy who had lost everything at Béziers! He was at Béziers, for sure, but on the side of the wicked Abbot and his Crusaders, watching as the city burned and all the hapless souls within were massacred! Azalais had been right. Somehow she had known that Guillaume with his silky ways and his big eyes was not to be trusted. Oh why, oh why had she not listened to Azalais? Her stupid pride had been surely punished this time. For hadn't she allowed herself to imagine even in her deepest daydreams that Guillaume was her knight errant and she a fair lady, never free to receive his love in an earthly way, but desperate to hear his words of devotion and praise. For even Constance, raised in a house of good women, knew the stories and the songs of courtly love. From time to time old troubadour friends of Azalais would pass by the house and stay for a few days, singing in thanks for their bread. Azalais would forbid any song that might incite an earthly passion, but some nights her guard would be lessened. The other good women could see the pleasure on her face as she heard the long notes of the harp and she would forget to stop the performer as they sang an old song of sweet love, so pure and impossible that it would leave them crying.

Constance felt her own tears hit the hands she had crossed on her lap and suddenly jumped up. She had a task to complete and people to care for. She pinched herself. She had better to remember that all those true lovers of song were also deceivers, just as was Guillaume. She would not be a fool again.

Constance felt her way around the cellar in the dim light. There were still some old roots and vegetables that they could eat raw, though almost everything else in the cellar needed to be cooked with water. She gathered what she could find into an old basket at the foot of the stairs. There must be more wine in this cellar, for surely respectable burghers such as this family would have stored many barrels. Constance headed further into the darkness until she finally found what she was looking for. She opened the spigot and felt the cool wetness on her fingers. Constance immediately lay down and placed her mouth under the spigot drinking and choking as the cool wine spilled into her mouth. Constance drank until she could drink no more and then sat up, feeling very light-headed and strange. She dragged a bucket over to the spigot and filled it up, before carefully turning off the spigot, making sure not even a drop escaped. Constance dragged the bucket and her basket of vegetables over to the stairs and began hauling them up, trying to ignore the giddiness in her head as she slowly made her way up the stairs, some of the wine sloshing out of the top of the bucket with each step.

Constance's back ached, but she finally made it to the top of the stairs. She closed the cellar door to keep it cool and took a deep breath before beginning her next climb. Suddenly, she heard a crash of timbers from next door. The Crusaders had started the bombardment again. She heard the little girl Aude shrieking and quickly made her way up the stairs.

The old man had managed to get out of his bed and was trying to comfort his little granddaughter. Beatritz sat by the window, still moaning. When she saw Constance, she suddenly jumped up and began shrieking.

"Heretic!" she screamed. "Now I recognize you, you fool blasphemer! You are one of the girls in the house of heretic women. I knew I had seen your face before. You are no refugee. It was you who brought this misery upon my family! Murderer!"

Beatritz jumped forward and grabbed Constance by her shoulders, shaking her so that Constance dropped the wine. It pooled out in blot of red, spreading quickly over the floor and dripping down the stairs.

"See, how the blood of Christ was spilled and yet you mock him! This is all your fault!" shrieked Beatritz. "And you, you slut, you tried to corrupt one of our Lord's own holy priests. Don't deny it. I saw the way you looked at him, you little hussy! You wanted to ensnare in him your heretic rites! How come you are not sick when so many who are true Christians have died? It is because you are in league with Satan!"

Beatritz kept pushing Constance closer to the top of the stairs. Constance tried to push against her, but lost her footing in the spilled wine and started to lose her balance. Suddenly, Constance felt the pressure release on her arms and watched as Beatritz slowly dropped to the ground. Her father stood behind her, clasping a wine bottle in his hands.

"She will be fine, but this should keep her from waking for a few hours," said the old man. "Hopefully, she will have calmed down by then."

Constance knelt to touch Beatritz' face. She was still breathing deeply and did not appear to be hurt. Constance dragged her up to the nearest bed and then helped the old man back to his bed. His face had turned deathly pale. Constance ran back to the cellar for more wine and gave some to him. He fell into a deep sleep as did the little girl after Constance gave her wine and assured her that her mother would be fine.

Constance listened to the crash of the stones in the buildings around her and heard chanting from the monks across the river again. She looked at the three sleeping forms surrounding her in the stifling heat and poured herself another mug of the wine. She sipped it slowly.

DAY 13 OF THE SIEGE OF CARCASSONNE

Thursday, August 13, 1209

Bernard

Thursday, August 13, 1209, morning

As I suffered, I tried to remember the trials of all the apostles and all the saints and of our Lord Jesus Christ himself. I knew that I would be blessed with eternal life and that I should be joyous that I was given this chalice to bear, but my being was consumed not with forgiveness for those who had wronged me, but with hate for my foolish, proud brother who thought himself higher even than the Abbot himself.

Guillaume groveled at the feet of the mason, who spat on him and tried to kick him with his shackled feet and beat him with his shackled arms. Imagine that Guillaume, who was only doing the bidding of God's representatives here on earth, should want to beg forgiveness of that foul blasphemous sinner! It was as if the last days are come and the world was turned upside down and Satan ruled here on earth.

At least we were no longer in the cell with all the other prisoners. The three of us were in a tiny cell deep in the earth, where the walls sweated moisture. This was fortunate because I feared that the Viscount and his guards had forgotten us. I tried to quench my thirst by licking the walls, and blessed the most Holy Lord for his infinite mercy in providing for his faithful servant, as the cool wetness passed my lips. The water tasted of the earth and plants, but it was wet and that was all that mattered.

We had been alone for what seemed like days and I did not know what to fear more - the return of the guards to torture us or have us drawn and quartered or to die here, forgotten for however long it took to die. I turned back again to the great fear I harbored for my soul, for I did not want to go to my death without confession. My sins had been legion, though they had all been for the greater good of these ungrateful people. How horrid if I would have to endure the pains of purgatory when all I wanted to do was save those who had in danger of hell fire. Guillaume would have to be called. I was not likely to see another priest before my death, which could come at any time. I looked at my brother, who sat next to the mason, his head bent in prayer.

"Guillaume," I whispered, for I did not want to wake the mason. He had finally fallen into a deep slumber, breathing raggedly through his broken nose. I did not want him to hear my confession.

"Guillaume," I said, a bit louder.

Guillaume moved his head and looked at me.

"What do you want, brother?" he asked.

"Guillaume, we must prepare for our deaths," I said.

"That is what I am doing," said Guillaume. "I am trying to make my peace with God."

"No, we must confess each other," I said. "Quickly, before the guards return."

"I have already confessed my sins," said Guillaume. "I am trying to do penance and ask forgiveness of those I have grievously wounded."

"But, you did not confess in the formal manner of the sacrament," I said. "We need to do this so we do not suffer the fires of purgatory."

"I am sure that is the least of what I will suffer, my brother," said Guillaume.

"If you do not care for your own soul, at least think of mine, brother," I said. "Please hear my confession."

"Very well," said Guillaume.

I crossed my self and kneeled in front of Guillaume. I was beginning to mistrust his state of grace, but blessedly the Lord allows even those priests who have sinned to perform the sacraments. His power is so great that their sins mean nothing and his mercy is all.

"Bless me, Father, for I have sinned," I began. "It is one month since my last Confession. I accuse myself of the following sins. I have lied and deceived, but only for your greater power."

"And what else?" said Guillaume.

"And I have given in to the sin of gluttony. Though I have eaten nothing for days, I can think only of banqueting halls and rich wines, when I should be thinking only of your glory and the rewards of heaven."

"And what else?" said Guillaume.

I searched my soul, for surely I wanted to be clean of all sin before my execution.

"Lust," I said quietly. "I have lusted in my heart after that foul heretic girl. She is Satan's seducer, a siren to lure men to their destruction, Eve's foul, diseased daughter. But, I was too weak to withstand her wiles and have corrupted the temple of my mind with wretched desire."

I felt great shame, but also anger that this witch had robbed me of my dignity. Guillaume merely smiled and I wanted to hit him.

"And I have felt anger towards my brother for his actions," I said.

"And is that all?" asked Guillaume.

"That is all," I said. "For these and all the sins of my past life, I ask pardon of God, penance, and absolution from you, Father."

Guillaume smiled.

"Oh brother, I think you forget your must constant sin of all," he said.

"I have done nothing else," I choked. "And all I did was for the glory of our Lord, himself."

"For do you not remember your Proverbs: Pride goes before destruction, a haughty spirit before a fall," asked Guillaume.

I wanted to smack Guillaume for his insolence, but remembered that sometimes wisdom can come from the mouths of fools.

"If I have been guilty of the vice of pride, it is only because I remember what I represent - our most holy order of Cistercians, our lord Abbot, and our Lord's representative on earth, Pope Innocent," I said.

"After what I have seen on this Crusade," said Guillaume. "I wonder truly who is innocent."

I gasped. Guillaume had gone too far, but I needed his absolution.

"Give me my penance and absolve me, father," I said. "For I cannot rest and I am weary."

"Very well," said Guillaume. "You have only one penance. You must ask and receive the forgiveness of the mason before I give you final absolution."

I moaned and leaned back against the cell wall. I would spend an eternity in Purgatory before I asked the forgiveness of that foul fiend of Satan. Guillaume had gone mad and I could do nothing to save him. I felt engulfed by despair, but tried to remember the words of the apostle, "We are hard pressed on every side, but not crushed; perplexed, but not in despair; persecuted, but not abandoned; struck down, but not destroyed."

I said to myself the comforting words of the psalms: "Deliver me from my enemies, O God; protect me from those who rise up against me. Deliver me from evildoers and save me from bloodthirsty men."

Gauda

Thursday, August 13, 1209, night

I sat by the bed of Agnes, softly playing for her on my harp. She looked as if she were gazing out the window to the far hills, though her small window was dark, and she could only see the blackness of the night. I shifted and felt the small vial of poison dig into my hip and knew that my time was rapidly running out. I had been spared my task last night for Trencavel had never called for me, either too filled with grief over Agnes' illness or too consumed with the details of the siege to waste time with me. All I knew was that my final trial had been put off for at least another night. Perhaps I would be spared it yet again tonight.

A shadow crossed the threshold of Agnes' room and I did not need to look up to recognize the gait of the servant always sent for me by Trencavel. I stopped playing and looked up.

"The Viscount calls for you to play for him," said the servant.

"Please tell the Viscount I will be there as soon as I have finished caring for his wife," I said.

The servant looked shocked, but dared not argue with me. He quietly left the room.

Agnes woke up from her reverie and looked at me with a sad smile.

"I forgive you, cousin," she said.

Agnes grasped for my hand and I held it tight. Finally she pressed my hand one last time and let go.

"You must not keep him waiting," Agnes said. I could see the tears forming at the corners of her eyes and as she turned her head away I knew that she loved him as much as he loved her. Probably the only pair of true lovers actually married in all Christendom and even they could not be together. Fate is cruel. I knew that better than anyone.

I stood up with my harp in one hand and walked slowly to the door. I turned one last time, but Agnes was facing away from me. I walked into the hall and down the corridor. As I did I felt the all too familiar sensation of someone silently walking along behind me. This time I did not even start, for I had been expecting him for so many hours. I stopped, still facing ahead though I longed to turn and face my tormenter.

"You know what to do," said the voice. "I will be waiting for you afterwards."

He silently glided away and I continued on my way to the Viscount's chambers. I entered and saw Trencavel sprawled on his chair, his wine goblet in his bejeweled hand. Despite the heat of the night, some breezes seemed to enter the room from the high, small windows.

"How is she?" he asked.

"As well as can be expected," I said. "She regrets very much all that has happened."

"Oh, Gauda, play for me," he said. "They loved her all - every troubadour that came to this castle would fall for her and I loved to watch them as they tried every subterfuge, every form of flattery, but nothing every worked. I knew that she would never love any one but me. We were the happiest of lovers in all the land. Who would have ever thought our parents could have chosen so well? But it must have been something else - fates, divine intervention. But we were too happy and proud and scoffed at all the poor fools who did not have our good fortune. Beautiful young ladies married to ogres three times their age trying to steal moments with their young lovers. We had to deal with none of that. We must have tempted the fates with our joy. But the saddest is that I love her even more now that I can not have her, ever again."

"Oh Gauda, I want to remember," said Trencavel. "Play for me all the songs that have been written for her, of her beauty, her youth, her nobility, her gentleness."

And I knew them all, for Agnes had made sure that I learned of every canso ever written for her, every stanza that glorified her beauty and her grace. I was forced to sing them night after night, while Agnes corrected my words in one line or my melody in another in her flat nasal voice that could not hold a tune and would make even the deaf cringe. To be honest, the vast majority of these chansons were dribble. Mediocre poetry set to mediocre melodies by itinerant troubadours who never made a name for themselves and rightly so. But, never had Trencavel asked me to play these horrid pieces for him when I played for him alone. For Trencavel knew music and poetry and had a preference only for the most refined of troubadours - Jaufre Rudel, Bernart de Ventadorn, and Raimon de Miraval.

And Trencavel had asked me to play my own songs, the cansos I had composed over the years, the tensos I used to sing with Raimon de Miraval. If he had enough to drink, he would even take the part of the male troubadour, in his untrained but solid voice, and we would sing into late in the night. For two years I had shared his bed and shared my music with him, songs I had played for no one else, songs I thought he would understand. Even I was no fool as to think our physical couplings meant anything more to him than a release, but still my heart had fallen for him, for his youth and beauty and strength. And for the way he looked at me and listened when I played my harp and sang to him. More fool I to think it had only been lust on my part. I couldn't even fool myself anymore.

And tonight he would have me play nothing but songs of her! And then he would take me to bed as always, though tonight he would be rough as he always was when drunk. And then he would fall deep asleep while I slowly, quietly untangled myself from his limbs, taking care not to wake him. I would slip out of the curtained bed and place my bare feet on the floor while I carefully dressed in the dark room, praying his guards would not wake and see my nakedness. I would walk slowly back to my narrow cot in his wife's room and bear the shame of being little more than a whore who slept with her kinswoman's cousin. But I was ashamed most of all of myself. For though I tried to tell myself that none could resist the overtures of her liege lord and I was not to blame, I knew that I would have done it anyway, even if I were the Queen of Aragon and he my vassal. What had this man driven me to?

I sang the words that glorified his wife, but I marveled that

Trencavel could not see the spite that underlay each stanza. I almost spat out each word, but he seemed not to notice. He sat, his glaze drunken. His wine glass was low. It would be so easy to offer to fill it from the pitcher on the table, as I had done so many times before. So simple to slip the poison into his glass as my back was turned to him. So easy to forever silence this man who did not love me and never had and never would. And how I would be rewarded! The city would surrender without a leader and I could finally escape to the Count of Toulouse to claim my lands!

"Gauda, fill my wine for me," said Trencavel, lifting his glass up drunkenly.

I put down my harp and walked over to him. I looked into his eyes as I took the glass. They were red from crying. I despised him.

I walked back to the table and took the vial from my hip pocket, as soon as my back was turned. I topped up his glass of wine and poured another for myself. I lifted the vial and pulled the stopper, but something stopped me from pouring it into his new glass of wine. I had become a spy and a deceiver because I wanted to regain what was rightfully mine. I had become an adulterer because I had no choice, even if I reveled in it. Would I let myself become a murderer too? Where would I stop?

I poured out the vial of poison onto the floor. I could not do this. I would take my chances. I carefully stopped the empty vial and placed it carefully back in my tunic. I picked up the two glasses of wine and gave one of them to Trencavel. I took my own and set it on the table, after taking a long, deep gulp. I walked over to Trencavel and knelt at his side, my hand upon his arm.

"My Lord, please excuse me," I said. "I must visit the privy, for I have drunk too much wine. Think of what you want me to sing for you next, for I will return shortly."

Trencavel took a deep draught of his wine, his hand wavering as he held the cup and his eyes bleary and red. He caressed my face with his hand.

"Don't be long," he said. "I don't think I want to hear any more songs tonight."

He held my head and kissed me firmly on the mouth. I kissed him back deeply and strongly. And then I got up to leave. As I walked out the door I realized with a pang that I would not be able to take my harp with me. My father had given me that harp as a girl and Azalais had taught me to play and sing and compose on it. I had carried it with me on all my travels, but I would have to leave it now. Tears filled my eyes and burned past the lashes.

In the corridor, I ran into the hooded man and thrust the empty vial into his hands.

"It is done," I said. "I will not be found at his side when it is discovered."

I turned and walked away. I had to leave and quickly. I headed down the stairs towards the main hall of the castle. I passed several guards at their posts, but none questioned me. They were used to my nocturnal wanderings in the corridors. I silently stepped over the bodies of the sleeping soldiers in the great hall, praying not to awaken anyone for my presence would not be expected here in the middle of the night. I had to leave the castle and lose myself in the streets of the city. At the entrance to the castle the guards were awake and alert. They stopped me with their hands resting on their swords.

"What need have you to leave the castle at night?" the captain of the guard asked. "It is dangerous to walk these streets at night. Only spies and thieves go abroad."

"My Lady the Viscountess is ill again," I said. "I need to go find medicines and help."

"And she would send you about on a night like this?" asked the captain.

"I have no choice," I said.

I did not know how long the poison was supposed to take to work but I assumed it would be fast-acting. I assumed the guards would be expected to hear Trencavel's struggles and would raise the alarm. When this didn't happen, the hooded man would realize I had betrayed him and come after me. I expected to hear his footsteps come up behind me at any second.

"I must leave," I said again, my voice becoming high and tight.

"Very well," said the captain. "But I will send two guards with you."

How was I going to get rid of them? I did not know, but only wanted to leave the castle as quickly as possible. I allowed myself to be escorted from the castle gates across the broad plaza and down the narrow city streets. I had not left the castle for many days and I could not believe the state of the city, which resembled more a painting of the Last Judgment and the sinners cast into the furthest circles of Hell than it resembled the bustling market town I knew so well. The wounded lay in the streets, their flesh rotting, drunk with thirst and delirious. The exhausted sick, old men and young mothers and little children, lay piled up in houses we passes, doors open to the street, their bodies covered with flies they were too weak to swat away, the dead lying alongside the barely living. The guards' torches cast a red, flickering light over every scene of horror we passed. Rotting carcasses of skinned livestock lay everywhere joining with the odors of the dead and dying to create the most horrendous stench of decay I had ever smelt in my life. The city had truly been turned into the Gates of Hell.

I tried to cover my face with head scarf, to ward off the vile odors. A delirious man came running up to us, begging for water. The guards brusquely knocked him away and he fell to his feet, screaming in pain. I let the guards take me to the doors of the house of good women and I banged on the shuttered windows. We heard nothing, but finally the small window at the top of the door slid open and I saw a familiar face.

"Oh Eleanor," I said. "Please let me in."

Thankfully, Eleanor did not ask any questions and merely opened the door. I turned to the two guards.

"I will be here a while. It is best if you return to the castle. I will send a messenger when I want to return."

The two guards turned to leave.

"Thank you for your help in guiding me here," I said.

The guards nodded and left.

My plans for escape were foiled. Anyone could simply ask the guards where I had gone and come get me for my punishment. It was only a matter of time before the hooded man discovered my betrayal and the Viscount learned of my spying. I would have only hours. At least I was here with Azalais and could make a good end. I would take the consolamentum and become a good woman, at least for the short time before I died. I had sinned much, but all would be forgiven and I would soon be in paradise.

DAY 14 OF THE SIEGE OF CARCASSONNE

Friday, August 14, 1209

Azalais

Friday, August 14, 1209, morning

Azalais winced as the doctor cut deep into her arm, slicing the skin open and letting the blood pour into a basin at her side. She knew that like cured like, and the best way to counteract the bloody flux was to bleed the poisons out of her system. She thought of the souls she had seen leave this world by the endura and envied them their peace - no doctors cutting them open or sticking hot glass on their backs to draw out the foul humors. They simply decided not to be part of this world anymore. They allowed no material substance to pass their lips other than water to relieve their thirst and they were taken on to the spiritual world, free of their flesh, in such a quick, quiet way.

The doctor left and someone else entered her room. Azalais groaned as she rolled over on to her back burned by the doctor's ministrations. It was Gauda. She seemed paler than usual and her hands were trembling as Azalais reached for them.

"My child, you have come," said Azalais. "What a blessing."

"I did not know you were sick, my teacher," said Gauda.

"It came suddenly," said Azalais.

"But why are there doctors here?" asked Gauda. "Do you not perform the endura?"

"My child, I was not yet ready to die, but I feel that I now I am," said Azalais.

Azalais smiled deeply at Gauda. There had been no word of Constance and Azalais felt herself growing weaker, despite the efforts of the good women and the doctors. Maybe she was not meant to see Constance again in this world, but at least she had been sent Gauda, quite unbidden. To see in the woman the face of the girl she had taught so many years before gave Azalais so much pleasure and so much pain.

"Azalais, I want to make a good end," said Gauda.

"But my dear child it is not yet your time," said Azalais.

"I cannot explain all I have done, but the Viscount's soldiers could come for me at any moment," said Gauda. "They will take me away to my death. Please let me make a good end."

Gauda was crying and she held Azalais' hands tightly in her own.

"I cannot believe that you would have done anything to merit such a punishment and I know the Viscount to be a just ruler," said Azalais. "Surely whatever has happened can be explained, for I know you to not be evil, my dear."

"I have done many things of which I am ashamed, but what I did tonight, I did for the good," said Gauda. "But, it will not be seen that way. I have played a dangerous game and lost."

Azalais noticed suddenly how very cold she felt, a cold deep inside - in her bowels, in her blood, in her bones. It almost felt like a relief after the unrelenting heat and misery of these weeks. But the cold cut too deep and Azalais knew she did not have much time left.

"Gauda, my child," said Azalais. "I would not see you take the consolamentum like this. It is for those who feel compelled to live as if their flesh no longer existed, so hungry are they for the world of the spirit. You are not ready and whatever you say, I do not think you will come to an end, bad or good, anytime soon. Remember that God is merciful and even if you are suddenly taken, you will just be reborn into this veil of tears again. You will have many lives and many chances to attain salvation and heaven. Remember too that there are beauties, however fleeting, of this material world that help us to imagine the glories of the next, spiritual world. Maybe your role is to create this beauty. When you are truly ready to take the consolamentum, you will do so, but the desire will be born out of joy for the spirit and not out of fear for the flesh. "

Gauda started to speak again, but Azalais gently covered her mouth with one finger.

"Gauda, sing for me," said Azalais.

Azalais closed her eyes and let the gentle melody float over her. Gauda's voice was as fine as ever and she had chosen to sing an old song by Raimbaut of Orange. Azalais smiled to herself as she felt her body grow colder and she felt the very blood slow in her veins. It was not a very good end for a Good Women to be serenaded by a song written by the great earthly love of her life, he who had given her such pain and such pleasure. Azalais gave herself a few moments to remember those earthly passions and then tried to focus on the freedom of spirit and joy she would soon enjoy, far from this earthly world of pain and suffering. She had even let go of Constance. She had to entrust the girl to the care of God and trust that she would be brought to a good end, however tortuous her path. Azalais thought back to the child she had borne and how she had laid it in the ground so soon after its birth and she longed to see that spirit again, for she knew she would always recognize it no matter where it had traveled in the time since it had left her.

Azalais was finally ready to let go. She breathed one more time the air of this earth and after she breathed out, she breathed no more.

Trencavel

Friday, August 14, 1209, noon

Trencavel felt unnerved by the silence. The siege engines had been quiet all morning. He had become so accustomed to the crashing of rocks against the city walls over the last two weeks that the quiet seemed unnatural. Trencavel sat with Cabaret in his chambers. Bertrand entered the room and came up slowly to the table. His wound had not healed and he hobbled into the room, angrily pushing away a servant's hand when he stumbled and almost fell. Bertrand steadied himself with his arms and lowered himself to a chair, letting himself down with a groan, his face daring either Trencavel or Cabaret to comment. Neither did.

"Have you gotten any more information from the Abbot's spies?" asked Cabaret.

"No, the fools know nothing of importance," said Trencavel. "I will have them drawn and quartered."

"And your own spies?" asked Cabaret.

"They tell me nothing solid," said Trencavel.

Trencavel's clerk Pons brought them wine and sausage. Pons poured each man a mug of wine and stepped back from the table. Trencavel lifted his mug and was about to put it to his lips, but Bertrand's hand stopped him.

"Why has this man never brought us wine before?" asked

Bertrand.

Cabaret put down his mug. Pons continued to move away from the table.

"Stop, man," said Bertrand to Pons. "Come back here. I don't think I know you."

"Sure you do," said Trencavel. "This is Pons, my clerk. He has been with me for several years and does his work well."

"I am sure he does," said Bertrand. "But never in all the time that I have visited you here do I remember a clerk pouring your wine. It's usually a rather lovely serving wench, if I remember correctly."

Trencavel thought for a moment, his head aching and his dry mouth desperate for the cool wine.

"Pons, why are you serving the wine?" asked Trencavel.

"My Lord," said Pons. "The serving girl was ill and the day so hot, I thought it would be quicker if I brought it myself."

Trencavel looked at Pons. He was sweating and had the look of a hunted rabbit. Trencavel held out his mug towards Pons.

"The day is so hot," said Trencavel. "Why don't you refresh yourself with some of my wine?"

Pons gingerly took the mug in his hands, slowly raising it to his lips. Then he suddenly dropped it to the floor and turned to run, but the guards at the door held him.

Trencavel walked over to Pons. He pulled his sword and held it at the man's throat.

"You will tell me who sent you, you betraying serpent, or I will kill you now myself," said Trencavel.

Pons began to make the sign of the cross.

"Oh father in heaven," said Pons. "Have mercy on me, forgive my sins."

Trencavel dug the blade into skin and a trickle of blood fell to Pons' shirt. Pons eyes jumped out of his head.

"You should be begging me for forgiveness," said Trencavel. "Now tell me who sent you or I will take you to the rack myself and find out the hard way."

Pons turned and spat in Trencavel's face.

"You foul heretic scum," said Pons. "You are hated and surrounded by spies. Even that foul slut singer with whom you commit adultery is against you."

Trencavel kept his knife at the man's neck, but looked around him slowly at Cabaret and Bertrand.

"Whom else do you accuse, spy?" said Trencavel.

"I was sent by the Lord to avenge him. You can kill me, but others will come. The Lord Abbot will prevail and the blasphemers will be made weak before the forces of truth and light. You can trust no one! You are alone now and you will be alone in hell for all eternity!"

Trencavel slit Pons throat in one quick movement. The man fell to the floor, blood gushing out of his wound. Everyone stood quietly.

"Guards, get me Gauda," said Trencavel. "I must speak to her of this accusation. But do not hurt her, for I know not whether to trust any of the words from this liar's mouth until I can ask these questions myself."

The guards left and Trencavel turned to Cabaret and Bertrand.

"I do not know whom to trust anymore," said Trencavel.

Bertrand shook his big head and looked sadly at Trencavel.

"I raised you as my own son," said Bertrand. "It is you who have betrayed me by your lack of faith in me."

Trencavel came forward and put his hand on Bertrand's shoulder.

"Forgive me, old man," said Trencavel. "Forgive me."

"You are wise to trust no one," said Cabaret. "For that is the first truth of those who hold great power. Trust makes you weak. But, now you must decide what to do for now we have more information. The Abbot risked a valuable spy in a bid to kill you. This is the move of a desperate man."

Trencavel turned to Cabaret, his heart beginning to feel less weary.

"The Abbot wants this siege over before his army leaves," said Cabaret. "Already there must be men who have served their due.

They only hold on to see what the booty will be, but once their sins and debts are cleared, they will not stick around for a drawn-out siege into the fall and winter."

Suddenly, a guard entered the room.

"My Lord," said the guard. "There are men outside the gates who want to parley. It is a Lord who claims kinship with you and thirty of his men."

"It must be Pierre Bermond," said Bertrand. "They want to negotiate and they know he is the one man in that Crusader camp that you will talk to."

"It is a chance to end this all," said Cabaret.

"Why negotiate now?" said Bertrand. "If half their army is ready to leave, we can wait them out. It could rain any day now."

The three men looked out the courtyard at the cloudless, blue sky, burning under an unremitting sun.

"And it could not rain for weeks," said Trencavel. "I would have no city and no people left to rule by that time. If they are nervous, now is the time to negotiate. Get one hundred of my knights and meet me at the gate."

Trencavel turned and headed to his chambers to change. Trencavel would meet his negotiators as an equal.

Trencavel walked down to the courtyard. His squire held his finest Arabian steed and Trencavel jumped onto his back. Already Cabaret and Bertrand waited at the front of a hundred knights, all on their fastest horses. They waited as the drawbridge slowly dropped and then marched across, Trencavel in the lead.

Trencavel stopped in front of Pierre Bermond, their men arrayed behind them in the hot wind. No one spoke and the only sound was of the flapping of banners in the breeze. Trencavel looked at his old boyhood friend, and thought how sad it was that this man, of all others, would be fighting in the army that came to take his lands and his castle. Yet, he knew that this man loved him as a brother.

"Sire," said Pierre Bermond. "I am your kin, may God watch over you and over me. I have a great wish to see you healthy and safe of this trap. You must accept a negotiated surrender. If you could count on some kind of prompt aid, I would heartily approve of your desire to defend yourself, but you and I both know that all hope is in vain. Accept therefore the good will of our Pope and these noble Crusaders. In truth, sir, if you oblige us to take you by force the massacre will be equal to that of Béziers. So, content yourself with saving your life. At least there will remain for you a bit of chance."

"Sir, I put myself under your protection" said Trencavel. "I will go to hear what these Northerners have to say, if you promise me that I can cross the Crusader camp without fear."

"Sir, on my honor," said the knight. "I will take you there myself and bring you back here, back among your men safe and sound, I swear it."

Trencavel turned to choose the men he would bring with him. Cabaret and Bertrand stepped forward.

"Cabaret, I will you to stay here and lead the men while I am negotiating," said Trencavel.

Cabaret nodded.

Next Trencavel looked at Bertrand, whose face was a mask of pain and who sat atop his steed none too steadily, holding his wounded leg with one hand.

"Do not ask me to take you with me," said Trencavel.

"I will obey you, my liege lord, even though I do not want to," said Bertrand. "I will always be your loyal vassal."

Trencavel clapped Bertrand on his back.

"I will be back soon, old man," said Trencavel and smiled at him.

Trencavel and Pierre Bermond headed towards the Crusaders' camp, followed by Trencavel's nine vassals and Pierre's thirty men. As they entered the camp, knights and sergeants rushed up, crushing each other, wanting to see Trencavel and pointing out the man and elbowing each other, their eyes round. Trencavel arrived in front of the pavilion of the Count of Nevers, where they held the counsel of the Crusade each day. As he dismounted, he thought, I will see what their offer is. Perhaps it will be one that I can bear. For after all, what honor is there in ruling over a land of the dead?

All of sudden, men burst out of the Count of Nevers' tent and jumped on Trencavel, pinning him to the ground and stripping him of his sword. Just as quickly, Trencavel's nine men were surrounded.

Pierre Bermond jumped to the side of Trencavel, his sword in his hand, ready to fight. Just as quickly, he was disarmed and thrown to the ground as well.

"What treachery is this?" screamed Pierre Bermond, trying to throw off his attackers. Finally he was overcome by the other Crusaders and held next to Trencavel and his nine knights. "My brother, I did not know," said Pierre. "I know," said Trencavel. "I know."

"Have you no shame?" bellowed Pierre Bermond at the knights of the Crusade gathered outside the tent of the Count of Nevers.

No one answered.

Constance

Friday, August 14, 1209, night

Constance gently closed the eyes of the old man. At least he had gone in his sleep. He had been kind to Constance and she was glad he now had peace. For Constance surely believed that she would have gone mad in this house of death without his even, calm presence.

Constance looked around her. She was not even sure how long she had been here. She picked up the jug of wine. It was empty again, but she dreaded walking down those stairs to the cellar, past the pile of the dead. They were all gone. The mason and Guillaume rotting in jail if they had not been hanged already. Beatritz's whole family gone.

Except for the little girl Aude. Constance believed, through who knows what miracle, that the little girl would live. She slept now, peacefully, her color better and her fever gone. Constance had cleaned her many hours ago and she had not since soiled the sheets. Perhaps she would be one of the blessed who had survived this horrid flux.

And except for Beatritz herself. She sat in the corner snoring, her hair matted and her face streaked with dirt. When Beatritz had awoken from the knock to her head she remembered nothing.

Constance had kept her supplied with plenteous wine ever since and, fortunately, the woman had slept most of the rest of the time.

Constance clumsily walked over to the window overlooking the street. She threw open the shutters, but the air outside was as foul as that inside the house. Constance felt a wave of nausea sweep over her. She placed her shaking fingers on the edge of the window and looked out. Her throat felt parched, but the thought of drinking more wine to slake her thirst made her stomach turn.

Constance looked down at the people in the street and she noticed that something had changed. Still the wounded lay moaning in the streets, but others were moving. Voices wafted up to her.

"Trencavel has been taken," shouted one man.

"The Crusaders are waiting at the gates to massacre us all," screamed a woman.

"We tried to flee, but the gates are closed," said another.

Soon, those who could move were doing so, even though there seemed nowhere to go. Constance was glad that she was locked in a house with a cellar, even though nowhere was safe from fire. Suddenly, she felt hands grab her throat from behind and start to choke her. Constance grasped hold of the hands and tried to pull them apart, but she could not. Then Beatritz let go and swung her around, shaking her by the shoulders.

"You foul heretic bitch," said Beatritz. "What are you still doing in my home, befouling it with your presence?"

"I was just trying to care for your family," said Constance. "They were sick."

"And you killed them all with your foul spells and your necromancy," screamed Beatritz. "Look, they are all dead!"

The little girl woke up and sat up in her cot, her eyes wide as she stared at the mad woman her mother had become. She began to scream.

Beatritz turned deathly white and began shaking.

"Look it is a foul ghost come back to haunt us," whispered Beatritz. "It is the devil himself who has taken on the corporeal presence of my dead daughter."

Beatritz looked wildly around and finally put her hands on the empty wine jug. She started to move forward, the wine jug over her head. Her small daughter screamed even more in her terror.

Constance quickly jumped on Beatritz from behind and brought her to the ground, kicking and screaming. Constance had to escape from this house. She jumped up and ran to the cot to pick up the screaming child. Beatritz came up from behind, grabbing at Constance's tunic.

"We must kill the devil," screamed Beatriz. "Don't you see? Or are you blinded? Or in league with him, you foul fiend!"

Constance kicked hard at Beatritz who fell to the floor, clutching her stomach. Constance held the little girl tight and ran down the stairs. She heard Beatritz shrieking behind her, but did not stop to look as she ran to the door and struggled to lift the heavy wooden beam that braced it from inside, the little girl hanging on to her and screaming. The beam was swollen in place and Constance could not budge it. She heard Beatritz' heavy step on the stair. Constance put the down the screaming child and looked wildly around her for something to use. She saw the mason's mallet in the corner and tugged it from its place. She placed it under the door and swung upwards with all her might. The beam nudged a bit. Constance swung again and finally the beam was loose. She pulled it out and held it in front of her, holding back Beatritz as she pushed the little girl behind her back.

"We will leave this house," said Constance. "And you will be free of all heresy. But do not leave this threshold or I will tell my master the devil to send his minions to torture you and carry you down to Hell.

Beatritz stopped and made the sign of the cross, slowly moving backward, her mouth mumbling the words to prayers she did not understand anymore.

Constance reached down and picked up the little girl, who did not move or speak a word, her eyes open like bright deniers. Constance walked out the door, shutting it firmly behind her. She only hoped Beatritz would listen to her words and not leave the safety of the house. The streets were no place for a mad woman.

Constance looked around her. These streets were no place for any woman, let alone one carrying a child. More and more people moved about, and each rumor was worse than the one before. Constance turned and headed toward the house of good women. It was time she went home.

Walking through the streets of the city of Carcassonne, Constance wondered what this Hell was that these Catholics imagined for surely it could not equal the Hell they had created here. Everywhere the sick and wounded moaned while the hot sun burned down on them. Crows pecked out the eyes of the dead. The stench of decay pervaded the very earth and all was suffering or terror as the hapless victims ran through the streets. Constance almost fainted with relief when she saw the sturdy walls of the house of good women. She banged on the door and was happy to see the face of Eleanor. She could hardly wait for the old woman to open the door and fold her in her arms.

"Oh, my child, it is the blessing we were all praying for," said Eleanor. "You are come back to us, to join the fold."

Then Eleanor looked into the eyes of the little girl hiding next to Constance. The old woman was so tiny that she barely needed to lean over to talk to her.

"And what is your name my little bird?" asked Eleanor.

The little girl had still not spoken since they had left her grandmother's home and she did not now.

"She is called Aude, but she has seen much that no one ought ever to see," Constance said.

"Very well, Aude, my bird," said Eleanor. "You will stay with us and we will care for you."

Eleanor held out her hand and Aude went to her, surprising Constance.

"Constance, you need refreshment," said Eleanor. "You look as if you have seen even worse than this little one. We do not have much, but there is still some cheese and we have the smallest rations of water left."

"I must see Azalais," said Constance. "Before I eat. There are things I need to tell her."

Eleanor looked sadly at Constance and placed her hand on the girl's arm.

"For this you will need to wait, my dear," said Eleanor. "Azalais was taken from us this very morning. She is now in peace."

Constance felt as if she would faint. She knew that she would be punished for her pride, but she never imagined the punishment would be so cruel. Constance started crying, but she saw little Aude's face start to pinch up again and forced herself to stop.

"Can I see her?" asked Constance.

"There is nothing more to see," said Eleanor. "Her spirit has passed on to joy. You do not want to see the earthly vessel she left behind, for it is already stacked with the other empty vessels. Truly, without the spirit, the material vessel becomes a rotting manifestation of the evil it represents."

"Of course," said Constance. "She would not want that. I will go with you to eat. Please take me to the others."

They walked past the hall where still the good women cared for the ill who had not yet succumbed to their wounds or the flux. Though herbs burned everywhere, the sick smell of decay permeated the entire house. Eleanor led her past the kitchen and up the stairs.

"The air is a little better up here," said Eleanor. "As long as a breeze blows from the mountains. I do not understand why the miasma and foul humors take some so quickly, but leave others as if their pestilence was impotent. We have lost two others besides Azalais, but the rest of the good women remain well."

Constance sat at the table with the other good women, little Aude finally sleeping on her lap. The Viscountess's lady-in-waiting Gauda also sat with them. Constance remembered her from her visits to Azalais. She seemed pale and shaken and kept looking over her shoulder at the slightest noise. Constance tried to follow the talk as all tried to guess what would happen in the morning, but as soon as she had eaten her fill, Constance felt an enormous exhaustion fall over her and she took Aude with her to the floor, where they slept on unrolled blankets. Constance did not know whether she would live or die tomorrow, but that did not keep her from the deepest sleep of her life.

DAY 15 OF THE SIEGE OF CARCASSONNE

Saturday, August 15, 1209

Constance

Saturday, August 15, 1209, morning

Constance woke to feel the warm sun on her face. She felt strangely at peace, with the warm Aude snuggling into her side. Suddenly she heard motion downstairs. She tensed up, afraid that the soldiers were already here, but the noise did not sound full of terror, only very busy. She woke up the sleeping girl who immediately began to cry, but Constance shushed her, picking up the child in her arms and heading down the stairs. The hall was open to the courtyard and the street was full of people teeming past, heading towards the gates of the city. Only the sickest still lay in their pallets in the hall. All who could walk must have left the house already and joined the throngs in the street.

She looked around, but could not find the rest of the good women. She went into the kitchen and found them all there, stuffing coins under their belts.

"Do not make it obvious," said Eleanor. "We do not want to be stopped by the guards. Take only enough for food along the way."

"What is going on?" asked Constance.

"The Viscount has been taken, but there will be no massacre, thanks be to God," said Eleanor. "But every citizen of Carcassonne must leave today with only the clothes on their backs."

"Those thieves!" said Constance. "We would just leave everything here that we worked so hard for?"

"But it is only material goods," said Eleanor. "How can it matter? Even were we to be killed this morning, it would not have mattered to us, for it is all only earthly and passes as the wind."

"How can you say that?" screamed Constance. "Would you have just let the soldiers kill you if they came? Wouldn't you have fought back?"

"And risk my eternal salvation by raising my hand in violence?" asked Eleanor. "Why would I risk freedom for all eternity for a few more minutes of earthly existence, miserable and brutish as it is?"

"I would have fought them till I died and I would have come back in the next life to hunt them down," said Constance.

The other good women all stopped what they were doing and stared in shock at Constance.

"My child," said Eleanor. "It seems that you are no longer ready to be a good woman. For you know how we must live - never to lie, never to take an oath, never to eat the flesh of any creature, and never to raise a hand in violence. We spend our whole earthly existence waiting for this time of trial to end. While we are here, we work to feed ourselves and we care for others, but this is all unimportant. Our earthly existence is like sand blowing in the wind, it passes quickly and we do not even know where it is gone."

"You may stay with us, Constance," said Eleanor. "But you are no longer one ready for eternal salvation. You must take your own path and the infinite mercy of God will bring you back to him eventually."

"Come," said Eleanor to the other good women. "It is time to go. We will saddle the donkey and carry the sick that remain with us in the cart."

Constance stood looking at the women. They were kind and they would care for her, letting her stay with them as long as she needed. But Constance already knew that this path was not for her. She stepped forward to Eleanor.

"I am sorry, good woman," said Constance. "I am not ready. But please take Aude and care for her. Her father is gone and probably dead and her mother is mad. And I cannot care for her now. I know she will be safe with you, as safe as anyone can be now."

"My child, you will always have a home with us," said Eleanor. "And watch that this bitterness does not poison your earthly existence as well as your heavenly one."

Constance nodded.

"Where will you go?" she asked. "How will I find you?"

"We will head towards Toulouse," said Eleanor. "My family is from there and there are many houses of good women. We will be taken in. I will keep Aude by my side. The good men and women will know where we are."

Constance went around the room to each of the women and said her goodbyes, returning to hug Eleanor one last time and give Aude a kiss on her forehead. The child cried quietly, but she already clung fast to Eleanor's tunic.

Constance left the house of good women for the second time that week. She did not know where to go but aimlessly joined the throngs heading toward the gates by the Viscount's castle. She could see guards on either side of the open drawbridge as people filed out of the city. Many ran immediately to the river and slurped greedily from its banks. Others were slower and tried to hide some silver or tools in their tunics. They were stopped and whipped and then sent on their way naked. Constance watched as thousands of people streamed out of the city. They wandered numbly in all directions, on the road to Toulouse and the road to Aragon, and just across the burned fields. The crusaders began to assemble, ready to enter the city and take their loot. It was time for her to leave.

But instead of leaving the city Constance stopped in the courtyard. Everywhere was confusion. Knights stood talking to the horses they would have to leave behind. Archers streamed off the walls of the city, leaving their bows cluttering the ground. In the far corner of the courtyard, prisoners slowly moved out of door that must lead to the depths of the castle. Some were still in chains. All were blinking in the hot sun. Finally, Constance saw three figures that she barely recognized. She called out and the mason looked up and came over to her, as fast as he could, his feet chained together. The two brothers saw her, but they turned to each other, speaking heatedly.

"My family," said the mason, his voice creaking with thirst. "What happened to them?"

"I am so sorry," said Constance. "They are gone. All except your wife, who is mad, and little Aude."

The mason's face crumbled.

"My wife hates me now," said the mason. "I know she will never talk to me again. Damn those filthy lying priests to corrupt her so. She was once a kind woman, hard- working and a joy. She is now dead to me. And what of Aude?"

"I could not leave her with Beatritz. I feared what she would do, so I have left her with the good women. They will take her to Toulouse and take good care of her."

"That is more than I can do for her now," said the mason. "I have nothing, not even my tools. Not even my good name."

"What will you do?" asked Constance.

"I will fight these bastards until they leave our lands or until I die," said the mason. "If you see my little girl again, tell her I love her and I will come for her someday when we are free again."

They heard the clanking of iron on an anvil and the mason looked up. In the confusion, the prisoners were using the abandoned blacksmiths' tools in the courtyard to remove their chains.

"I must go, Constance," said the mason.

Constance watched him walk away and join the others waiting anxiously to be free of their chains. Already the streets of the city were starting to empty and Constance could see across the opened drawbridge that the Crusaders were beginning their march towards the city gates, the Abbot and his monks leading the slow procession, chanting and burning incense. She would have to leave, for she had no intention of remaining behind when the soldiers entered the city. Constance looked again at Bernard and Guillaume and started walking quickly to the open drawbridge. When she reached the gate, she turned back one last time to look. Bernard and Guillaume were still arguing, but finally Guillaume turned away. He looked at Constance. She stood still.

Guillaume walked towards her.

EPILOGUE

Bernard

September 1, 1209

I find that I sing the words of the psalmist much these days for there is much joy in my heart. "I will praise the Lord at all times; his praise will always be on my lips. My soul will boast in the Lord, let the afflicted hear and rejoice. I sought the Lord, and he answered me; he delivered me from all my fears."

It is as it was written. For a leader rules in righteousness and the eyes of those who will see are no longer closed and the ears of those who hear now listen. The city of Carcassonne is free of the stain of heresy and is like unto a shining city on a hill. The blasphemous Viscount Trencavel is chained in his own dungeon! A true warrior of Christ now is lord of this city and these lands. The Viscount Simon de Montfort is a man so honorable in his strength, so firm in his beliefs, and yet so humble, as befits the truly blessed. The Abbot Arnold, together with the Count of Nevers and the Duke of Burgundy, had to beg Simon de Montfort to take this burden. The noble lord refused, claiming to be unworthy of the honor (when there was never a more worthy man than he!), but finally succumbed to the authority of the most Holy Father in Rome, as passed through his legate here, Abbot Arnold. I count myself doubly blessed, for I saw this great warrior of Christ perform one of his many heroic deeds. Lo, the day that I watched a brave knight rescue a fallen comrade from the walls of the city and marveled at his bravery and his strength, I did not know it, but it was the great Simon de Montfort!

So, I remain here in Carcassonne, a city now full of grace and joy. The cathedral rings with the sounds of the monks chanting. The streets are now filled with those who speak the Northern tongue, which I am quickly learning to understand, harsh and ugly as it is. The noble Lords and knights are all now returning to their homes in the north, their forty days of service for the Cross fulfilled, their ears deaf to the righteous pleas of my Lord Abbot to stay and finish the fight. For truly, were this magnificent army of thousands upon thousands to stay but a little while longer and finish the task of conquest and salvation it had started, this whole land would be under the control of the Crusaders and made free of the blot of heresy in but a blink of an eye. But, even as I chafe at this injustice, I marvel at the magnificence of heaven. For surely, the most powerful almighty could have subdued these lands with his forces quickly and completely. But, in his most infinite justice and mercy, the Lord has decreed that this conquest will go slowly so that the heretics have time to confess their sins and reach a state of grace. For the longer this war lasts, the more souls can be saved! Oh, blessed, merciful God, infinite in his wisdom!

So the magnificent warrior Viscount de Montfort and his loyal followers remain to keep this land safe for the one true faith, whatever the price they must pay in leaving their own homes unprotected. Their task is great, for many enemies remain. Though, I must admit that many of the other Crusaders who have stayed behind, I find to be villains of the lowest order - criminals, prostitutes, and mountebanks. But I caution myself to have patience for even our Lord Jesus Christ consorted with the Magdalene, and these Christians are the ones who most deserve the attention of those who have been blessed with greater faith.

I caution myself much these days, for my sins weigh heavily on my soul, though I finally received absolution as soon as I escaped from the city and found my way back to the Abbot Arnold's camp. It is a blessed glory to see the Lord of Montfort installed as Viscount of these lands and I know that my actions played a small part in that wondrous event. I think of how many souls will be saved by the Viscount Montfort as he rids this land of the scourge of heresy. But, yet I feel unsettled. For what of the mason and all the others who have fled the city? How will we reach them and save their souls?

I worry that my Lord Abbot concerns himself too much with the things of this world and not enough with the things of the next. I hear much of the young Spanish priest called Dominic Guzman who has wandered these lands, preaching barefoot and begging for alms, concerned only with the souls of his listeners. I went looking for him in Prouille, where he has a convent for woman blessedly converted away from the houses of heretic women. I did not find him, for he was out spreading the most joyous word. I did, however, see the mason's wife, living a life of prayer, fasting, and reclusion for her many sins. I blessed her, but she did not speak to me. Apparently, she speaks to no one.

Maybe Dominic will help me save the soul of my brother, Guillaume, for I fear that he is lost to us and that his soul would rot in hell for all eternity were he to die unshriven at this moment. Guillaume, most loyal brother monk, has fallen for the foul heretic girl, that Eve wrapped in her serpent and offering the apple. He claims they live in a state of pure chastity. He claims they search together for the true path to salvation, but I know it all to be falsehoods. I know he lies with her and spills his seed into her foul body, a mockery of the temple of the Lord. I see them fornicating in my mind and I know what evil she is. But now I cannot even find my brother to try to save him. There were living in a small village nearby, but when the Viscount Montfort went to set the inhabitants free from their heretical overlord, we arrived to find the village deserted.

But know this. I will find my brother and save him. I am my brother's keeper and I will always be.

Gauda

November 1209

I sit now at the head of the table in the great hall where my father once sat, the fire roaring behind me and the remains of a great feast spread in front of me. Musicians play and sing and I hear drunken laughter from the men and women seated around my tables. It is all as I imagined it and yet it is not. For the land is at war. Though we are not yet touched here in the lands under the control of the Count of Toulouse, thanks to his wise and rather convenient decision to take the cross and join the Crusaders, I wonder how long it will last.

It is odd how one behaves when one is sure to die, but unexpectedly finds oneself living. The guards came for me at the house of good women, as I expected. But they treated me with deference and, in my surprise, I said nothing, only stopping to kiss the cheek of Eleanor as I left with them. They placed me in a locked room in the castle, but it was comfortably furnished and food and water were brought to me. I waited for what seemed an eternity, sure that every footstep I heard was that of my executioner. But nothing happened. There was no window, so I could not tell how much time had passed, but eventually a guard came to unlock the room. He was a man I had never seen before and he told me only to leave with only the clothes on my back. I did not stop to question him.

When I came out in the light of day I saw the city disgorging its citizens into the valleys around. The siege had ended, though I did not know how, and we were not to be massacred. I followed the tide of the broken and wretched and almost naked towards Toulouse. When I arrived in that city, I looked for many days until I found the house of good women where Eleanor and the others had been taken in. Even though they were crowded with refugees, they let me stay. I lived with the women for a month and Eleanor offered to give me the consolamentum so I could join them. I thought about it for I had grown quite fond of the little girl Aude, whom I imagined to be like the daughter I was never blessed with. But I never did join them. Something else seemed to be waiting for me and I remembered Azalais' final words to me and I would not betray her commands.

One day, I heard that the Count of Toulouse had come back to his city. I went to Toulouse and waited in line with all the other supplicants. I waited a long time, but the Count kept his word and I was given my reward for my services. When I came with the Count's men to reclaim my castle and lands from my hateful stepsons, I expected to feel the sweetest revenge and joy as I watched them driven away from my castle. Instead, I felt nothing. It was good to have my lands back and my father's old servants were glad to see me and made me feel most welcome in my old home. I checked accounts and saw the villagers, performing the same tasks I used to perform every day before my husband's death, but it was all hollow.

Only a week ago, I received word that the Viscount Trencavel has died, a prisoner in his own castle. They say it was of the flux. I knew Trencavel better than most and I cannot believe that such a healthy, vibrant young man is dead like that. After he was taken, we all thought it would only be a matter of time until he could be ransomed. Pierre Bermond, sick with guilt at his unwilling role in the treacherous betrayal, had collected vast stores of coin and treasure, enough to pay the ransom of a king. We all thought Trencavel would come back to reclaim his rightful lands from this usurper from the north. They call him Simon de Montfort, but I call him a larcenous second son who knows nothing of honor. To grab a lord who comes to parley under a safe conduct, steal his lands, and lock him in his own prison? And then to poison him before he could be ransomed? These northerners disinherit all their sons, save the first, and everyone else must pay the price, as their second and third sons storm far-away lands, burning vineyards and fields and stealing titles they do not own. I don't know why I feel this, but I hope that Trencavel never believed that I had betrayed him and that if he thought of me before he died, it was only to think of the music I played for him.

Agnes must mourn him, though she is safe and cared for. I think even the King of France was shocked and alarmed at what his vassals did there in Carcassonne. For to strip a man of his feudal rights and lands in such a manner threatens to shake the very foundations of our society. So Agnes is provided for by the King of France. I only hope she is able to find peace. Their young son, the last Trencavel, is safe in the mountains with the Count of Foix. He is only two, but maybe he will be a hope one day for this land, if we can ever get rid of these usurpers.

The Lord of Cabaret continues the fight, from his three fortresses perched high in the mountains above Carcassonne. I am sure that Bertrand de Saissac would be there with him, but the old warrior died shortly after the end of the siege. The Crusaders came to take his castle only weeks after they had taken Carcassonne and he died soon after, his body no match for his rotting wounds and his broken spirit. But, there is hope. Now that the thousands of Crusaders who came only for their forty days of service are gone, Montfort and his men are weak. For every town they take, three renounce his sovereignty and vow to fight against him. The winter will be a long one for Montfort, but I fear that the summer will bring more second sons from the north, butchers anxious to escape their debts and fight for what they think will give them a straight shot at heaven.

But for now, at least, I am safe here in my castle. I listen to the sweet music and let myself feel peace. For I know that Azalais' words are right, one loses much more rapidly than one wins.

Acknowledgements

I have been lucky to have a wonderful, large, and supportive family. I thank you all, especially Edna Malik, my grandmother, who taught me to love books, and my parents, Walter and Margaret Cook, who always believed in me.

I would like to thank my friends and family who read the first draft of the novel and provided valuable feedback or helped out in other important ways: Emmanuelle Bresson, Kathleen Callaway, Elizabeth Cook, Fred Cook, Jane Cook, Margaret Cook, Walter Cook, Kate Donohue, Anouk Lavoie Orlick, Tony Hayward, Ellyn Hill, Nannette Kye, Neus Lorenzo, Manuela Luchtmeijer, Edna Malik, and Linda Menache.

The lovely cover design is by Elizabeth Cook and the title was suggested to me by Walter Cook. I would like to thank Erik Pezarro for permission to use the author photograph and José Fernando Álvarez for the cover photographs.

Dr. Franklin W. Knight, Dr. A.J.R. Russell-Wood, Dr. Gabrielle Spiegel, and Dr. Thomas Christopherson instilled in me a love of historical research. Sharyn McCrumb and Sharan Newman provided invaluable advice about the publishing industry.

Dr Gerard C. J. Lynch was very kind to provide technical information about medieval masonry. I would also like to thank the tour guides at Carcassonne and other Cathar monuments for their assistance. Of course, any errors that remain in the novel are solely my responsibility.

Finally, a huge thank you to my editor, agent, typesetter, and biggest fan, José Fernando Álvarez. This book would not have been published without his love and support.